THE BOOK OF HARD THINGS

The Book of

HARD
THINGS

SUE HALPERN

Farrar, Straus and Giroux

NEW YORK

FARRAR, STRAUS AND GIROUX
19 Union Square West, New York 10003

Copyright © 2003 by Sue Halpern
All rights reserved
Distributed in Canada by Douglas & McIntyre Ltd.
Printed in the United States of America
FIRST EDITION, 2003

Library of Congress Cataloging-in-Publication Data
Halpern, Sue.
    The book of hard things / Sue Halpern.—1st ed.
        p.   cm.
    ISBN 0-374-11559-1 (hc : alk. paper)
    1. Executors and administrators—Fiction.   2. Male friendship—Fiction.   3. Mountain life—Fiction.   4. Teenage boys—Fiction.   5. Violence—Fiction.   I. Title.

PS3608.A549B66 2003
813'.6—dc21   2003044067

Designed by Gretchen Achilles

www.fsgbooks.com

1   3   5   7   9   10   8   6   4   2

To Peter Halpern and our parents
and to Shawn Leary

THE BOOK OF HARD THINGS

S L A T E

"A dense, fine-grained metamorphic rock produced by the compression of various sediments" (Webster's); this is the place to begin; Webster's also says *"tabula rasa"* is hypothetical. This is important. We come into the world already written upon. Such is our burden. We are indelible.

Cuzzy Gage woke with sand in his mouth from where his head had strayed off the sleeping bag and onto the beach sometime after the girl, Amber-Rose, climbed out around midnight or one—nobody wore a watch. When he opened his eyes, there was grit in them, too, which he wiped away with the back of a hand that smelled like her sex, his beer. The beach was empty. He guessed it was before seven. The fire they'd lit the night before smoldered nearby. Cuzzy wrestled himself out of the bag and stood over the fire ring with his back slightly arched, waiting a moment, then watching his pee arc and land on the hot rocks, making them steam. He was wearing only a T-shirt that advertised a brand of sneakers, and he was cold. The thinnest skin of ice was beginning to form over the lip of the pond, and the swamp maples had already turned. It was September in those mountains, which is like December a little farther down the road.

He pulled on his jeans, which were warm from being jammed at the bottom of his bag all night, and his socks and steel-tipped

3

boots. There was a piece of candy in his right front pocket, a caramel he'd swiped from the Grand Union days before, and it had melted and hardened enough to make peeling off the wrapper a morning's work. He had nothing else to do—no job, no place in particular to go. On the other side of the lake was the county road, and he saw, in the distance, a yellow school bus coming closer. Amber-Rose's bus, he decided, though he didn't really know. Amber-Rose was seventeen and still in school. He had been out four months.

He liked Amber-Rose all right. He liked her more than he'd thought he would. She was skinny, scrawny almost, like one of the dogs he'd see sometimes, walking around the woods, who didn't belong to anyone. Amber-Rose belonged to him now, even though he had Crystal, like it or not, and together they had Harry. But Crystal was pretending not to know him; at least she had been the night he met Amber-Rose, as if pretending would reduce the swell of her belly and the life she felt in there. It was graduation night, the last day of May, and he was right here at the town beach, lighting M-80s and working on a case of St. Pauli Girl. She was wasted, too, Amber-Rose was, but not so much that when he asked a group of girls if they had a graduation present for him, she didn't hesitate to follow into the shadows, watch him unzip his one pair of good pants, and, without a word, reach inside. It was summer. It was something to do.

Then Crystal had the baby and called it Harrison Ford, and the only way he could see her was by going to the hospital after her parents had left for the night, and later by sneaking into their trailer-house when they were in bed, which he had been doing the year before. Marcel and Therese weren't Crystal's parents anyway, they were her grandparents, Marcel one generation down from Quebec, a logger as broad and muscular as the Shire horses with which he worked. He could have taken Cuzzy out with a single

4

punch, he could have killed him, but he had done the same thing himself once upon a time, fucking, fucking, fucking, as if, working on his father's farm, he didn't know what that would bring. That day, the day Therese told him, Marcel went to the woods and hauled out three cord by himself, then spent the next week cutting and splitting until his hands were raw and splintered. He sold it green, for firewood, and left the money on the kitchen counter in a grimy envelope. It stayed there a few days, and then he printed the word "kid" on it and the envelope disappeared. Crystal understood it was for her, that he was giving as much of a blessing as he could.

Therese, meanwhile, went from despair to a kind of ecstasy, for though she knew the baby's provenance, she chose in time to forget about Cuzzy's participation and considered Crystal's condition a miracle of conception, a virgin birth. She constantly talked about the baby and to the baby, crocheted countless hats and capes and tiny, doll-footed boots; and made sure she attended every prenatal visit with Crystal. If it was wishful, shutting Cuzzy out, it was a wish that came true. Five months into the pregnancy, just as she was starting to show, Crystal began to ignore Cuzzy. First she stopped sleeping with him, then she stopped letting him touch her, then she wouldn't go out with him, and finally she pretended for a while that he didn't exist and never had.

Crystal was two years out of school when Cuzzy first saw her, working road crew, flagging cars. It was August, and the skin of her neck and face and hands was brown and dry as old varnish, and like varnish, it was chipping. Her hard hat was yellow, and so was her hair, which wagged in the wind. Her face wasn't especially pretty, but when men looked at her, it was not her face they saw but her breasts, which rose from her chest like the Appalachians, steep and round. The guys on the crew called her Beams, short for high beams—not, they said, because of how they thought she looked but because other guys, driving by, would flash their headlights when they saw her. She didn't care. She was twenty and making good steady money.

When she flagged Cuzzy to a stop that first time, he rolled down the window of his truck and beckoned to her. He didn't know why. It was just something his hand made him do.

"You need something, Cuzzy Gage?" she said when she was ten paces from the vehicle.

Cuzzy, who was absently sucking the end of his middle finger, burned at the tip by the last scrap of a roach the night before, looked at her suspiciously. "How do you know my name?" he demanded.

She looked him over, her eyes traveling up his left arm, which was tanned from sticking out the truck window, to his shoulder, pumped from a summer of shoveling gravel, and up his neck to the curtain of lank brown hair that opened at the cleft in his chin, to his full lips and round, almost pretty cheeks. His eyes were chocolate, the color of pudding, doeish eyes ringed by long black lashes that made him look innocent, always, and surprised. Women, he was noticing, were drawn to his eyes, and to the tentative promise of those black lashes: like maybe he wouldn't be mean.

"You're from Poverty," she said squarely, as if that answered his question.

"So?" he said, challenging her. He didn't like it, didn't like the reference to Poverty, as though it was something he had done, being born and raised in that part of town (so named the day the child-welfare lady went door-to-door asking questions and, upon hearing the answers, declared, "Why, you're living in poverty!" So it was official: They lived in Poverty).

He looked at her directly, her khaki eyes, idling for a better explanation. Her face wasn't half bad, he thought. Prominent cheekbones, a bridge of freckles on her nose, and something—either ungiving or desperately honest—about the corners of her mouth. Why had he called her over? He had wanted to know what was happening down the road. He was bored and she was there. Her T-shirt said SINGER EXCAVATING across the front. He looked at it hard, not sure, pretty sure, certain, and grinned then with amazement: both the "I" in "Singer" and the "I" in "Excavating" were dotted from the inside out by the hint of raised flesh.

"Didn't your mother teach you manners?" she said when she saw him staring. There was another truck behind him, and the guy was right on his tail, nudging his bumper.

Cuzzy's grin fell like a shot duck. "She's dead," he said. It had been what, four years already? Blood clot in her brain. Born that way, the doctor said. No better reason than that. Every one of her seconds, from the moment she was born, was numbered.

"573-3184," Crystal said quickly, dismissing him with a broad sweep of her flag. He pushed into gear and rolled out.

"I know Joey," she shouted after him. He was in third by then and could barely hear her.

It bugged him that she knew his cousin Joey. Joey the pervert, not back from Laslow Village two months and working at the Nice n Easy where everyone could see him, sent away at sixteen for sticking it to his little sister. Funny thing was, nobody really thought he did it—at least they had doubts. But the girl had a disease down there that had shown up during the annual school physical, and the county health officer came poking around and checked out all the kids and found it wasn't only her. Their father was hopping mad— they made him drop his pants, too—and ready to skin his daughter, who did what she always did, she blamed it on her brother Joey.

"Fuck," Joey said in his own defense, "she's pissed from what she saw me doing with Skunky." Skunky was the dog. Joey said this to the police and to the papers and to the judge and jury down in Halcyon Falls. They sent him away then, thirty-six months in juvey, where he was not allowed to work with the animals. Typical Poverty, people said during the trial, even people who lived in Poverty, where everyone was related one way or another, where Cuzzy Gage, who had no brothers or sisters, only relations, got his name the same way a maple branch is made into a walking stick, by peeling and shaving till form gives way to function, all those "Hi Cousin Tommy"s and "Hey cuz"es whittling at the heft of his given name until it was left for duff. "Thomas" was the mistake new teachers made the first day of school, or what the sheriff said into his two-way radio the night Cuzzy and Joey were clocked driving the county road at eighty-eight.

So Crystal knew his cousin Joey, Cuzzy thought as he drove up Whisper Notch—where the rich summer people lived—to dump a second load of crushed stones; she knew they were cousins, and she didn't think he was a pervert, too, or maybe she did, maybe she liked that stuff, which made him laugh out loud, right in the truck, all by himself, and grab a look at himself in the rearview mirror, his lips turned up, his eyes in on the joke.

"3184," he repeated to himself, happy, as if the numbers were that week's winning Lotto, which gave him an idea, and he made a sudden turn onto Street Road and headed over the hill for the Nice n Easy, wondering if he'd play a dollar or a ten, or maybe go for this week's broke on a twenty.

And there she was again, sitting in one of the booths, alone on break, drinking a chocolate milk and reading *People*. Her nail polish surprised him. It was Popsicle blue. She didn't look up from the magazine at first, or didn't seem to, so he stood there looking down at her fingers, wanting to stick them in his mouth.

"Jeez Louise," she said at last, cocking her head in his direction. "Did you know that Princess Diana has an eating disorder?" He looked at her dumbly, mumbled a few words, and shook his head. "The same one that killed Karen Carpenter." Now *she* was shaking her head. "Can you imagine having all that royal this and that, like custard and whatnot, and not wanting to eat it?"

"I thought she ODed or something," Cuzzy said, trying to stay in the conversation.

"Princess Di?" Crystal exclaimed. "You're even more out of it than I thought."

"No, Karen Carpenter," he said sheepishly.

"She weighed like sixty pounds when she died," Crystal said confidently, tipping the milk carton up toward the ceiling and draining it. She had a faint brown milk mustache. He was enchanted.

"Didn't your mother tell you it was rude to stare?" she said sternly. "Oops, sorry," she said, embarrassed. "I forgot about that." She stood up, walked past him, and put the magazine back on the rack. He did not move. Couldn't seem to.

"Nice eyes," she said, pushing on the glass door with her shoulder and sending a throaty laugh in his direction. "But don't let it go to your head."

Cuzzy continued to stare at her dumbly.

"Eyes. In your head. Get it?" And she walked out.

So they got together, and she demanded one thing: no matter how they did it, he would have to keep his eyes open, even in the dark. He thought it was a little weird, like being a voyeur looking through his own bedroom window, but he was happy to oblige. Anything to sink into her. She was older and knew things. Tricks. Things he wasn't sure about and didn't want to be a wuss about, one way or the other. He wasn't used to girls telling him how.

"I want you to go to Florida," she whispered to him one night when they had spread a raft of blankets in the bed of her truck. She pushed at his head. He looked up, mystified. Why was she pushing him away?

"South," she said. "Like Jane what's-her-name, the exercise lady, in *Coming Home*." She looked at him like no girl had ever looked at him. It almost gave him the creeps.

"Fonda. The one with the tapes," he said, resting his chin on her belly.

She took her pinky and tickled his tongue. "Use this," she told him.

He didn't move. She pulled out her finger, drawing a line on his tongue as she did. Neither of them moved. It reminded him of the games of checkers he used to play with his mother, when the only way to open up the board was to let yourself get jumped.

"I must really like you," he said, heading in her direction.

That was August. She had her job, eleven dollars an hour plus overtime and benefits, and he was hauling gravel for his cousin Hank Gage, and for a few weeks, when the county road was getting paved and there was one lane open at a time, Cuzzy shunned all the detours, putting himself in her path four, six, eight times a day. Crystal, in her gimme tees, made those extra miles, with their discursive itineraries, worth it.

How long had he known her? His whole life, it seemed. Or it seemed as if his whole life had recently begun, that he had pulled anchor and she was the lapping ocean.

"What do you plan on doing when you get out?" she asked him one evening in bed, not sneaking, since her grandparents were away on their annual Labor Day fishing trip to Stover Lake, twelve miles west. They were sharing a strawberry wine cooler, passing it back and forth like a joint, and the fan was sending a rustle through the sheets, and the big, soft bed and open bedroom door tricked them into believing this house, this life, was theirs. "Out," Cuzzy knew, meant "out of school," which would happen, if nothing went wrong, at the end of the school year.

"Fucking you," he said easily, as if he had weighed all the options, like real estate and carpentry, and this was the absolutely right one for him.

"No, really," she said.

He put his head on her shoulder and didn't say a thing. He had a feeling she was asking him something else, something that had to do with the bed and the trailer and the smell of the bacon sandwiches they'd made for supper.

"You could work road crew," she said tentatively, then felt him frown against her skin.

"Everyone works road crew," he said. "It's like frigging welfare."

When he thought back on it later, he realized that this was the moment she began to turn. She was running the nail on her big toe down the back of his left leg, and she stopped halfway to the calf and took her foot away—not far but away—and her whole body shifted, leaving space between them. This gap was a revelation to him, like when he knew the second she leaned his way that morning at Nice n Easy, he would be spending time in her bed.

You are a fucking idiot, he said to himself. Why the fuck did you have to say that to her. He was back at school, for what that was worth; no Crystal; he could have been fucking this woman. He wasn't fucking anyone. Why the fuck did he have to open his fucking big mouth? How many times did he ask himself this? Why couldn't he have told her he was thinking maybe of being a plumber. Why didn't he say, Yeah, road crew sounds okay. Everyone worked road crew. The pay was pretty good, and the benefits. Eleven dollars an hour, and he'd be able to take her to the Meat Spot any time, not just for the early bird. "Fuck that!" he said out loud. He was in math class. He got a detention and spent a lazy hour thinking of her, thinking reels of porn thoughts that sent him twice to the boys' room.

But really, road crew? How many of his cousins worked road crew? How many guys from school and their fathers, too? Up at three to sand, plow all night, the stink of tar in the summer, unemployment in the spring. Though Cuzzy didn't know what he wanted to do, he was clear on what he didn't: no digging ditches to lay sewer pipes, for one thing. Prison work crews did that. He didn't want to do the same fucking job as those downstate brown boys he saw sometimes on the side of the highway.

Had he said this to her? He thought he had, maybe. They were pretty wasted by then, four wine coolers chasing the twenty-ounce malt liquor. She was on road crew herself. It had slipped his mind. How had it slipped his mind? Because lying in bed with her, he could not imagine her any other place but right there, in any other attire than blue percale, wrapped haphazardly around her naked body.

His father, a lay preacher in the Baptist church, had worked road crew. Maybe Cuzzy should have told her this. But he never talked about his father, ever, his crazy father, gone to the hospital in Newkirk with the razor wire around the perimeter, thinking he was Pontius Pilate and crying all day, sobbing, wailing, till they quieted him with drugs, which made him fat and caused his arms to jerk away from his body as if they no longer wanted to be associated with him. He went the summer Cuzzy was nine, taken away in the town ambulance, his feet blistered from the hot asphalt he poured over them as he tried to fasten himself to the road.

No clothes on, standing eastbound on Route 17, at one with the blacktop.

Cuzzy's mother followed the ambulance, signed the papers, came home, and told him his father was gone. Cuzzy had been asleep. "Evaporated," his mother said, sitting at the edge of his bed. "It's like that man evaporated." So a year later, when his physical-science teacher talked about the three states of matter, he listened up. Couldn't his father, who taught him how to tie a trapline and knew all the verses to "Amazing Grace," his father who'd turned to liquid—to tears—and vaporized, couldn't he be made solid again? This was Cuzzy's secret hope, and it seemed to be coming true the times his father would call from Newkirk and remember Cuzzy's name and the name of Hops, his rabbit, until those times became more common and they sent him home for a trial visit, overweight and distracted but still *there*.

It was Cuzzy who found him in the woods, red smears on his hands and shirt and the ends of his mouth, the mouth of the man who had been his father, ranting about blood sacrifice, the rabbit eviscerated.

Cuzzy ran, he ran hard, leaving his father cross-legged on the ground, his right hand jammed up the slit gut, tugging on the heart. He ran home and left his father there and almost crashed into his mother, coming home from her job cooking at the nursing home.

"Seen your dad?" she asked him.

"Nope," he said. He wasn't lying. That man was not his father.

"You're an orphan now, pretty much," his cousin Hank told him after they put his mother in the ground, and he guessed, even though his father was technically alive, that he was. Cuzzy was almost thirteen. Cuzzy and Laura had been staying with Hank and his five kids for about a year then, so Cuzzy stayed on. People said Hank went through women the way a growing boy goes through blue jeans, though when Cuzzy and Laura moved in, Hank was between females, and Laura, Hank's cousin by marriage, cooked and cleaned and took care of the kids. The whole time she was there, Hank didn't bring another woman through the door, and Poverty talked about that, too. Then she died, and five weeks later Charlotte moved in to help out. She was fifteen, the daughter of Hank's brother's best friend, and Cuzzy liked her. She let him watch her wash her thick black hair. Their secret. She had other secrets, too, though not for long. In March, right after her sixteenth birthday, she gave Hank his sixth child, a girl named Little Cynthia, who was "slow."

Crystal turned. She turned away from him. It was subtle, and he didn't notice at first. It was a body thing. Her body was no longer completely open to him. And a muscular thing. Her muscles were ratcheted down by disappointment and whatever came to fill the place formerly occupied by the belief that her life—their life—was going to be different from the lives she saw around her, the small, hard, unsurprising lives of her grandparents, and of her mother, young enough to be her sister, dancing in a casino bar up north. How glamorous that had seemed when Crystal was little, to have a mother who was a dancer. Crystal had seen Debbie Allen on TV and imagined her mother like that, energetic and beautiful and all legs. At six and seven, at nine, ten, eleven, she told everyone she was going to be like her mother, a dancer. She told especially her grandparents, who were strict and uninterested, told them in a way she intended to be a reproach for their own unimaginative and boring existence, till one day, exasperated, her grandmother told her to stop it once and for all, and explained that her mother danced on men's laps and they stuffed money *up there*. Then her grandmother slapped Crystal, right under her eye with the back of her hand, livid. But Crystal didn't feel it. What she felt instead was insulated from the lives around her, which were hard as rock. Not rock like granite, riddled with lines that *went somewhere,* but hard like slate—all gray and dull and brittle.

The new *People* was on the magazine rack the day she met Cuzzy. Maybe that was the source of the feeling that things were going to be different with him. His chin was like John Travolta's. She checked her watch. She liked to know exactly when she'd had what might turn out to be a very significant thought. Just so she'd remember. She had seen Cuzzy at 10:18 at mile twenty-three of the county road. Not that seeing him was significant or anything. She just happened to look at her watch right then and calculated that she'd be on lunch break in twenty-two minutes. An hour later to the minute (on the store clock, which was three minutes slower than her watch), she saw Cuzzy Gage walk into the Nice n Easy, which was sign enough, but there was more. Cuzzy walked in right as she turned the page and saw the headline—"John Travolta, Family Man"—saw the dent in his chin, which reminded her of Cuzzy's, and there, miraculously, he was!

There he was. His hair hung like a curtain around his face, revealing his features stingily. She wanted to see more. She wanted to pull the cord and see his cheeks, his ears, the chicken-pox scars on his forehead. She tilted slightly in his direction. She wanted to give him a sign, too. But she wanted to give him a sign without really giving it to him, and then she wanted to know that he had gotten it. She looked up at him expectantly. And caught him staring at her chest.

Fuck, she almost said. Instead, she said what she said about Princess Di. She loved Princess Di. She felt sorry for her, stuck with that cheating creep of a husband. What unnecessary despair. Crystal identified with her, with an actual princess. It tickled her, but in a sad sort of way.

"Did you know that Princess Di has an eating disorder?" she asked him. Of course he didn't know, and she didn't much care— about that. What she cared about was his knowing she knew about the royal family, and thought about them, and even cared about them (not that it mattered to them; she knew it didn't, really). So he would understand right off that her frame of reference was bigger than Poverty or South Stover or even Halcyon Falls. She wanted him to believe, like she did, that their lives could be more like the lives in *People*. Not more beautiful or glamorous, exactly, but more possible.

Later on, she taught him the lottery game. They were on the swings down by the town beach. Cuzzy was facing east, Crystal west, and she was on his lap. His hands were in the back pockets of her jeans, and he was using them like handles to rock them back and forth.

"What would you do if you won a million dollars?" she asked him.

"Get a blue Chevy Silverado 2500 with an awesome sound system and a custom fade on the hood," he said.

"And?" she prompted him. "That's like what, thirty grand?" She used her feet like brakes. She stopped swinging and sat there. An owl hooted, and then another, closer.

He had to think. Maybe it was then. Maybe that was when she began to turn, because he had to think, and the owls were hooting, underlining the silence. "A camp up on Stover Lake?" he said tentatively. "Those cost a shitload of money."

"It's not about money," she complained.

He was confused and a little hurt. What was winning a million dollars about if it wasn't about money? "I don't get it," he said.

Now she was a little shy. "It's about dreams," she said in a small voice.

He laughed. He couldn't help himself. It was a nervous laugh, and it fell out of his mouth. He knew she was pissed. Girls were so mysterious. But he had to say, he liked that about them. Their furry emotions. Their odd, unbidden sounds that reminded him of walking through the woods at night. It always surprised him that porcupines *screamed*.

He took her to Burger Time to make up, and bought her a cheeseburger club, large fries, and a black and white milk shake. They ate in his cousin's truck. He liked how the smell would linger when they did that, how he'd get in the cab the next day and there it would be, and it would follow him around all day like a puppy.

"What if you won a million bucks?" he asked. She took a couple of his fries. She had finished her own, and her milk shake, too, and was eyeing his, which she swiped as soon as she began to speak. She looked happy again, unclouded. Girls were like weather.

"Well," she said eagerly—gratified, it seemed, that someone had asked—"I wouldn't quit my job. I know everyone says this"—she laughed—"except the ones who say fuck this shit, but I like my job, and it pays real well, and the benefits are great."

"You wouldn't need benefits," Cuzzy said. "You'd be rich."

"Even rich people need benefits," she said sagely, and she pushed the last scrap of food into her mouth and reached at the cup holder for Cuzzy's milk shake, which wasn't there. Like a blind person, Cuzzy thought, surrendering it to her.

"I wouldn't quit," she said again, "but maybe I'd work part-time. My own hours. I'd tell *them* when I was going to work."

"No benefits," he told her. "You don't get them when you go part-time."

"You just told me I didn't need any frigging benefits. I'm rich," she said, punching him playfully in the arm.

"Yeah," he said.

"So the first thing I'm going to do, I'm going to move out of that trailer, and I'm going to get a room at the Red Roof Inn," she said.

"You're going to live at the fucking Red Roof Inn?" he asked, incredulous. "You can't live at the Red Roof Inn."

"They don't have beds at the Red Roof Inn?" she demanded. "They don't have bathrooms? I can live wherever I fucking want. I'm loaded."

He didn't say anything.

"Warren Beatty lived in the penthouse of the Beverly Wilshire Hotel. John Belushi had a bungalow at the Chateau Marmont in L.A." She felt superior. She knew her stuff. She held out the milk shake as a kind of exclamation point.

He took the shake. "The Red Roof Inn is a motel off the fucking interstate," he said, and punctuated his own declaration with a long, loud draw on the straw.

"I'm only going to be there a couple of months," she said, "while my sixty-seven-hundred-square-foot log home is being put together on Whisper Notch. Plus the heated indoor pool and Jacuzzi." She had, he thought, a look of rapture on her face, a deep and spreading happiness that reminded him of her torso when they made love, and how it would redden, the blush traveling south to north over the height of land at her chest and up her neck, ringing it with a sawtooth necklace. Sometimes it was a slow traverse, and patchy, other times as quick and forceful as water released from a dam, and he had given up wondering, worrying, if the difference meant anything.

"If there's any money left over, I'm going to split it and use half to play Win 4 and the other half to buy a savings bond for our little girl. 'Cause I sure as hell don't want her growing up to work on that goddamned road crew," she said.

It was in this way that Cuzzy Gage learned about the baby, Harry. Their baby. She just assumed it was a girl. Another one of her dreams.

A G A T E

"Agates are made from quartz crystals too small to be seen with the naked eye," Ross, Gemstones for the Ages; *Persian magicians used agates to divert storms (Lux,* A History of the Lands of the Bible*); there is magic everywhere if we don't insist upon seeing it: intuition is magic talking quietly to itself. Knowledge begins before knowledge is acquired.*

uzzy squatted, hands on his haunches, breathing in the last heat of the fire. Another school bus passed by, and then another, and he followed their distant traverse along the county road as if they were jet trails or meteors; he reflexively made a wish about the weather. He stood up abruptly, and began kicking dirt on the smolder. Satisfied that it was out enough, Cuzzy balled the sleeping bag into a plastic garbage sack and stashed it in the woods. This was home, and had been for two weeks, since Hank kicked him out of the house and fired him all in the same day for disrespecting, he said, his wife. Only she wasn't his wife, she was his culvert, his sluice, and she was pregnant again and didn't want to be, and cried on Cuzzy's bed, and made him do it to her hard to shake it loose, but it stayed. And stayed some more, and either Charlotte told Hank, or he somehow knew, and either way Cuzzy had to leave.

"Get your own piece" is what Hank had said, not real mad,

and pulled five twenties from a roll of bills in his pocket and handed them to Cuzzy.

"What's this?" Cuzzy asked.

"Wages," Hank said, rerolling the money and securing it with a thick red rubber band, the kind used to bind broccoli stalks.

"You owe me more than this," Cuzzy said.

Hank pointed to Charlotte, sitting impassively at the kitchen table. "You already spent it," he said.

One hundred dollars can last a pretty long time when you're living in the woods and your girlfriend loads up her knapsack most days during school breakfast and school lunch, restocking your larder by midafternoon. Cuzzy had a trash bag filled with saltines and packets of cocoa and little tubs of peanut butter and jelly and silver tubes of cream cheese that he'd ribbon onto his tongue and wash down with a shot of V8. And Joey was at the Nice n Easy, where Cuzzy was headed now. He could always get stuff off Joey.

Not much traffic on the county road. A backhoe on the opposite shoulder, the occasional Corolla or Jeep cruising at sixty, and quiet in between. A log truck sneaked up on him, not on purpose, whacking Cuzzy on the back with a huge blast of air, its sound delayed, like an afterthought but loud. He jumped sideways, startled, fighting the wind, and gave the guy the finger. His cousin Christine went by—she drove the Poverty mail—and five minutes later Hank's oldest girl, Tina, a nurse's aide, coming off the lobster shift at the hospital in Halcyon Falls. It must be near to eight o'clock, Cuzzy thought, as she honked and passed him.

He wished it had been Crystal. He knew if he walked the road enough, she'd eventually go by, but no such luck yet. She stayed home most of the time and didn't want to see him in any case.

Five hundred more feet, and there was the MADD/DARE

shrine, a white wooden cross planted in the ground a foot off the shoulder, marking the exact spot the Baker brothers lost control of their vehicle, crossed the center line, and slammed into the cab of a trucker who was out taking a leak. There was a girl in the car, too, and all three of them were completely incinerated: no need for the jaws of life. It was assumed they were drunk, or high, or both. The girl had been a neighbor of Amber-Rose's, and even though they didn't know each other, Amber-Rose came here sometimes and freshened the wildflowers people left in beer bottles, even though it had been a couple of years.

The truck driver lived. The explosion carried him twenty-two yards downwind, and he landed sideways in the marsh followed by a rain of glass that cut him up so badly the paramedics said it was like 'Nam. The high school held a memorial service for the Baker brothers, who were basically bad boys, and the girl, who had been thirteen and ran with them, and all the kids were asked to raise their right hands and pledge that they wouldn't drink and drive, and Cuzzy's hand went up with the rest because the trucker was right there in the auditorium, all banged up and in a wheelchair, and it seemed right. Cuzzy heard that the guy killed himself a year to the day later, but he didn't know for sure and couldn't see why. As far as anyone knew, he'd never been back to Stover or to Halcyon Falls, where he'd spent the better part of three weeks in the ICU, and if he had returned, Cuzzy thought, he might as well have died.

Cuzzy turned up Bypass Road just as his father's brother-in-law, Frank Cole, the school custodian, took the same turn, driving the town trash hauler.

"You need a ride somewheres?" Frank called out to him. Cuzzy waved him on. "Where you heading then, Cuzzy?" Frank said, slowing to Cuzzy's speed.

"To the Nice n Easy," Cuzzy said, blowing on his hands.

Frank nodded and scooted ahead. For a moment Cuzzy wondered if he had meant it the way Crystal would have meant it—where was he *heading?*—then decided no, the future was a pussy thing.

Traffic picked up, and so did the wind, which was coming in cold from the north, lifting every piece of trash off the ground, the coffee cups and cigarette boxes, spinning them in circles like kayakers caught in a wash. Cuzzy's hands were iced, and he jammed them in the pockets of his jeans, rubbing them on the fabric in there, which made him think of Crystal, he couldn't help it, and how she liked to do that, too, to come up behind him and put her hands in his pockets and hold onto him there.

A Snap-on Tools van passed, and a propane truck, and Cuzzy knew both drivers. The ambulance went by, but slowly, no lights, and then the minister, Jason Trimble, who doubled back and motioned for Cuzzy to join him. Cuzzy kept walking. He wasn't interested in a sermon from Trimble.

The minister dogged him, and Cuzzy looked straight ahead, slowing his pace so Trimble had to take his foot off the gas pedal and creep, his rusted Subaru moving in fits and starts.

"Can't we talk, Cuzzy?" Trimble said, leaning toward the open window.

Cuzzy turned his head and smiled. "I hear a truck coming, Reverend Trimble," he said solicitously, and sure enough, when Trimble glanced in his mirror, he saw an eighteen-wheeler not far behind. He floored the gas pedal, and Cuzzy saw him crest the rise ahead and disappear, the big rig bearing down on him.

"Thank you, Lord," Cuzzy said, and kicked a can.

Over the rise himself, and he could make out the Mobil sign at the edge of the Nice n Easy lot. Any minute and he'd be able to see that sign, too, blue underscored by yellow, and the double row of gas pumps lined with wire baskets of antifreeze and pyramids of wiper fluid. He didn't see them yet, it was all a blur, but like the constellations on a cloudy night, he knew they were there, which is another way of seeing.

Then he could make out Joey's Chevette, and a maroon pickup with a gray cap over the truck bed, and the Frito-Lay supplier parked diagonally, and a green car, most likely a Taurus, pulling up to the pumps. Cuzzy kept his eyes fixed on the store windows as if vision alone could draft him there. LARGE EGGS, $.99 DZ, BRACH'S CANDY, 2-4-1 SALE, BUD, BUD LIGHT. He almost missed seeing the silver Porsche at the far end, a two-seat convertible, parked in the same spot where watermelons were piled in summer.

He knew this car. He had seen it a couple of weeks before when he went with Amber-Rose to the Health Center so she could get one of those birth-control patches stuck up her arm. He had seen it; it was so sweet, that car, and the second Amber-Rose went into the examining room, he was back outside, stalking the car, checking it out, running his palms over the fenders, fingering the grille, till it was too much and he climbed in and slid down the back of the leather seat like he was getting dressed, and took hold of the steering wheel. It didn't move, but he ran his hands over it anyway, left and right and left and right, as if he were on one of the rides they had outside the Grand Union that cost a quarter but not a cent to pretend. There were two marbles in the ashtray, cloudy blue agates, and Cuzzy thought about pocketing one as a souvenir, but they looked perfect there, the way peaches do on a summer table, so he left something of his instead. In the waiting room, holding Cuzzy's arm to steady herself, Amber-Rose noticed that the friendship bracelet she had made for him was gone from his wrist, and she made him crawl around the rows of chairs, patting the carpet, even though he knew it wasn't there.

So here was that car again, sitting outside the Nice n Easy, all closed in. Cuzzy circled it once to make sure it was the same one, then peered inside through the zippered windows. The two marbles were there, and his bracelet, too, ringing the shifter. He opened the door, reached in, and grabbed the bracelet. The green-handed clock said 8:39 A.M.

"Shit, Cuz, you've got to see what I've got!" Joey called as Cuzzy walked into the store. Joey made him laugh in the clown uniform they made him wear—red pants, red-and-white-striped shirt, a red baseball cap, and a badge that said, I'M JOE! I PLAY BACKUP MANAGER ON THE NICE N EASY TEAM! All that was missing, Cuzzy thought, was the big red nose. Joey didn't mind. He said it was better than Laslow Village, where they had to wear piss-yellow jumpsuits that didn't have pockets.

The store was crowded and steamy from all the talk. People hung out either here or at the Gotham in town, but the Gotham had a minimum, so it was mostly here. Sander teams came in on breaks, and guys working construction, and anyone who wanted to read *The News of the World* and not pay for it, and the girls who cooked at the nursing home, and people passing through wanting gas. There were always some of these, and they always looked different—cleaner and softer, as if they had a higher thread count. There were the regulars, too, guys on disability or unemployment or both, who sat in the back booth playing five-card draw and nursing a single cup of coffee half the day, unmoved by the Little Debbie cakes and Lucky Strike cartons that the manager carefully arranged to encourage them to add to the bottom line.

Cuzzy wasn't surprised to see Joey's cousin Ram Pullen there, sitting with a kid Cuzzy thought he recognized from Amber-Rose's bus, and Ram's constant companions Squint and Larry Miller, half brothers (same mother, different fathers) whom everyone called the Sylvanias because of the shape of their heads. Maybe they used to mind, but they had long since stopped caring and called themselves that, too. When Joey drew morning shift, it was as if Ram and the Sylvanias drew it, too. They could have punched the clock, showing up regularly at half-past seven to suck on Slim Jims and loudly study the wildlife in the *Asian Brides* or *Hustlers* that Joey could not afford not to sell them. When Ram told people the three of them were the northern posse of a gang from L.A., no one chose to dispute him. What if they were wrong? Ram had a thing for guns. His road kill was prime.

Cuzzy knew Ram was dealing. He was the one who could be counted on to pull a twenty from his billfold. He was the one driving a pretty new truck. It was pot, mostly, some speed and coke, pills off the street. The Sylvanias, perpetually working on their equivalency diplomas, still sold him their Ritalin even though they could have gotten more selling it themselves. That would have meant crossing Ram, who was both bridge and raging sea.

Cuzzy said hey to them as he worked his way to the coffee machine, and nodded to the back-benchers, who were thick into their game. He poured himself a large coffee, laced it with three sugars, and looked for a place to sit down. All five booths were occupied, so he leaned against the ice-cream freezer, waiting for a seat. He had time. Time was what he had.

"Straight!" said one of the old-timers, slapping his cards across the table.

"Oh, nelly, nelly!" said one of his companions, folding. No matter that it was a tired old joke. They said it every day, all day.

An older couple in the front booth stood up to leave. Leaf peepers, Cuzzy decided; the man had a pair of Leica binoculars hanging from his neck. The woman was reapplying her lipstick.

"Ready," the man said. His wife stood up. People were always leaving Stover.

"So Cuzzy, would you look at this," Joey said, pulling out a box from behind the counter. Cuzzy reached out to take it.

"Don't look!" Joey said. He was holding the box to his chest.

"Jesus, Joey, you just told me to look," Cuzzy said.

"Put your hand in here and feel it," Joey said.

Somebody whistled. "If it's round and firm, I want to cop a feel, too," Ram shouted. Cuzzy put his hand in. It *was* round and firm, slightly canted, cool. Joey looked on expectantly.

"A plate?" Cuzzy asked him.

"Not just any plate," Joey said. "Take it out."

Cuzzy tipped the box, and out slid an eight-inch dinner plate with a picture of a redheaded man holding a baseball bat in the middle.

"Rusty Staub? A Rusty Staub plate?"

Joey beamed. "It was only fifty bucks. A Rusty Staub *commemorative* plate. Do you know what this is going to be worth in ten years?"

Ram snickered. "Sixty bucks less than you paid for it." Cuzzy fiddled with the bracelet in his pocket, absently slipping it over his wrist. It felt good there. He took a last swallow of the warm sweet liquid and let it drip slowly down the back of his throat. He smiled at Ram. His throat was a tunnel to happiness. He felt better now. The chill was off, so thoroughly that he went over to the cooler and grabbed a lemonade and a bottle of Rolling Rock.

"Put it on my bill," he said to Joey, who was still admiring the plate.

27

A man came out of the bathroom, a man in his thirties, with short, curly black hair, poodle hair, Cuzzy thought, and oddly translucent skin, white with a cast of blue that hinted at a possible map of veins underneath. Though he was tall—well over six feet—his features were delicate and elfin, especially his nose, which was small for his face and ended uphill, not down. He was wearing black jeans, sneakers, and a holey navy and white sweater. A red wool scarf was draped around the back of his neck and shoulders like a stole. Sunglasses sat on top of his head like frog eyes.

"Good morning, Michael," one of the old-timers said to him.

Michael smiled. He had expensive, perfect teeth. "How are you, Gus?" he said. "How's Molly doing? I thought I might see you at church yesterday."

Was this the new minister? Cuzzy looked him over. Did ministers drive Porsches?

"Her sugar was acting up," Gus said. "Had to take her to the doctor's down Halcyon Falls."

"Well, tell her I hope she's feeling better," Michael said, nodding at the other men with a tip of the *New York Times* he was carrying. He took a pint of milk from the cooler and looked for a place to sit. Cuzzy had grabbed the last table when the leaf peepers left, and now Michael was odd man out and holding *The New York Times* to clinch it.

"Mind if I join you?" he asked Cuzzy, who was busy pouring beer into a cup that was half filled with lemonade. "In England that's called a shandy," Michael said, pointing to Cuzzy's drink. "I'm Michael Edwards. My friends call me Tracy."

"Tracy?" Cuzzy asked, looking up.

"Or Tray," he tried.

"Tray. As in cafeteria?"

Tracy laughed.

"Très," he said sitting down, "for three. I'm Michael Edwards the third. And you must be . . . Cinderella?"

"Huh?" Cuzzy asked.

"The bracelet," Tracy said. "I've been looking for the owner."

"Sorry," Cuzzy said sheepishly. "That would be me." His cheeks burned.

Ram leered. "Watch out, Cuzzy, he may be your prince." Now it was Tracy's turn to blush. Ram came over, nudged Cuzzy's shoulder to push him over, and sat himself down.

"Great car," Cuzzy said. "Incredible car."

"Want to take it for a ride sometime?" Tracy asked.

"No shit?"

"None."

Cuzzy eyed him doubtfully. What was the deal? "Do I know you?" he asked quickly, worried that Michael-Tracy-Tray would withdraw the offer.

"Not yet," Tracy said amiably, "though I heard someone call you Cuzzy."

"Yeah," Cuzzy said. "Cuzzy Gage."

"As in *becuz* he's such a loser," Ram said, but no one was listening. The old guys were deep in their game. Squint and Larry were comparing ads in *Soldier of Fortune*; the high school kid, if that was what he was, had left; and Joey was in the stockroom. Tracy, who had spread out the *Times* on the tabletop when he sat down, was absently wiggling the flap on his carton of milk to get it open.

"Nice neck warmer," Ram said to Tracy, pointing at the red scarf. "Did you make it?"

Anyone would know that this was an insult, Cuzzy thought. Anyone but Tracy, who seemed so clueless as to be flattered. "It is nice, isn't it? A friend of mine got it in Ecuador." He pushed a straw into the opening and took a drink.

"Ecuador? Where the fuck is that? New Jersey?"

Tracy laughed so hard that a little milk dribbled out of his mouth and down his chin. He rose to get a napkin. "That is very funny," he said appreciatively to Ram, who was looking at him hard, unsure whether Tracy was making a fool of him or being a fool himself.

"So where *do* you live?" Ram said defensively. He took hold of Cuzzy's beer bottle and played it like a drum.

"Now? Tamarack Road. Up past Whisper Notch." Ram nodded. Everyone knew that address. Tamarack Road was code for the Larches, which itself was short for the Shoreham Estate, seventeen outbuildings and a private hunting lodge tucked into 587 acres of forest, stream, and pond owned by the heirs of Caleb Crown Shoreham, the man who at one time held more prospecting leases and mineral rights in the Southwest and California than anyone else in the country. Even the road was heir to his largesse, paved with tailings from his mines, hauled north in the beds of coal cars.

"You a Shoreham, then?" Ram said. He was trying to seem unimpressed. Cuzzy could see that. But the Shorehams never came to town. *Their people* came to town.

Tracy winced, snorting softly. "Only by association," he said. "Like you."

"I don't know none of them," Ram said dismissively, as if it were by choice.

"I once dropped two ton of gravel on their access road," Cuzzy broke in.

"Exactly," Tracy said, his smile brightening again. "That's exactly the kind of association I try to get my students to make when I teach. When I taught."

"You dropped a load of rocks on the Shorehams', too?" Ram asked, incredulous.

Tracy's single "ha" hiccuped across the table. "Not at all. I'm doing some work up there this fall, that's all."

"Work?" Ram said.

"Work," Tracy said, gathering up the newspaper and folding it neatly into quarters. He stood up and dropped his milk carton into the trash. "It's good to meet you," he said to Ram. "You coming, then?" he said to Cuzzy.

"Is he always so charming?" Tracy asked, when they were on the other side of the door.

"Ram?" Cuzzy asked, surprised. "Oh. I don't know. I guess I'm just used to him."

"Where to?" Tracy asked, when they reached the car.

Cuzzy shrugged. "I'm easy," he said, and for the second time he got in and slid down the car's seat, feeling the leather as a caress.

They circled the town once and were cruising along the river that edged its western flank, heading toward Stover Lake, where Cuzzy went sometimes with Hank—used to go—to pull up sunnies and perch, just for fun. Ducks were overhead, flying in formation, mallards surfing the cool arctic wave that was heading straight, it seemed, for the Gulf of Mexico. Cuzzy couldn't hear them over the growl of the engine, but he imagined their honking and made a wish, like he always did, when he saw any flock in the air on its way to somewhere else. Let this car be mine, he wished, make it mine, and looked sideways at Tracy, who was unaware, talking about how where they were driving reminded him of New Zealand, the south island.

"You live in a beautiful place," Tracy was saying. He'd had acne once. Cuzzy could see it. His skin was cobblestoned, but underneath, as if it had been paved over.

"Yeah," said Cuzzy unenthusiastically. People were always saying that, as if he personally had something to do with it. As if he were the lucky one, blessed with a wealth of bark and leaves, and not the poor suckers from down below, the ones who paid for their finite terms in paradise—last two weeks in August, President's week, July 4—with gold cards and wads of cash.

"Do you mind?" Tracy asked. Not waiting for an answer, he pushed a cassette into the tape player. The machine clicked and whirred, then the oddest music Cuzzy ever heard filled every available space between his body and the car. There were drums, lots of them, and people wailing deeply and people singing so fast it would have been impossible to know what they were saying even if it was in English.

"Ladysmith Black Mambazo," Tracy said, as if this meant something. But he, too, it seemed to Cuzzy, had been reduced to talking nonsense. Smiling and talking nonsense as if he were perfectly understandable, and for a moment Cuzzy thought of his father and then, just as quickly, put him out of his mind.

Two kayakers were bobbing in the water. Both Cuzzy and Tracy saw them, bouncing along a chain of hydraulics called the Crabby Sisters, and Cuzzy was sure they were going to flip, and was going to say so when one of them did—went underwater and rolled and came back upright like a weighted toy.

"That looks cold," Tracy said over the music. "Have you ever done it?"

Cuzzy shook his head, then brushed the hair from his eyes. He'd gone down in an old inner tube once, and in a metal canoe, with Hank and Charlotte and one of Joey's many brothers. And one time on a dare, in nothing but cutoffs and socks. It had been a hot day, and the water was low, and when he got out, the seat of his pants was completely worn away, and his skin there was polished ivory, though later it turned purple and blue.

"We should do it sometime," Tracy said, as if they were friends.

"You can't do it now," Cuzzy said. "You have to wait till the spring, when it's safer. If you're here then." But Tracy didn't answer.

The car started up the long hill to Stover Lake, vibrating at the clutch but taking in the pavement smoothly, climbing with little effort. Cuzzy glanced over at the odometer. Eighty-two. He would have guessed fifty-eight, sixty, at most. There was nothing but trees on either side of the road, even in the abandoned railroad bed where poplars had sprouted between the ties, spindly saplings that were overhung by big old weepy hemlocks and red and yellow pine, old trees that long ago might have sheltered an Iroquois or two. Mountains broke through, rocky islands rising from the green sea, the nearest one a full day's walk. Mountains, trees, and so little sign of human life that it seemed less a foreign country than another sort of place altogether, one that existed independent of borders and boundaries and the notion to draw them in the first place.

Cuzzy was tapping his foot. He looked down and saw it bobbing in his boot, his left one, like it had nothing to do with him, like that other part of his body, which made him smile a self-conscious smile, but happy, too. The music was weird, but he liked it, and he liked how the day had changed, how he had started out walking and now he was in a Porsche—who could have predicted that? He glanced over at Tracy and was surprised to see that he didn't seem to be registering the music at all. Both hands were on the steering wheel, no fingers drumming. His face was serious, especially his eyes, which were squinting, even while his sunglasses perched on his head. For the briefest of seconds, Cuzzy felt something like fear—who was this guy?—but the thought was so small that it passed through his mind before he could dismiss it. The car sailed effortlessly over the pavement, it wasn't even straining, and it was easy to forget he was in a stranger's car because everything out-side was so familiar.

"Have you ever been up north before?" Cuzzy asked, and no-ticed Tracy's right hand start rubbing his thigh as if it were cold. But it wasn't cold. The car was a solar magnet, pulling in the day's brightness and converting it to a warm and spreading heat. Or maybe Cuzzy's heart was doing that: he loved riding around in this car, loved its muscular intimacy, the way it commanded the road.

"A few times," Tracy said, turning down the music. He didn't move his head and spoke in a measured way that abruptly made Cuzzy nervous and more alert. Who was this guy? A guy with a Porsche.

Before he could pursue this thought, something low to the horizon caught on the edge of his vision and pulled it that way.

"Check that out!" Cuzzy said, pointing.

"What?" Tracy tried to follow the line of Cuzzy's finger.

"Loon. At one o'clock. A pair. They came over maybe four feet above the roof. They're not great fliers. They're great swim-mers. Incredibly fast. But they've got to get out of here before everything freezes. They go to Mexico or someplace warm like that. I don't know. Florida, maybe. Over at the ranger's station, they have a white one. They get winter feathers down south."

These were the most words Cuzzy had strung together in Tracy's presence; they were a speech, almost, and their effect seemed to slow the car. Tracy was easing off the gas.

"I don't know anything about that stuff," Tracy said, pulling onto the turnout and stopping the car. "I'm always impressed by people who do."

Cuzzy guessed this was a compliment—at least he felt flattered, even though he didn't entirely want to. It was no big deal, know-ing the woods. He fixed his eyes on Tracy's right hand, the long and oddly colored fingers, red as if he'd been sucking them, and watched Tracy turn off the ignition and pocket the keys. They were maybe a mile or so short of the lake, in the midst of nothing but forest and the long taffy pull of road in front and in back, and *who was this guy.* Normally guys like this didn't worry him at all. They'd order a load of gravel, and when he'd dump it out, they'd stare at it, as if staring might knock it back.

"I won't be long," Tracy said, cracking his door and nodding toward the trees. It took Cuzzy a minute, and then he got it: Tracy had to pee. He was already halfway to the trees. Cuzzy watched him disappear amid a stand of white pine, then turned his attention to the interior of the Porsche, rubbing the tips of his fingers across the polished wooden dash to the glove box, which he popped open. Inside were a pair of leather driving gloves and a flashlight, and under those a photograph of a blue-eyed, black-haired young man, thin, with angular features that Cuzzy thought he vaguely recognized, wearing a green T-shirt, cutoffs, and flip-flops. His hands were cupped together as if they held water, and extended out in front of him like he was making an offering.

Tracy emerged from the trees, still working his zipper, and waved to Cuzzy, who closed the glove box and waited. But Tracy must have heard something—people said there were mountain lions up here, and a few moose—because he turned on the balls of his feet and walked slowly back the way he had come. Cuzzy opened the glove box again and stared at the picture. Something was familiar. He looked at the open hands and was surprised not to have seen them the first time, the two agates resting in the well of the palms. But maybe that was because they looked so much like the man's eyes, as if his hands were merely small reflecting pools. Here, he seemed to be saying, you take them. See what I see.

"You found the picture," Tracy said. He was standing alongside the car, looking at Cuzzy through the passenger-side window. Cuzzy hadn't seen him walk up, hadn't heard his footsteps, and he felt cornered.

"I guess so," he said, only that.

S C H I S T

You want to know how we get from the incontrovertible—from the actual tangible physical world, the world of schist and other metamorphic rocks—to minds that see the rock as something else or not at all. In fact, we don't get there. It is inherent. Schist, schism, and schizophrenia come from the same Greek root, skhistos, *to split.*

Then they drove. Cuzzy was quiet and uneasy, embarrassed to have been caught looking. Tracy was quiet, too, driving with both hands on top of the steering wheel, eyes locked ahead, jaw set. It was a rich man's jaw, Cuzzy thought, all straight lines. Cuzzy turned away. Another perfect stand of aging ash, and then a clear-cut where the forest had been shaved to stubble, a quarter mile of this, too exposed for any wildlife except the crows in the air, which had few places to alight. Then they were past it, to where the trees were still standing, their top leaves tipped red, like matches. Cuzzy thought to point this out, but the car was traveling slower than their silence, which they couldn't seem to catch, and which felt like a crevasse that needed ropes and ladders to cross.

Cuzzy shifted in his seat, feeling the warm shiver of the engine move up his spine. Still, he was chilled, even his feet were chilled, especially the first three toes on his right foot, which had poked through the sock and rubbed against the rough of his boot till they felt numb. Cuzzy concentrated on this little puzzle: if they were numb, how could he feel them? He remembered a verse from Hebrews his father was fond of, that faith was the evidence of things not seen. His father, for whom nothing was unseen except what was completely visible: his wife, for instance, and his son. And what about that son? His toes were numb.

"I'm going to walk," Cuzzy said. He looked over at Tracy, who didn't turn to face him. The speedometer said seventy-two. Then it said seventy-five. He needed to be gone from this man, from this *stranger.* "Walk," Cuzzy said again. "Stop the car." He paused, then said once more, "I'm going to walk," as if explaining his intentions to a child, and this time Tracy aimed for the shoulder, slowing down.

"It's seven miles to Stover," Tracy said. His way of asking Cuzzy not to go. He braked sharply.

Cuzzy clicked the door handle and pushed, swinging his feet to the ground. "Thanks for the ride," he mumbled, as if this had been planned and he was at the place he meant to be.

"Right," Tracy said, and even that one word sounded strained.

Cuzzy unfolded his body from the car and stretched in the open air. There was not a blessed thing around. Nothing he could see, anyhow, except for trees, and so many they might as well not be there. He walked away from the car, hearing first its idling motor, and then, after it faded, the scuff of his boots along the pavement and the words "what the fuck" playing in his head over and over, a backbeat to his footfalls, and then he didn't hear the Porsche at all. He turned, expecting to see it parked where he had left it, a silver coin glinting on the pavement in the sunlight, but it was gone.

Cuzzy picked up speed. There was only one way back, and it was long, and it was cold, and he was hungry. He fingered the caramel in his pocket, rolling the cellophane between his fingers, loosening it. He thought about a guy he'd seen on TV whose car had rolled into a ditch during a snowstorm and was buried under a ton of snow when a plow inadvertently dumped its load on top of it. That guy had survived a week on snowmelt and a box of Milk-Bones. "Do you think he ate them one at a time," Cuzzy asked Crystal when he told her, "or in handfuls?" "Definitely one at a time," she said, as if she knew for sure. "Wouldn't you?"

He didn't know, couldn't say, though he was good at waiting. Waiting was something he could do, was doing, all the time. Waiting for her, and waiting for him, his father, camouflaged like a hunter in a duck blind, where no one could see him.

Food was different. Food was like sex. Cuzzy fingered the caramel. He could taste the buttery lump of sugar on his tongue, feel it melt and stick to the roof of his mouth. Cuzzy guessed it was around ten. The beer and coffee and lemonade in his stomach were no longer there. He wished he had a Milk-Bone. The caramel stayed put. His shoes scraped along the pavement. His mother would complain about this, how he went through shoes, and was appeased briefly when he could step into his father's size ten-and-a-half Herman work boots that stood upright in the mudroom for years like a dog waiting attentively by the door. He didn't want them to fit, but they did, perfectly. One year in his father's shoes, holding his breath, and then, thankfully, his feet grew.

Cuzzy picked up a pinecone from the side of the road and rolled it between his hands as he walked. It was soggy from last week's rain, but its pitch had dried into small white half-moons at the bottom of each scale. From the tight braid of those scales, Cuzzy guessed the cone was spruce; the cones of white pines flared and looked more like women's skirts. Cuzzy crushed the cone and let it trail after him like crumbs. When he was younger, he and Joey used to smoke the crumble because somebody said it would get them high.

Half an hour later and a car was coming, the first one. He heard it behind him, its engine muffled by the distance. A little closer, then closer still, and Cuzzy stuck out his left thumb without even turning around. Hope required too much energy. He'd keep walking—wouldn't give the driver the pleasure of checking him out before pulling away.

The car came closer. Cuzzy stepped more securely onto the shoulder and tensed himself for the backdraft as the car flew by. Instead, it pulled up behind him and rode the shoulder, and then the engine quit. Cuzzy turned, thinking something was wrong—a flat tire, probably—and saw the silver Porsche, and Tracy leaning out the window. "Hop in?" he said, the last word curling up at the end into a question.

Cuzzy didn't want to, but he was practical, and his ears burned from the cold, and he was hungry and at least two hours by foot from his stash. Led by his stomach, Cuzzy walked over and got into the car. "It's fucking cold out there," he said, blowing into his hands. Tracy nodded. Cuzzy thought he might have been crying. His eyes were red, and there was a bloom of tissues in the ashtray.

"Sorry," Tracy said at last. Cuzzy said nothing.

"No, really," Tracy said. "I shouldn't have let you leave."

Cuzzy shrugged. At least they were moving again. Sixty-four miles per hour. Not more than eight minutes till peanut butter and jelly on saltines. He sat still, watching the clock count down the seconds. Tracy cleared his throat, seemed about to speak, and then didn't. He cleared his throat again, opened his mouth, shut it. Cuzzy picked at a thread on his jeans, winding it and unwinding it around his finger, watching the finger turn white at the tip and striped where the string cut into his skin.

"I'm really sorry," Tracy said at last. "You probably think I'm crazy."

"No," Cuzzy lied, shaking his head and the curtain of hair around his face, which moved as one piece.

Tracy took a deep, audible breath. Cuzzy sank down into the seat again and looked hard out the window. A Ryder truck was lumbering up the other side of the road, and then a postal delivery truck, and then nothing. If Cuzzy squinted, he could make out a turn in the river, the top of the "S" running mackerel gray and disappearing, as if it had gone down a drain. Revelation made him squirm. Those baptismal Sundays with his father, a different stretch of this very river; clothes stuck to the skin, the skin shining through. He didn't want to see, to hear. Didn't care. He was curious—yes—but indifferent. Whatever Tracy had to say was none of his fucking business. He was hungry.

". . . my best friend," Cuzzy heard. Tracy was talking about the man in the photograph. ". . . inseparable in a way, even though he traveled so much." Cuzzy did not think he needed to hear this. "But that's the thing about death, isn't it. It's the Great Separator." Tracy turned to Cuzzy, who was turned away, looking out the window. "That's something people your age don't know yet. That death lasts forever."

But Cuzzy knew. Of course he knew. They went past the sign for the public boat launch. He knew, but why say so? Tracy was still talking away, like all-news radio, perfect reception but on in the background, where it was just noise. "Bailed out before the wedding. Left my job. Literary executor. Beneficiary." Crystal would do that, too, talk and talk about this or that, and it got so Cuzzy could look at her and see her mouth moving and hear, instead of her voice, his own groaning desire.

". . . got his Porsche."

Cuzzy perked up, tuned back in.

"In his will to me," Tracy said.

"He gave you his car?" Cuzzy cut in. "You didn't have to buy it? He just gave it to you?"

"You make it sound so easy," Tracy said, and then he said no more. They sat in silence again, Tracy lost in thought, Cuzzy confused, even angered, by Tracy's sudden withdrawal.

"Fuck," he said under his breath.

"What?" Tracy said. His voice was oddly diffuse.

"Nothing," Cuzzy said. His stomach growled. He guessed it was a mile to the town beach. His stomach growled again.

"Omelettes!" Tracy said loudly, a manic edge lacing his voice. "Let's get omelettes. They'll have omelettes at the Gotham, won't they?" He turned sharply off the county road onto Main Street at the last possible moment, so that the tires squealed and tipped up before falling back to earth with a quick bounce.

Main Street was three blocks long, long enough for a pharmacy, a liquor store, the Grand Union, the lawyer's office next to the jail, two clapboard churches and one made out of stone, the Gotham, and the hardware store. The other buildings were boarded up: the old train station and the movie theater and the butcher shop and the bakery. Not enough people for all that commerce. There used to be more—people and commerce—back when the forests were virgin and mills and tanneries lined the shore of the river and its tributaries, back when there was more work than could be done in a day, more even than in a lifetime of hauling logs and driving them downstream or stripping bark or milling lumber or curing hides. More work and more people and more life to this little town than anyone, a century later, would ever see here.

"Damn," Tracy said, pulling up to the diner. The OPEN sign was off, and a piece of paper was taped haphazardly to the window. GONE HUNTING, it said.

"It's closed," Tracy said. "And it's not even hunting season."

"Turkey," Cuzzy said. "I think it's turkey season. Or maybe it's bear-dog season or muzzle-loading season." He was disappointed. That omelette had sounded better than he could say.

"We'll have to go to my place," Tracy said, flooring the clutch. "I've got eggs."

As he put the car in gear, a thin, chinless man with gold wire glasses leaned over the curb and gave a thumbs-up, smiling broadly. He was looking at Tracy, who smiled weakly. It was Jason Trimble.

"I hate that guy," Cuzzy said when they were in motion again.

"Isn't 'hate' a strong word?" Tracy said.

"Now you sound just like him," Cuzzy said, pouting. He picked at the thread of his jeans. He did hate Trimble. The guy was always on his case, suggesting they do stuff. As if Cuzzy really wanted to hang out with Jason Trimble.

They were out of town in minutes, on the other side of the county road and heading up the mountain. Macadam turned to dirt, and the Porsche clattered over bright loose stones, kicking them up like a trail horse. Cuzzy had been this way before; he had been here the day he met Crystal. A sign—maroon with gold lettering—said ENTERING WHISPER NOTCH, AN EXCLUSIVE PRESERVE, and when they had passed it, they were in a different place. In here the trees were so old, their trunks so thick and the branches so broad, that even shorn of leaves, they made the sky seem impossibly far. There were houses tucked in here somewhere, the mailboxes and driveways hinted at that. But these were like kite strings on a windy day, the thinnest wisp of evidence.

"Deer," Tracy called, and sure enough, Cuzzy saw a buck crash into the understory, and then another came leaping across the road, and then another, like overgrown rabbits. Only a few weeks of freedom left, Cuzzy thought, and then the woods would be crawling with guys in blaze orange, though not these particular woods, which were posted. A stone wall ran low to the ground, corralling part of the forest as if it could be broken and tamed. There had been farms here long ago. Even now Cuzzy would walk through the woods and come upon old house foundations covered with weeds, or trip over tin cans that had rusted to filigree, a whole pile of them, or chimneys rising from hearths that themselves rose from bare dirt. Lost civilizations, he used to think, imagining the pioneers who had beaten back the forest by hand—had tamed it—taking down trees and pulling up stumps and rocks as though they were weeds. All this until they had made pasture, made it themselves where it had never been. Success was measured by attrition, by how many trees were gone, by how empty the land was.

Cuzzy's own ancestors, his mother's side, had done this, pushing back the forest as if it were the sea, pushing and pushing against the tidal force of gravity and new growth, clearing the land only to find the soil thin and alkaline and at best a begrudging home to the seeds they had carried with them across the ocean. They tilled the earth, and the earth yielded boulders. It broke their plows. It gave them roots. The roots tripped them up. They couldn't work hard enough. All around them the forest was constantly returning to its metabolic set point. Three generations later, and this was what was left to show that people had been here, had made their lives here: a mossy necklace of flat stones, intentionally laid, the occasional slag of rotted cans, and a road that once went somewhere.

As a boy, Cuzzy liked these best. He'd follow one as far as it would go, deep into the woods. The paths started out wide enough for a horse-drawn wagon and were still rutted where the weight of those wheels had laid down their lasting impression. Before long the path would narrow, as if the intentions of the road builder, while good, had grown more realistic and practical. The road would be just wide enough, which was hardly wide at all, and then it would peter out altogether. It would end as if it had never been there, as if someone had had the idea—"road"—and then thought better of it.

When he was younger, Cuzzy had assumed that this was where the house had been. At the end of the road. He'd dig through the weeds looking for signs—brass doorknobs that couldn't possibly decay, or shards of crockery, and wouldn't find them. Then he'd backtrack, taking the path to where it made its widest gesture to the land, and often he'd discover something there, some small acknowledgment of a time before. This was where the house had been, where lives were lived. He would imagine those people on that very spot a hundred years earlier—women with thick ankles and plaited hair and sour expressions, and their pock-faced men. It was always the same for Cuzzy. No matter which road he followed in, whether it was hung over by birch or maple, whether he saw hop vines tangled in the branches or neat rows of stone underscoring the tree trunks, it was always the same. The people were long-suffering and tired. And they were ignorant, yet, that the future had no room for them. Nature would reassert itself: the trees would grow back. The experience of those people would be mulched to obscurity.

Cuzzy knew the lineage. His own great-great-grandparents were recruited from Ireland to tend a patch of scree like this. His great-grandparents, born to the land, a team of oxen, and a sickly Brown Swiss. His grandparents and their siblings, more ambitious in their way—unwilling to scratch out a living from the land, they moved to town, where they were still poor but no longer exactly, precisely, *dirt* poor.

"We're getting close," Tracy said, then laughed. "Relatively speaking. The road in is a good three miles."

45

They came to a substantial wooden gate—cedar, it looked like—into which THE LARCHES had been carved and painted black in relief. Tracy slowed, and Cuzzy opened his door, intending to jump out and get the gate, but Tracy called him back.

"Electric," he explained, punching numbers into a small keypad built into a post they were idling beside. The gate sailed open, and they rolled through. Tracy checked the rearview mirror to make sure it swung shut again. "Good," he said when it had and they were safely tucked into the property. But Cuzzy was uneasy.

Around the next turn, and both men saw that a silver aspen had come down and was blocking part of the road. Again Cuzzy seized the door handle, ready to jump out and move it, but Tracy didn't stop the car, he skirted around the tree instead, the top branches slapping successively across the side of the car door like baseball cards clothespinned to bicycle spokes.

"Gus'll get that," Tracy said in an offhand way, as if Cuzzy of course knew who Gus was, and then he realized that yes, indeed, he did. Gus Meacham, from the Nice n Easy. The one whose wife was having trouble with her sugar.

"Isn't he like eighty?" Cuzzy said.

"You've got to let a man do his job," Tracy said, as if it were a benevolent act, letting Gus take his chain saw to the tree. "He's seventy-three," he added. Then he looked up. "What's that red bird?"

Cuzzy didn't see it. "Tanager, probably," he said. "Must be on its way out of here."

At the next turn in the road, the steepness leveled out, and it felt to Cuzzy like they were getting somewhere. Tracy pointed out Gus's "cottage," a three-car garage with an apartment overhead and a yellow backhoe, its snowplow at the ready, parked out front. That was a Labor Day tradition—take the docks out of the water one day and put the snowblade on the next, and it was not unheard of for snow to fall the night in between. Next to the cottage was a small pond that was stocked each spring with brown trout and brookies. Tracy said it was almost impossible not to catch one.

"You should come up here whenever you want and fish," he told Cuzzy. "No one would mind."

"You have to know the code," Cuzzy said.

"Oh, I don't know," Tracy said. "Fly-fishing's an art, but it's not really a code. You have to think like a fish, you have to know what's going to make them jump. I don't know. I'm not very good at it. But maybe that's it. Maybe I don't know the code, either."

Was he being serious? Sarcastic? Cuzzy couldn't tell. "The gate," Cuzzy said. "You have to know the code to get in the gate."

"It's unlocked most of the time," Tracy said, looking disappointed. He had been serious, Cuzzy decided.

The house rattled him, the way it appeared in the woods as if hidden among the trees, three stories of leaded glass and massive blocks of schist that seemed to balance one atop the other like the most accomplished gymnasts. It was not only the biggest house Cuzzy had ever seen in his life (not counting the ones on *Lifestyles of the Rich and Famous* and *Dallas*, which he watched sometimes with Crystal, who was faithful even to the reruns), it was the most beautiful. No building had ever brought him up short the way a girl might. This one was stunning, especially the windows, which were set at acute angles and caught the light like prisms. Even the stepped roofline and the copper gutters, green with age, disarmed him. And the weathervane, a big, shaggy conifer, that was cut from copper, too.

"We're here," Tracy said, though it was obvious.

Cuzzy nodded. He was thinking about Crystal and her lottery game, and how it was hard for him to know what he'd wanted before he had seen it.

"Did he give you this, too?" Cuzzy asked, looking up at the Larches the way he remembered looking up his teacher's skirt when he was in kindergarten, lying on his mat during nap time as she'd tiptoed among them, making sure they were all asleep. She'd stand over him, looking the other way, and he'd catch a glimpse of her slip and the inside of her calves, and wonder that her head seemed so remarkably small and faraway, and that he, too, felt so small in proportion to her. It was that smallness he was feeling now in relation to this big house.

"No one gave it to me," Tracy said. "It's not mine. I stay out back, in the guest house."

They were approaching the building, walking along a hop-scotch of flagstones patrolled on either side by massive tamaracks, yellowed and tousled, like large, unkempt dogs. Cuzzy trailed a few steps behind Tracy, who was taking the stones two at a time. God, Crystal's going to be jealous, he thought, not unhappily. So he didn't have a job or a plan—he had the Larches. Okay, it was an exaggeration, he knew it was, but he knew, too, that she wouldn't see it that way. Just getting through the gate would do it for her. Touched by greatness, she'd say.

"I'm putting together his archive," Tracy said, his head turned slightly over his shoulder to speak to Cuzzy, who looked back at him blankly.

"Sorry," Tracy said. "His. Algie's. My friend. From the picture. This is his family's house."

Still, that hardly clarified things for Cuzzy, who was unacquainted with the concept of either papers or archives. There was no library in Stover, and Cuzzy had been in the one at Halcyon Falls only five or six times, on school trips. He was confused by the name, too, which he had thought meant "pond scum," but guessed, in this case, it did not.

"He was an ethnomusicologist," Tracy continued. "He traveled to incredibly exotic foreign places and studied the music there and collected instruments and made a lot of recordings. His specialty was initiation rituals. You know, like Native American vision quests or Apache sunrise ceremonies."

No, Cuzzy didn't know but didn't say.

Tracy opened the carved oak front door—more buttons and codes—and pushed into the house. It was dark inside, yet even before Tracy flipped the light switch, Cuzzy could make out deer and moose heads lining the walls. Lights on, he saw a full-size black bear, wearing a floppy rain hat, and a cub on all fours next to her, grimacing fiercely.

"The big one is called Teddy," Tracy said as they admired her. "Not for the obvious reason, but because Old Man Shoreham was with Teddy Roosevelt when he shot him. The bear, not TR. This was before he became president."

Cuzzy listened but was looking everywhere else: at the chandelier, which had actual candles in it, at the mullioned gun cabinet stocked with an arsenal of antique weapons, at the massive oil paintings on the wall. The place was a museum. "People live here?" he asked.

"Not anymore," Tracy said. "Christmas. Summer. The family's pretty scattered. Algie liked to come up during hunting season for the colors."

"Like now," Cuzzy said, though the leaves were coming down fast. Outside, framed in the distance, the branches of birch trees, balding in the wind, looked soft, like dandelions gone to seed.

"Oh, you're right," Tracy said brightly, as if it hadn't occurred to him before. Cuzzy stepped up to a portrait of Old Man Shoreham. He saw that the man had a cowl of fat under his chin, which rested on a pair of hairy jowls, and hooded reptilian eyes.

"It killed him," Tracy said, pointing to the rings of fat around Shoreham's neck. "Turns out there was a goiter under there that no one could see."

The next portrait, Tracy said, was Shoreham's daughter, Augusta, a handsome woman with narrow green eyes and rolling blond hair topped by a garland of daisies. She was wearing an emerald-green evening gown that matched the color of her eyes, and what Cuzzy at first thought to be a gold belt was actually a gold chain on which a scabbard hung, cinching the dress at the waist.

"Amazing hunter," Tracy said when he noticed what had caught Cuzzy's eye. "Didn't believe in guns—said they gave humans an unfair advantage. So she studied tracking with a real Indian her daddy found for her in a jail out west and brought back here and set up as a guide. Till she killed him."

"Till she killed him?" Cuzzy repeated.

"Yeah. Isn't that wild? Said she thought he was a cougar. Apparently it's late at night, and she hears this noise outside her tent and rushes out, knife first, and the blade pierces his carotid artery. In the morning, after he'd bled to death, she drags him out of the woods about three miles down the trail, and when she can't go any farther—he was a big man—she field-dresses the guy."

"Jesus," Cuzzy said. "What did they do to her?"

"Not a thing. Think about it. It was her word against his, and he was dead. Later that year she had a baby, and not long after that, she walked out of the house one day and disappeared."

"What about the baby?" Cuzzy asked.

"Algie's father," Tracy explained. "James Blackfoot Shoreham. It should have been Shoreham Blackfoot—that's what the birth certificate said, but when Augusta took off, the old man turned the name around to suit himself. After he died, Algie changed it back and dropped the 'foot.' Later, when there was all this Native American pride going on, he thought about using it again but said he didn't feel comfortable. He was kind of like his grandmother. Said it was inauthentic."

"What about Algie's father?"

"James?" Tracy smiled and shook his head. "He was really into horseshoes."

"Horseshoes?"

"Yeah. He was obsessed with them. He had this theory that the sport was a direct descendant of discus throwing, and therefore it should be an Olympic sport. He basically dedicated his life to petitioning the Olympic committee, writing memos and letters and reports about it. He wrote the definitive history of horseshoes, not that it got published, and collected old horseshoes from around the world. He wanted to start a museum, which is why there are so many horseshoes and these things that sort of look like horseshoes and sort of look like miniature discuses all over this house and the cottage. They're called quoits. You can't miss them. He was sort of a nut, but that's where Algie's collecting gene must have come from."

Cuzzy looked around. He did see them hanging off the walls, like hoofprints on the wallpaper: dull silver horseshoes of various sizes, and round flat doughnuts of metal, blackened with age, that he figured must be the quoits.

"That's how he died," Tracy added.

"Playing horseshoes?"

"Oh no, he didn't play," Tracy said. "He went over to judge a contest in England—he was the trig man, the person who looks for foot faults—and he caught a cold that turned to bronchitis and then to pneumonia, and he got stuck in one of those National Health hospitals, and after that no one knows what happened. He just got sicker and sicker, and then he died."

Cuzzy looked around for a place to sit. There wasn't one, except for the high-backed carved dining room chairs that reminded him of the chess set Reverend Trimble kept in the parsonage as part of his scheme to improve their small, inbred lives. The dining room, where they were, was long and narrow, like a crypt, with a vaulted ceiling crisscrossed by thick, dark beams. The ceiling was high, the room drafty. Cuzzy could imagine animals living there—bats hanging from the eaves, or a red fox staking out a corner of the walk-in ceramic fireplace, which was large enough to fit a double bed. Maybe it was the absolute absence of people, maybe it was how deep in the forest they were, but the house, substantial as it was, seemed hardly able to keep out the outside.

"Come look at the pool room," Tracy said, leading Cuzzy into a room so big and deep that it swallowed the Steinway concert grand that sat in the center and spat it out like baleen. There were instruments everywhere. Guitars that didn't look quite like guitars but more like cellos. Panpipes the height of small men. Flutes carved from bone. Conga drums. Violins, or something like violins, with two and three strings.

"Algie brought these back," Tracy explained. "These are bombos from Ecuador." He ran his hand around the side of the drum. "This is a wancara—a drum from Bolivia. This is a transverse flute that comes from the Andes. And check this out." He pointed to a stringed instrument in the shape of a horse. "It's a morin huur from Mongolia."

"This place is weird," Cuzzy said, taking it all in. What he meant was that the house felt empty as well as more than a little haunted by other lives.

"I used to think so, too," Tracy said. "I guess I've gotten used to it. I read somewhere that humans were the most adaptive creatures on the planet."

Cuzzy shook his head. Still, he was the one who called a sleeping bag and the sand beneath it home.

COPPER

This was the first metal used by humans (The Matter of Anthropology, Pransky and Price). We used it to make tools. That was how we defined ourselves: the animal that makes tools. That was how we helped ourselves become what we are. We made tools, we shared tools. There appear to be many motivations for making and sharing: mutual aid, fear, altruism, ability, creativity, goodness, cunning. Do not be fooled. *The engine of civilization is, and always has been, death.*

"'This is the saddest story ever told,'" Tracy said. He was facing the stove, tilting a frying pan right to left as if playing pinball. Smoke rose off the surface like ground fog, enveloping his head, then clearing. When the butter was melted, he rested the pan on the burner and reached to the refrigerator and began pulling things out of it—eggs, cheddar cheese, onions, a jar of something Cuzzy couldn't make out, milk, paprika. Under Tracy's sweater, his muscles moved purposefully. Cuzzy thought they looked like small, burrowing animals.

"That's a quote from Ford Madox Ford," Tracy said. "Algie liked to say it a lot. He thought it was funny. Like anything could be the *saddest* story. Though, ironically enough, his turned out to be. Not that he knew it."

Tracy was chopping onions and sniffling. Maybe he was crying. Cuzzy couldn't see and didn't care. He was hungry, and he was thinking about Crystal. How he could call her up and say, "Boy, do I have something to tell you," and she wouldn't be able to hang up.

Tracy pushed the onions into the pan, where they sizzled, releasing a sweet and woody scent. His back was still turned. He cracked an egg into a bowl, and then another, six altogether, and began to turn them with a wire whisk. Cuzzy watched attentively, like a dog under the table, and though Tracy couldn't see him, he must have felt the wanting eyes, because he said, "There's toast." Not "Would you like some toast?" or "We could have toast" but a simple, unambiguous, declarative sentence for which Cuzzy was grateful.

Cuzzy stood up immediately, nearly banging his head on one of the cast-iron skillets hanging from a ceiling rack like charms on an oversize bracelet. He stepped back and just missed knocking a quoit from the wall. It was a small room. One step across the pine planking that someone painted gray long ago, and then another, and then, blessedly, food. He fished out three pieces of bread and dropped two into the toaster. He squeezed the third in his hand and surreptitiously jammed the whole thing into his mouth. He swallowed so fast, it hurt going down. He was sure he could feel it expand in his stomach like a sponge. Then the toast popped up a perfect caramel brown, its yeast released like pollen to the air, and he breathed deep and swallowed that, too.

"Done!" Tracy said, turning to Cuzzy and showing off the contents of the pan. Could three eggs folded like a letter be beautiful? Cuzzy, who had never thought so before, was sure of it. Tracy tipped the pan and delivered one omelette to one plate and one to the other, motioning for Cuzzy to deal out the toast.

There were piles of books on the table—*A Century of Ethnomusicological Thought* and *The Ethnomusicologist* and *Musicologic Notation*—that Tracy pushed aside to make room for the two of them. He laid out straw place mats and napkins and cutlery heavier than any Cuzzy had ever held between his fingers. Fork and knife felt awkward in his hands, the way his father's old dovetail saw did, except the saw was so small, it was his hands that were unwieldy. Remembering that, Cuzzy cut into the omelette like it was soft wood, and the loose belly of melted cheese ran over his plate.

The first bite was so good, he was reluctant to let it down his throat. But then there was another bite, and another, and he consumed each one as deliberately as the first, sweeping his tongue around his mouth, urging it into the salted folds, which reminded him of, he couldn't help it, the most private parts of Crystal and Amber-Rose. Tracy, too, was eating as if he were alone, looking down at his food, saying nothing. All of his exuberance was gone, and he seemed tired.

What is the saddest story ever told? Cuzzy wanted to ask but didn't, because he didn't know how. With the guys he knew there was always something to talk about—Joey had all the gossip, Ram was good for girls, and Cuzzy could never get his cousin Hank to shut up once he got started in on welfare cheats and tax fraud. People like Tracy, he guessed, were different. He guessed they guessed you and they knew so much already, why waste breath. Like who was Ford Madox Ford, anyway?

"It's snowing," Tracy said after a while. "I saw a couple of flakes." Cuzzy turned and looked out the window. As far as he could see, there wasn't any snow. The sky, though cloudy, was clear.

"Dander," Cuzzy said. It fell out of his mouth, and he couldn't take it back.

Tracy looked at him quizzically.

"My father used to say that God's dander was up when it snowed," Cuzzy explained. He never talked about his father, not on purpose, so he was surprised at how readily those words—"my father"—slid out of his mouth. Cuzzy was usually so vigilant. It was like the tree in the forest: if he didn't talk about Leo Gage, did he still exist? But Tracy was a stranger—maybe that was it. Tracy didn't know Leo Gage, his history; he could assume Cuzzy's father was as normal as everyone else's. What Cuzzy wanted.

"My dad would say 'snow,'" Tracy told him. "He didn't believe in metaphor. Snow was *snow*. Snow was ice crystals formed directly from water vapor when the temperature was below freezing. But it could get too cold to snow. He liked to tell us that, too, as if it had significance. You know, as if that was wisdom itself."

"What did he say about rain?" Cuzzy asked.

"Rain? That's easy. Water falling in drops condensed from drops in the atmosphere. If a drop is less than two tenths of a millimeter, it is called drizzle."

Cuzzy laughed. "I guess he liked facts," he said.

"You'd think so," Tracy said. "You'd think that was a good enough reason to like his kids."

"What was?" Cuzzy asked.

"Oh, I don't know," Tracy said. "The fact of four of us. The fact that we are made up mainly of water. The fact that we have tendons and bones, which are made up of their own facts.

"Basically he's one of those guys people admire but don't especially like. He doesn't even try to be nice. He always called Algie 'your friend the fag,' and it didn't do any good to ask him not to, since it was true. A fact. Unimpeachable."

Cuzzy took it as a sucker punch right between his ribs. He felt the adrenaline charge through his veins, rushing through his heart and lungs and out to his fingers and toes like a hook-and-ladder company responding to an alarm; he was sure that this was a setup: the car ride, the food, the house in the woods where no one could find him. He had heard about things like this. A guy lured another guy someplace and did things to him. The adrenaline was in his head, in his ears.

"It's not what you think," Tracy said, sensing Cuzzy's discomfort. "We weren't lovers."

The word rattled him. "Lovers." It was too graphic, even modified by "weren't." What was that? Two guys getting it on with a slash through what they were doing.

"He was my best friend. We met in high school." Tracy laughed, but to himself. "At Boys' Congress, of all places."

Cuzzy nervously pushed the crumbs around his plate with his finger. He felt disoriented, sort of dizzy, no longer in immediate danger but not out of it, either. What kind of place was this Boys' Congress?

It had been Tracy's teacher's idea for him to attend. She was the one who wrote the letter nominating him, calling Tracy "a most judicious young man whose eagerness to consider every side of the issue is exceeded only by his zealous commitment to fairness, a boy of earnest goodwill." Still, even she was surprised when he came back from the state capital with the grand prize, a trip to the national Boys' Congress in Washington the following month as one of the two "senators" from the state of Pennsylvania. An official "election" letter the following week told him that the "senator" from Maryland, Algernon S. Black, was to be his roommate.

Algie was already in the room when Tracy got there, and though it was for only a week, he had taped a poster of Nina Simone to the wall above his bed, and plugged in a Lava lamp, and was listening to Brian Eno on a cassette. Tracy felt like he was intruding.

"Oh, great!" Algie said when Tracy walked through the door. "I've been waiting for you."

Algie was an enthusiast. That was the first thing anyone noticed about him, how enthusiastic, how curious, he was. Tracy, who still mumbled when he was feeling shy, was disarmed.

"Unpack your stuff and let's go to Georgetown. There's this great record store there."

"Is that allowed?" Tracy asked.

"It isn't not allowed, if that's what you mean," Algie said.

Another lawyer, Tracy thought. Half the boys at Boys' Congress, the joke went, were planning legal careers, and the others were planning to sue them.

Tracy still had pictures from that week—boys in suits and ties, or with their jackets off and sleeves rolled up, huddled around conference tables; boys lined up behind a podium, fanning themselves with index cards; boys on the floor of the real Senate, shaking hands with real senators; boys in the Rose Garden, drinking iced tea. Algie was in these pictures, but no more or less than anyone else. Back home, Tracy looked for evidence that their friendship was more, that it was different, but he could not see it.

This, Tracy decided, was because it grew at night, in the dark, in their stifling dorm room. It was too hot to sleep, and they'd lie in their separate beds on top of the sheets, gratefully anticipating each lukewarm breath of air across their sweating chests as the fan huffed left, then right, then left again, and they would talk. They talked about the writers they admired—Jack London, Ernest Hemingway, Mark Twain; and the books they had, until then, been sure no one else knew about, like *Siddhartha* and *The Stranger*. Tracy suggested that now that William Faulkner was dead, J. D. Salinger might be the single greatest living American author; he thought so, at least. But Algie said he was suspicious of Salinger, that Salinger might be the biggest phony of all time—it was a feeling he got from reading *Nine Stories.* Tracy loved *Nine Stories,* and he thought Algie was being cavalier. "You don't always want me to agree with you, do you, Très?" Algie said, and Tracy said he guessed not, even though, in fact, he did.

They talked music and poetry, too, as if music and poetry mattered, as if they were all that mattered. They talked about Dada and de Stijl. They talked about Woody Allen and James Agee. Words, words, words—they all went into the dark. In other rooms, other boys were talking about sex, how it was done, how they were going to do it. In Algie and Tracy's room, the world itself was erogenous, and the mind was aching to mount it. Night after night, talking, till the ellipsis of someone's breathing, regular and soft, intervened.

In the morning they put on their suits and riffled the papers in their briefcases to make sure they were all in order, then walked out the door looking like the men in pinstripes and seersucker filling up the sidewalks of the District of Columbia at that hour, only younger. The conversations of the evening were left behind with the bedclothes, though for Tracy, who had been assigned to the working group on interstate commerce and spent the days drafting legislation to regulate articulated truck hauling, they stayed in his mind. Through endless debates on axle construction and container size, through dissertations on infrastructure and bearing weight, Tracy remembered what Algie said about Billie Holliday ("You have to accept that the drugs are part of her greatness") and whether Rainer Maria Rilke was right about literary criticism (ignore it), and whether he had time to go to the bookstore and buy Algie *Letters to a Young Poet* and what Algie would say about it if he did.

When the week ended, with Tracy being drafted secretary of commerce and Algie declaring to the assembled that he would not seek another term so he could devote more time to his family and finish the novel he had shoved in his desk drawer twenty years before (he was then seventeen), they promised to write, and they did. Tracy wrote almost every day, trying to keep the conversation going in his head, if not on paper. Algie did not try to match him. He fielded a few letters, then wrote back in his considered architectural hand, using a Rapidograph with the finest of points. He sent *New Yorker* cartoons and quirky items from the newspaper that fell out of the envelope like confetti. He wrote, "Tell me, what was the fuss about Andy Warhol—give me Rembrandt any day," and Tracy would take him literally, and go to the library, and look things up, and compose a response.

Tracy would also comment on the state of their friendship—how wonderful, how much of a relief, it was to have someone in his life who cared about the things he cared about. And Algie would say yes, a relief, and quote Aristotle (he was thinking of going to a college that specialized in the classics) and sometimes Emerson (a concession, since Emerson was, in the opinion of that college, a modern): "I can get politics and chat from cheaper companions. Should not the society of my friend be to me poetic, pure, universal, and great as nature itself?" They decided to meet in New York in December, under the clock in Grand Central Terminal, Algie's feelings about Salinger not withstanding.

It was a cold night in New York City. They walked around awhile, impervious, talking about school and books and music and politics. They were happy. "You two are looking good," a homeless man said as they passed him talking loudly about D. H. Lawrence. Algie stopped and gave him a dollar, and the man said, "You take care of your friend," and Tracy thought, Yes, it's true. They walked to the East Village, stopping to buy each other books on St. Mark's Place, and tapes from a man who had set up shop on the sidewalk, laying out his merchandise on an old army blanket. They were two minds intersecting. They were Carlyle and Emerson, Fitzgerald and Hemingway, Johnson and Boswell. No, not Boswell, Tracy decided. Boswell was a jerk, even if he did write a famous book.

"Let's go to Washington Square Park," Algie said, and crossing over there, they were both surprised to find, at that late hour—it was after ten—a crowd of people gathered around four extremely

tall men beating on steel drums. THE TRINIDAD AND TOBAGO MARCH-
ING BAND, their sign said.

"I love this," Algie said, taking a seat on a bench. At the other
end was a girl with three earrings in her left ear and a joint between
her teeth. Tracy sat down, too, and the three of them shared the
bench and the smoke and the music. It was a fat joint that kept going out, and every time it did, the girl put the whole thing in her
mouth, then drew it out slowly, to get it wet. Algie didn't notice,
but Tracy did. He thought it was exquisite. He studied how she
clamped her mouth around it dry, and how it would come out
dampest where it rode her tongue. He imagined he was the joint
and that she was smoking him right there, in the cold, on that
bench, with all those people. He was high, and he was happy. He
was grinning foolishly, and his grin was like a cockeyed hat. He was
happy. He was high. He was with his best friend in a park in the
middle of the night listening to music, and a girl with a sexy mouth
was sitting next to him. He wanted to say something to her but
couldn't think what. And then she got up and drifted away without a word, disappearing into a fold of darkness.

Tracy could not remember how long it was after that. The
band was playing up-tempo Christmas carols, "God Rest Ye Merry
Gentlemen" in five-eight time. Tracy shut his eyes so he could let
those sounds enter him through his skin. Algie asked if he was cold,
and he did not even open them to answer. "What is cold?" he asked
dreamily.

That much he could recall: the feeling of it more than the de-
tails or the chronology. He knew they played, "Hark! The Herald
Angels Sing," but he couldn't remember if that was before "We
Three Kings" and after "Silent Night" or the other way around.
His heart was light. He was with his friend. They were having an
adventure. Algie leaned over and explained how he had seen men
in the Caribbean hammering steel drums out of old oil cans. In

that light, Algie's eyes were the color of the sky before the sun. He told Tracy that they could tune the drums in different keys depending on where they hammered. His hair fell across his forehead. His lashes were long. He said that technically they were not called drums, they were called pans. "I love it," Tracy said. Algie smiled at him. He had a playful, winning smile.

"Wouldn't it be great?" Algie said a little later, when the musicians were packing up and the crowd was receding like a tide, taking the two boys with it.

The tense was wrong, Tracy thought. It *is* great. "What?" he said.

"To live here. In that building over there"—he pointed to a plain brick building. "For us to go to NYU and live there and come to the park whenever we wanted." This was pure fantasy. Algie had already heard from the college in New Mexico.

"Yeah," said Tracy. "It would be amazing." Maybe he'd go to school here himself, and Algie could visit.

They were walking along Washington Square West, going nowhere in particular. The sky was purple, the way it often is at night in a city before it snows. They stopped so Tracy could tie his shoe, and when he stood up, Algie reached out and put a mittened hand on the back of Tracy's neck and drew him in. They were exactly the same height, and standing on the sidewalk, eye to eye, not six inches apart. Tracy felt Algie's breath on his cheeks. It was a warm current, parting left, parting right, over the bridge of his nose, as if his face were an island. A fire truck turning the corner threw red light on the wall above their heads, taking Algie's eyes with it. Tracy stepped out of Algie's grip and started walking down the street again.

"I wonder where the fire is," he said. But he knew: Algie had wanted to kiss him.

"So," Tracy said, turning to Cuzzy, his voice full of false cheer, "I've told you my secret. What's yours?"

Cuzzy felt a blush pepper his face. What, exactly, was Tracy's secret? "Me?" he said.

Tracy nodded.

Cuzzy shrugged. It wasn't that he didn't have secrets. He didn't live anywhere and he had a crazy father, for starters. His feet curled in their boots, getting ready to stand and grip the floor, but when Tracy spoke again, the toes went flat, as if they'd been ordered to lie down.

"Jason Trimble says you have a son," Tracy said, and Cuzzy lifted his eyes and looked at him hard. How did he know this? What was he doing, talking to Trimble about him before they'd even met?

"I don't get it," Cuzzy said. "Why would Trimble tell you . . ."

"He's concerned about you, Cuzzy," Tracy said. "That's all."

"So this whole thing is a setup," Cuzzy said. It was a different kind than he'd thought at first, but it was a setup all the same.

"A setup?"

"Trimble put you up to it."

"Trimble put me up to what?" Tracy said. He was standing very still, like a hunter in the woods who knows that any stray movement, even an eager heart, may be startling. "He didn't put me up to anything, Cuzzy."

Cuzzy's skin tightened on its frame. Was he supposed to believe that? He wasn't an idiot. Why were they talking about him—whose business was that? But it was a small town. People talked. He knew that.

"His name is Harry," Cuzzy said after a long pause. "The baby." Here was another fact, offered neutrally, like an item on an inventory. And when it came right down to it, what more was that little boy to him?

It wasn't that Cuzzy didn't think about him. Harry was like the North Pole or Orion's Belt or even New York City—Cuzzy knew he was there, and he knew the boy shaped his own world, but he couldn't say exactly how. It occurred to him that maybe Crystal was testing him by keeping him away, but if this was a test, he had no idea how to pass it. Should he leave her and Harry alone, like she asked, or not? He didn't have a clue, and he wasn't sure it mattered. Just because Crystal was a mystery to him, did that mean he had to solve her?

He thought he heard Tracy say something, and looked up, surprised to see him walking over. Cuzzy tensed, waiting for Tracy to put his hand on his shoulder or pat his back, but Tracy passed like a light breeze and went to the refrigerator to extract a quart of milk.

"I'm making latte. Want one?"

"I've got to go," Cuzzy said. He had never heard that word, "latte," but guessed it was gay for coffee. He took his coffee black, with sugar—nothing faggy about that. He wanted to leave, to get back to the beach, to stretch out in his sleeping bag and do some girl, it didn't much matter who.

"It's freezing out," Tracy said, but he wasn't arguing. "You might as well have one of these before you go."

Cuzzy stayed seated, resigned to this one last thing, unable to stop the slide show that came into his mind—unable because he didn't want to—images of Crystal, every part of her, every which way. Tracy put a cup of milky coffee in front of him, and the foam was her foam, warm and sweet. A tentative peace settled in around them like the snow that was falling in earnest outside, broad mainsails of water vapor tacking efficiently to the ground. The snow caught Cuzzy's attention, and though he was thinking about Crystal, he was watching the snow falling, flake by flake, watching it gather on the windowsill like grains of sand in an hourglass, and before long, with his head resting in the cradle of his own arms, he was asleep.

When he woke, he wasn't sure he had been sleeping, but the coffee mug was nearly full and stone cold, and there was a mohair throw across his back. Steam was smoking out the spout of a kettle on top of the woodstove, a fire rumbling in its belly. Through the open doorway, he saw Tracy in the next room, leafing through the pages of a black composition book. When he saw that Cuzzy was awake, he smiled at him and said, "You snore."

"What time is it?" Cuzzy asked sleepily. He had no idea.

Tracy pointed to a big oak clock engraved with the Shoreham coat of arms on the wall behind him. "Three-twenty-one," he said.

Cuzzy stood up abruptly, crashing into one of the hanging pans. "Jeez," he said. "The Shorehams must have been midgets." He sat back down.

"The Shorehams rarely came to this cottage; the servants did."

"Three-twenty-one," Cuzzy said. "Then they were midgets."

"Three-twenty-two now," Tracy said. "Are you late for something?"

Just about now, Amber-Rose would be getting off the school bus, eager to show him her haul. She was like Joey before he went straight and became store manager, which was pretty much a joke, given his ability to walk out of a place with things down his pants—a salami once, and about a dozen cases of Coke over the years if you added all of them up. Amber-Rose was good, too. The first day of school she came back with an unopened box of cornflakes, and last week she lifted a jar of nondairy creamer. Every day she'd bring him Oreos, which they ate when they were done in the sleeping bag.

"This girl I know," Cuzzy said vaguely, "on the bus."

"The school bus?" Tracy asked, and though it didn't seem to

be meant one way or another, Cuzzy was suddenly ashamed to have a girlfriend who still rode the bus.

Tracy pointed to the radio. "They closed school an hour early because of the snow," he said. "A lot of power lines are down. I think the school might have lost power. I know the nursing home did."

Cuzzy looked out and saw that Tracy was right. The snow was thick and steady and heavy on the leaves of the trees. He thought he should go, but where, now that the beach was no longer an option?

"I don't have snow tires on yet," Tracy said. "This was so unexpected."

A tree branch cracked, and they both saw it streak by the window, snow cartwheeling off of it in all directions, and then they heard another sound, like ripping, and they both knew it had pierced the roof of the car. Cuzzy jumped to his feet. "Did you hear that?" he asked, hurrying to the door. Tracy rose and followed slowly.

It was like one of those accidents in which there are no outward signs of injury, the face and body are unblemished and the victim still looks lovely and appealing, so how could she be dead. From the porch, the car looked perfect, exactly the same as the day the will was out of probate and the lawyer handed Tracy the keys.

Cuzzy was on the other side of the car, inspecting the damage. "Not too bad," he called out to Tracy, who was standing in his socks in the snow. "Just a small tear. The branch went through like a lance. Duct tape. It won't look real good, but it'll keep out the moisture."

"There's some in the closet by the door," Tracy said, but he made no move to get it. This is where it starts, he told himself. This is where the car belongs to me and not to Algie, and it saddened him.

The patch job was simple. Cuzzy did it from the inside, where it wasn't too wet, making a cross with the tape directly above the driver's seat, and then another cross, so the whole thing looked like an asterisk.

"It will be fine till you can get it sewn," Cuzzy said. Tracy nodded. They were sitting in the car, snow accumulating around them. "It could have been a lot worse."

People were always saying that, Tracy noticed. They said, "It could have been worse, he could have lingered," or "It could have been worse, it could have been a brain tumor." But why could it have been a brain tumor? He hadn't even had cancer. And what would have been so awful about sticking around a little longer?

"Better go back inside," Cuzzy said, and Tracy obediently got out of the car and headed for the porch. But before he got there, he turned and stood looking at the Porsche.

"It's snowing out," Cuzzy reminded him, but Tracy did not budge. "Suit yourself," he said, climbing the stairs himself. He wanted to leave, and now he wasn't going to get to.

Tracy came in then, snow thick on his eyebrows and lashes, snow in the coils of his hair. Without a word, he stripped off his socks like an excess of skin, and laid them on the hearth next to the woodstove. His bare feet were white in some places, red in others. Cuzzy pretended to read a magazine, a *Time* from the year before. Malibu was on the cover. Crystal would like this, he thought, except that the houses were all sliding down a steep muddy hill toward the ocean. He should have left when he had the chance. He heard Tracy walk into the bathroom, then the shower turning on, and he thought he heard Tracy groan, going under.

It was after five, though the sky would claim that it was later. Gus Meacham called to say that the road into the Larches was too soft to plow, there wasn't any frost in it yet. "Don't look like you're going anywheres," Gus said, "but it's not so bad—" Then he proceeded to tell how he'd struggled to get the plow on the truck that afternoon, and about the new blade and the hitch with the wrong diameter, but so close that he thought a little axle grease would do it the way it did in '65, that big storm in August when ten of the town's twelve trucks were in the shop and the plows they had weren't built for Fords anyway, and they had to spend the night welding new hitches, and it started to rain and they had to haul sand off the town beach and— Cuzzy held the phone away from his ear, listening to the sound of Gus's voice, not his words. This yammering was a habit of north-country men, something to do with the long winters, his father had surmised after spending an ungodly amount of time backed up against the dairy case in the supermarket listening to one or another of his male congregants catalog the ruts along South Stover Road, segue into the benefits of night crawlers over mayflies, detail the problems a cousin's wife had chewing, now that the mouth cancer had caused her to lose half her lower jaw. Cuzzy, taciturn by nature, did not have this trait, nor did his father.

"If I ever go on like that, you'll know I've been possessed," he once told his seven-year-old son after forty-five minutes in the hardware store, where he'd gone for a single sheet of number 80 sandpaper and found himself on the receiving end of a one-way discussion about the broken S joint under Arnie Shepard's kitchen sink. At the time Cuzzy had no idea what that meant, but it came back to him time and again the next year, when his father began to mutter incessantly.

Tracy looked better after the shower. His skin was pink, as if he'd just come in from walking the dog, if there had been a dog, and his eyes were lit again; the sadness had been extinguished.

"Gus called," Cuzzy told him. "He says the road is too soft to plow."

"Meaning?"

"Meaning that it will get all torn up if he tries to plow it. Basically he'll take out the road."

"I wondered about that," Tracy said.

What he didn't say was that Cuzzy would have to stay. Cuzzy didn't mention it either. Why make it obvious, he reasoned, even though it was. He followed Tracy back into the kitchen and fell into what was fast becoming his regular chair. Tracy, however, stood in front of the opened freezer, taking stock of its contents. "Frozen pizza," he reported to Cuzzy. "Two bean burritos. Toaster waffles. Baby peas." He dug farther back, clearing a path with his hands. "Half a loaf of sourdough." He paused over a plastic container coated with a rime of ice. "Something unidentifiable—" He held it up to the light. "Probably one of Algie's famous stews," he concluded. "He would make these stews where he'd throw in whatever he had around: tomatoes, navy beans, merlot, chicken necks, bay leaves, lime juice, spinach, cumin, balsamic vinegar, noodles, maple syrup—'It's not stew without maple syrup,' he'd say—and salt pork and did I say bay leaves? He loved bay leaves. He'd have them express-shipped from San Diego. Oh, and cayenne and turnips."

Cuzzy looked at him stupidly. He didn't think this stew, or whatever it was, sounded very good at all.

Tracy shoved the container to the back of the freezer, sandbagging it with the frozen peas. "So it won't be going anywhere anytime soon," he said.

"But you don't even know what it is," Cuzzy said, more petulantly than he'd intended.

"No, but I'm happier thinking it might be his. The possibility is so much more potent than the reality, either way. When I was in college, I read a short story about these two people, a man and a woman, and the man dies tragically and then one day the woman goes digging around the garage and comes across the camping mattress and all of a sudden realizes that it's his breath inside. He blew it up the summer before. If she opens the valve, she can breathe in his breath one last time, but if she does that, his breath on this earth will be gone forever. That really will be the end of him."

"But if she doesn't, it'll all leak out anyway," Cuzzy said, "and it'll still be gone."

"You know, Cuzzy," Tracy said, with a gravity that hung off him like an outsize coat, "I used to think like that, too. I thought the story was sentimental and stupid, the way it must sound to you now."

Cuzzy looked down at his hands. My mother had this hairbrush, he wanted to say. My mother had this *hair*. My father called it "the gift of the Magi." It was the color of new pennies, and wavy, and when she'd brush it out, the bristles would bump along like they were surfing. She'd do that after every shift at the nursing home, where she'd have to tie it up and net it. I have her hairbrush, and her hair.

But he didn't say this, he didn't say anything, though he would have liked to, and he found himself wishing, to his surprise, that Tracy would ask again, or prod him and draw him out. When he was a boy, and angry, his mother would say, "Use words." He wondered if maybe he had used them all up.

At suppertime they sat opposite each other again, eating burritos off of blue plastic plates. The snow had let up; there were maybe five inches on the ground.

"Tell me about Harold," Tracy said, chewing.

"Harold?" Cuzzy said. His mother had an older cousin, Harold Cotten, who ran a vacuum-cleaner repair shop in Halcyon Falls. When his father went to Newkirk, Harold sent them a case of number 21 vacuum-cleaner bags and a note saying that while he wasn't sure which kind of machine they had, number 21 was the most common, and you couldn't have too many vacuum-cleaner bags in your life, which perhaps was meant to remind them what they did have too much of. Cuzzy couldn't see why Tracy would want to talk about him.

"Your son," Tracy said. "Your little boy. Harold."

"Oh, jeez," Cuzzy said. "I thought you meant Cousin Harold. He fixes vacuum cleaners."

"I didn't know anyone fixed vacuum cleaners anymore."

"I guess so," Cuzzy said. "Anyhow, his name is Harry. His real name is Harrison. Harrison Ford."

"Uncle Harold?"

"Cousin Harold."

"Cousin Harold's real name is Harrison Ford? Like the actor?" Tracy looked genuinely mystified, especially when Cuzzy banged on the table and laughed so loud it made him laugh some more.

"The baby," he managed to say between breaths, and Tracy nodded gravely. "Crystal has a thing for Harrison Ford."

"The actor or the baby?"

"Well, both, I guess," Cuzzy said, "but I wouldn't really know. She doesn't let me near. It's like he's hers alone."

"Like you were the donor," Tracy said.

"The donor?" Cuzzy repeated.

"The sperm donor," Tracy said.

"I guess," Cuzzy said. "Sperm"—that was one of those health-class words that he never felt comfortable with, like "testicle." Who invented those words?

"I've always wondered what it would be like to be somebody's father," Tracy said. "But you know what scares me? What scares me is that then you'd have to forgive your own father for doing such a bad job, because you'd see how hard it is, and you'd probably make the same ridiculous mistakes."

The bed was soft and giving, his first bed in a while, and Cuzzy wrapped his arms and legs around it like a torso. His own blankness lay on him like the snow upon the leaves. Forgive your father? He hadn't realized how tired he was. For the second time that day, he was asleep in this stranger's house.

BONE

"One of the hard parts of the skeleton of a vertebrae," Routlege,
Biology 10; *not* the *hardest, though. Think about that. Where would
it be? Locate it.*

I f she drove, she might catch sight of him. Even though it was
November and cold enough in the morning to need the engine block to get her truck from neutral to reverse without
stripping the gears, the chance of him walking the county road
was going down with the mercury. She put Harry in his snowsuit,
a hand-me-down stitched to look like Dale Earnhardt's racing
ensemble, and strapped him into his car seat with a stuffed dog
(pink but he favored it) and a bottle. The gas tank was a little less
than half full, but she wasn't going far, just to where Cuzzy might
go: to town, to the store, to Whisper Notch where he was living
with that rich guy.

It bugged her that he made it up there before she did. That was
her particular dream, the big house up on Whisper Notch, not his.
He didn't even care, which was worse. Then there was that skinny
girl, Amber-Rose, whose spine was more prominent than anything
on the other side—that really ticked her off. He should have better
taste. The girl didn't have a thing to hang on to. Even if it was rude
to say it, it wasn't rude to think it: she was a dog.

She was history, though, that girl. That's what Crystal heard—

one day she hitches a ride in a snowstorm to where he's staying, a scrubby piece of woods behind the town beach for godsakes, because she's afraid he won't have enough food or matches and the snow is coming down fast, and when she gets there after skidding off the road not just once but three times for godsakes, after getting a ride in a truck with Cuzzy's uncle Hank, who thinks he's *entitled,* and Cuzzy is nowhere to be found, she goes berserk, totally, thinks he's already frozen to death, even though if she had any sense, she'd notice that his sleeping bag was empty and stashed in the woods. But to give her credit, whether or not it's due, maybe it's because the sleeping bag is unopened and there is not a single footprint to indicate that Cuzzy is even there and not with his new best friend, or whoever that guy is, Amber-Rose goes nuts. She loses her head. She charges over and pounds on the door of the nearest house, which isn't too near in any case, and when nobody answers, she breaks in and calls the rescue squad. She's on the phone when it dawns on her that there are people in the house and they are in the bedroom doing what people do when it's snowing hard, though not, apparently, Amber-Rose, who thinks the *wind* is shaking the wall, and goes to investigate and meets the lady of the house, who is preceded by a Remington 700, shouting, "Lois McCarty, Lois McCarty, you get out of here, you get out of here," and shoos the girl out the kitchen door and into the snow but not before getting off two good shots, one of which ricochets off the last hundred-year-old black walnut tree in the county and comes back and grazes Amber-Rose's shoulder. Pretty much the whole thing is heard by the 911 operator, who puts out two calls, one for an ambulance for the girl, and the other for a search-and-rescue team to sniff out Cuzzy, only the search and rescue never assembles, because one of the brighter members thinks to call Cuzzy's cousin Joey, who tells him not to worry, that Cuzzy is with the rich guy.

After that, Cuzzy drops the girl like a stone. Doesn't call, doesn't show up at the beach after school anymore, and Amber-Rose is sure it's because he was mad that she called 911 and made all that fuss. That's what she told people, that Cuzzy was pissed. But Cuzzy was not pissed. He'd moved on, and she was too young to get it. That was what guys did. Catch as catch can. She was too skinny, anyway.

The girl was gone, out of the picture, which was good for her, Crystal thought, even though she didn't want Cuzzy back, not for herself. She'd been reading in her magazines about "the *new* celibacy" going around Hollywood and New York. Women, and some men, were not having sex anymore, not even with themselves, so they had much more energy. Crystal could use more energy. Harry was going to start walking. She would have to keep up with him. That was where Cuzzy came in: the boy needed a father. Or, more precisely, Crystal needed him to have a father. There'd be another set of hands and more money. As it was, she was living off savings and unemployment, which was because Pete Moss, her boss, was kind enough to fire her, though it sometimes came down to the change she found behind her parents' sofa and what she got from returning beer bottles. Not that Cuzzy had a normal job. He had figured that one out, too. Joey said he was working for the rich guy, who was probably gay, so what kind of work would that be? Crystal didn't even want to think about it. Still, she had to admit that she kind of liked to imagine him living in that big old house. Everyone knew the Larches was the biggest estate in the entire state, at least this part of it, and even the servants' quarters were bigger than most double-wides. "Your daddy lives in a mansion," she would sing to Harry as she spooned rice cereal and puréed chicken into his gummy mouth. Two teeth poked out already, and more often than not these days, he was cranky and full of tears. "Your daddy lives in a mansion," she'd croon, not that it helped.

Oh, she had plans. Ever since she was a little girl, she had plans.

Lately they focused on New York City. She saw an article about game shows that gave the addresses for *Wheel of Fortune* and a new show called *Luck of the Draw,* where a gold key was hidden in a huge chest of drawers, and if you found the key, you could keep it (not really—the article explained that there was only one gold key, but if you decided to "keep" it, they'd give you a replica and a check for two thousand dollars) or use it to try to open one of their locked chests filled with cash and prizes. Crystal sent ten self-addressed stamped envelopes to both shows, and when her tickets came, she planned to go to Rockefeller Center and hang out early in the morning with a big sign that said POVERTY LOVES BRYANT, which, among other things, would show the world that people in Poverty were not prejudiced, even though she was not technically from there. She was pretty sure a sign like that would get her on the *Today* show and that everyone in Poverty would see her (because she'd tell them to turn it on), even Cuzzy, if he and the rich guy were not so busy "working" that they didn't have time for the tele-vision; and maybe her real mother, wherever she was; and they both would see Harry, whose hair would be parted to the left so that it came out on TV to the right, his best side. He'd look so cute and handsome and *telegenic*—she loved this word, it sounded so scientific, as if looking good on TV was encoded in his DNA—that the scouts who watched the show every day for this reason would discover Harry and make him the next Macaulay Culkin or Jodie Foster. Then they'd be rich, and wouldn't Cuzzy be eating it when he found out. As long as she told the agent to make sure he wrote the contracts so Cuzzy couldn't horn in on it.

If nothing else, she was practical. A cap for the truck would be good. Some downtime so she could get out more, and part-time work. According to Pete Moss, there was a three-week flagging job over near Osprey Pond, fifteen dollars an hour, twenty-three on the weekends, hers for the taking. If Cuzzy took the boy—if she could get him to take the boy—she would be set. A boy needed a father. Look at Christian Brando. Look at all those Kennedys, except for John-John. Michael Douglas and Charlie Sheen confused her. You would have thought they had strong fathers, but look at them, in and out of rehab for drugs and sex. It killed her that you went to rehab now because you had too much sex. Well, nobody could accuse her of that these days.

One problem with Cuzzy, and lately she had been thinking about this a lot—one problem, a big one, if you asked her, was his father, who was crazy. Everyone knew that. The guy was in a mental institution and wasn't coming out anytime soon. Even if Cuzzy never talked about him, it didn't mean they weren't still related. What if it was in his genes, the crazy stuff? She read about how it could lie dormant for years, like cancer, then bam! Usually it was because of stress or some life-altering event like moving, which turned out to be right up there with divorce and getting laid off, though Crystal could see how both of those could be two of life's great reliefs, too, and she felt vindicated some months later when the same magazine, probably *Glamour,* which was better, she thought, than *Marie Claire,* ran a piece suggesting the same exact thing. Not about moving, which turned out to be stressful even if you were pulling up stakes from Love Canal. And Cuzzy had moved recently, up and *beyond* Whisper Notch, which was saying something, and which completely pissed her off, though she thought it might be good for Harry. *If*—big if—Cuzzy Gage did not turn out to be insane like his daddy.

That was the other thing people talked about, how Leo Gage went like a traffic light from green to red—or red to green, Crystal decided, depending on how you thought about it. One day he was pretty normal, the next day he was peculiar, no yellow caution light in between. One Sunday he started in with the loaves and the fishes, and it was like his words became the loaves and the fishes, multiplying endlessly for thirty-eight hours before Leo finally fell down on the floor. Not that anyone, even his family, was there when that happened. The thirty-eighth hour was when his watch broke. People said that was when it happened, that his brain dried out, and it didn't matter how much fluid the doctors gave him at the hospital, the damage was done.

Crystal did not know when Leo Gage was put away. She was a girl, and people were talking about it at the Catholic church and at the store, how he was standing in the road completely naked (which always sort of thrilled her), and then people stopped talking about him, like he had been a serious weather event and now the sun was shining. Still, Crystal didn't forget. The image of Leo Gage naked in the middle of the street stayed with her till she wondered if maybe she, too, had seen him that morning. It made no sense—what would a twelve-year-old girl be doing there at that time of the morning?—but it didn't have to make sense, her memory was all the evidence she needed, and after a while she couldn't distinguish what had happened to her from what had happened to others around her. A test she took once in *Women's Day* (not her favorite magazine, but she was intrigued enough by the headline "How Well Do You Know Yourself?" to buy it) showed her to be "extremely empathetic," off the charts, actually, which she decided probably explained a lot about her.

She dreamed about him, all locked away among people who were truly crazy. In her dreams, he had dark, pleading eyes and fidgety hands and was dressed in a pair of blue cotton pajamas that were nearly white after years of institutional washing. Sometimes he was on the verge of getting out, and he looked happy in a sad kind of way, but most of the time he was completely bored. Once, though, she dreamed that he'd had another "episode" and had to be taken to a padded room in a straitjacket. (Which, in her dream, was a white overcoat without any sleeves.)

Of course she knew who Cuzzy Gage was—she had dreamed about him, too. (In her dreams, he looked remarkably like Michael J. Fox in *Family Ties*.) She always assumed that he would be more interesting than most of the guys she met, she just needed him to grow up so they could get together. He was almost famous; he was famous once removed. That was one of the endearing things about him, she thought—it hadn't gone to his head. He was so normal; he didn't even talk about his father. Not that he would have a lot to say, since he hadn't seen the man in years.

There was an eyelash in Crystal's eye. She dabbed her pinky into the corner, and the lash came out standing straight up, like an exclamation point. Crystal took this for a sign of good luck but couldn't make up her mind what to wish for. There was no reason to waste it wishing that Cuzzy would become Harry's father, she reasoned, because he already was. A house, she decided. Her own house up on Whisper Notch.

There was frost in the ground. She had felt it when she first stepped outside and the grass gave nothing back. She unplugged the engine heater and climbed in the truck, blowing her warm breath into the cold cab, where it turned visible. She switched the heat to high, then got out again. She liked it to be tropical before she put Harry into his car seat. It was a waste of gas, but it was the least she could do, she told herself, to make his life a little easier than her own.

"We are going on an expedition," she told the baby a good fifteen minutes later when she carried him out of the house. He gave her a sweet look, and she swung him around like they were on the same dance card and kissed him on the lips. He giggled and gripped her neck harder as she lowered him into his seat. "You are a handsome young man, Harrison Ford Gage," she told him, "and an excellent kisser." She peeled back his snowsuit and snuffled him, and he squealed with delight. Her breath left a dew trail along his skin. Crystal pulled away, and Harry's face clouded up. He wanted more. "Me, too," Crystal said, buckling him in. "Me three."

Whisper Notch was desolate. Not a car, not a truck, not a squirrel or a chickadee crossed Crystal's path as she threaded the pickup through the needle of roads. Rain and early snow and the rocks they dislodged had scoured the pavement and increased the grade, and they bumped and rattled along, which made Harry laugh and toss pink dog at Crystal's face in the rearview mirror.

"Don't do that," Crystal said sharply, also to the mirror. Harry did not look the least bit concerned. He stuck out his hand, and Crystal returned pink dog to his clutches.

"You love pink dog," she said sweetly. "Don't hurt pink dog. Pink dog is your friend, and now he has an ouchy." None of this appeared to register with Harry, who was busily chewing on pink dog's ear.

The thing was, she hadn't even gotten him pink dog. Marcel and Therese had, which ticked her off. She bought him a Pooh bear and a Tigger, and he didn't want anything to do with them. She bought him the indoor swing she saw on QVC, and a rocking horse that was controlled by phonics, and Lincoln Logs, the deluxe wooden set with 225 pieces plus the Indian Village. She was buying him trains on layaway; she figured he'd have the locomotive, a flatbed, a passenger car, and the caboose by the time he was five. Sometimes she imagined raking all of this stuff into a big pile and saying, "This is the mountain of my love, Harry, and you'll never get to the top of it." And he wouldn't, she knew, no matter how hard he tried.

"Stop!" she yelled. Harry, who was about to hurl pink dog again, put him down. "Good boy," Crystal said. "Why don't you look at the pretty trees."

They were pretty, she knew they were, but it was like a color-blind person knowing the traffic light was green: she didn't honestly think so. The trees depressed her. Once the leaves were gone, they reminded her of dead people reaching out for heaven, hoping God would choose them. The sight of them had made her morose every year for as long as she could remember.

"I bet I have that disease—what's it called?" she asked herself. "I read about it in *Prevention* or *Self* the day the computers were down in the supermarket and the line was so long. No, in *Mademoiselle*. I'm pretty sure." She addressed her words to the mirror, and to pink dog, whose reflection she found there. Though Harry was fast asleep behind pink dog, a thin line of drool connecting his mouth to the animal's collar, she talked to him, too. An article in *Working Mother*—which she planned to be sometime soon—said that talking to your baby the way you talked to your friends was the key to happy, healthy connections later on. Not that it even hinted at when "later on" was.

"Seasonal affective disorder!" she said proudly, as if she had coined the phrase and made the diagnosis herself. "SAD," she said. She thought it was weird the way people had to sit under grow lights as if they were plants, and weird that light could make you happy. Right now money would make her happy, though she'd have an easier time getting light. Money always cost more than its face value. What would Cuzzy want, for instance, when she told him he owed her child support? Time with Harry? Fine, that would actually save her money. Time with her? Why did sex always end up feeling like a transaction?

Boy, she was thinking, the houses up here are huge. Crystal had to slow the truck to get a look—every last one was screened by tamarack and spruce, as if they had come up from the forest floor, too.

Crystal liked the ones with cathedral ceilings and bay windows the size of billboards. Birch-branch chandeliers were popular, she noticed, as were the ones made from ten-point antlers that burned real candles. When she built her house here, she was having none of that. Rustic was for people who didn't spend anything but leisure time in the woods. Hell, her boyfriend lived in the woods, the same as a deer. (Past tense, she thought. Used to be her boyfriend. Used to live.) And Marcel, who wrestled all day with knots and boles and branches snapping overhead, wouldn't think of having a tree hanging in his house. Enough was enough.

Crystal found the next driveway and turned in. The sign said, HOLTS' BACKWATER. Crystal assumed no one was home. No one ever was up here. She followed the drive toward the house, and when she saw it, she stopped. She would do this sometimes. Pick a house or let a house pick her, then stop and look the way other people stopped at highway turnouts to admire the view. This one was big (of course) and covered in cedar shingles, with cedar shakes on the roof. Hand-split, Crystal figured. The door was painted red; there was a room that looked like a greenhouse, but it could have been an indoor pool. Crystal was going to have a pool.

She wished Cuzzy would come ambling down the road, though why he would be walking into Holts' Backwater, she had no idea. But walking fit into her idea of how they should meet today. This time she would be in the truck and he would be on the road. This time *he* would flag *her* down. This time the two of them would ride off together to the Nice n Easy. No, the three of them.

Bingo! That was the sign she was waiting for. The Nice n Easy. She started up the truck, knowing where it would take her.

"Hey, Crystal!" Ram Pullen called out before her right boot had crossed the transom. He had seen her pull into the parking lot. He had seen her tuck a blanket around Harry, who was still asleep in his car seat, and leave him there.

"Maybe you can help us." He patted the vinyl bench beside him and across the table from the Sylvanias. "Slide on in." Crystal sat down like an obedient child. Ram was a bully. She didn't like that about him, but she was attracted as well. There was nothing tentative about him.

"Five more words for 'Johnson' and we're in the running," Squint said, pointing to a magazine lying open between them.

"In the running for what?" Crystal asked, wondering if it was something she could get in on. Then she thought better of it. "Oh, never mind. I don't want to know." She stood up, and so did Ram.

"Stay awhile and visit," he said, but it wasn't an order, it was a request, and Crystal had no trouble denying those. She headed over to the magazine rack, which was filled with hunting magazines. Men wearing orange vests or camouflage fatigues and toting rifles graced their covers, when they weren't celebrating sleek German pointers on guard or jaunty retrievers with ducks in their soft mouths. It was hunting season, no question about it. Sonny Bono, on the cover of *Us*, was hiding among these magazines as if in a blind himself. He was standing on the steps of the Capitol with his arms around his second wife, Mary, with an inset photo of Cher, like a locket. Crystal took the magazine, laying three crisp dollars on the counter, and left without her change. Joey was in the stock-room, and she didn't want to stand there all day and listen to Ram drum his fingers on the Formica while the Sylvanias puzzled out synonyms so everyone could hear.

The knock on the windshield startled Crystal. She was deep into a story about two sisters, identical twins, who slashed their parents' throats in order to collect the insurance money and made it look like a double suicide—they had the forensics guy fooled, apparently—but got tripped up when the insurance agent read them the suicide clause, which caused them to change their story, each one blaming the other, and since it was one's word against the other's, and there were no witnesses, and the two of them were indistinguishable, it looked for sure like they were going to get off. But then the district attorney dropped the bomb that the forensics guy was in on the whole thing, so the three of them were serving two consecutive life sentences with no chance of parole. Also, Crystal was in the middle of a bite of Milky Way, and her teeth were gluey with that.

Shhh, she pantomimed. She didn't want Ram, who was standing there, to wake the baby. Ram, she noticed, looked surprisingly like the forensics guy, whose name was Lance Diebold, a name that should have tipped off the authorities right away, Crystal thought. Ram beckoned her out of the truck, and she went, closing the door quietly and not all the way. He was about her height, and she saw that his eyes were bloodshot, like he'd been reading too much, which was basically impossible, since he wasn't what she'd call a speed reader.

"Some good weed's come up from the city," he said.

"I don't have any money for that," Crystal said. "Hell, I don't have any money for anything." She licked the last bits of chocolate off her fingers and nodded toward Harry. "Seen his father lately?"

"Cuzzy? No. He's probably holed up with his rich boyfriend." Crystal let this pass. "But if you're really hard up, we could roll that guy and help you and him out both. Lighten his load."

"That's real kind of you, Ram," Crystal said sarcastically, but Ram either didn't notice or didn't care, because he bowed slightly and blushed and said thanks.

They stood there awkwardly. Ram shifted from boot to boot.

Crystal rocked heel to toe, and anyone watching would have thought they were listening to music or about to dance.

"This pot is so mellow, you're going to love it," Ram said, pulling Crystal by her sleeve in the direction of his truck. "It's called peace pot. Get it? Like Peace Pops."

The joint in the ashtray was already half gone, and its end was still warm to the touch when Crystal picked it up and ran it under her nose.

"Sweet," she said, holding it out for Ram to light. "Sweet," she said again after inhaling, holding the smoke and blowing it at Ram's face. Her head was light already, like a balloon. Better not open the window, she thought, and the image of her head floating away both frightened her and made her laugh.

She took another prolonged drag and sank it into her lungs. It was like free-diving in the lake, she realized, and closed her eyes. "This is nice," she said eventually, leaning back in the seat and letting her muscles go slack. They felt like guitar strings loosening. They felt like parrot fish and blue tangs swimming in tropical waters. They felt like— "Hey," she cried, sitting up, "what the heck are you doing?"

Ram smiled confidently. "Relax," he said casually, as if it was normal that his right hand was cupping her left breast and his thumb was passing over her nipple like a switch.

"I've always wanted to do that," he said, grinning. His voice was slurry. He closed his eyes. Crystal wondered if he was going to fall asleep. His hand and fingers kept working her all the same.

"Chew my bone," Ram said dreamily, pushing the lever next to his seat and easing backward.

Crystal snorted. "What number is that, Ram?" She tried to speak sharply, but her tongue felt too big for her mouth, like it needed to molt.

"Oh, come on, Crystal. I don't get blown every day," Ram said defensively.

"I meant what number. Remember, Johnson? The list. Get it?" she said.

"Oh," Ram said, comprehending and relaxing back into a smile. "I'm not sure. I think it was number eleven, right after whistle."

"Whistle?"

"Yeah. As in 'wet my whistle.'"

"That means something else," Crystal said, although she couldn't remember what.

"It doesn't have to," Ram said, "does it?"

His shut eyes looked like clamshells, she thought. It occurred to her that she could get out when he wasn't looking, push down the door handle and jump out before he could put a hand on her arm to keep her there. But she didn't do that.

"I don't know, Ram," Crystal said playfully, "what's in it for me?" Did she mean this? She didn't know. It was on her mind, and then suddenly, as if her mouth were psychic, it spoke those words: "What's in it for me?" She heard herself say them and she was impressed. She wondered what else she would say.

Nothing, it turned out. Ram reached into his shirt pocket and pulled out an accordion strip of Scratch 'n Win cards, tore one off, and slid it slowly into her breast pocket.

"Yours," he said, as if he had met the terms of their contract.

"That cost five dollars," Crystal complained. "Five whole dollars." She reached into his pocket and extracted the strip and tore off another card. Ram did not complain. He knew that she had given her consent.

She did everything she knew how to make it fast. Once he asked her to slow down, but she was in charge, so she didn't. When it was done and he was leaning back in the seat with his eyes unfocused on the ceiling, she took a dime from the cup holder and scratched the coating off the first card. Nothing. She ran the dime over the other.

"Oh my God!" she said. "I don't have that kind of luck." Crystal turned to Ram. He was fast asleep. She looked at the card again. She couldn't believe it; a full house. She didn't even need to turn the card over to know how much it was worth—she had studied the back of those cards for years—three hundred dollars, payable in cash. Crystal looked at it some more, basking in her good fortune, then slipped it back in her pocket and quickly exited the truck before Ram could snatch it away (not that he'd notice), running over to her truck to get Harry to bring him in the store for the payout.

Crystal looked twice, then three times, before what she was seeing made sense: Harry was not there. The blanket was gone, too, and so was pink dog. Crystal stood there, arrested by her panicked heart. The baby had crawled out, she was sure of it. He had wriggled out of his car seat. He had opened the door. He had opened the door? He didn't have to open the door, not all the way. She hadn't shut it. But he couldn't be that strong, could he? Someone else had opened the door. Harry had been stolen. Kidnapped. She was certain. Someone had taken her son. She should have locked the doors. She couldn't bear to think where he was, and with whom, and what sick thing they were doing.

She'd have to call the police. What would she say she had been doing? If they found out, would they take Harry away from her? But how could they, if the baby was already gone? She began to cry and shiver and walk slowly toward the store, and the phone, and the police, and the rest of her life. But what did it matter—Harry was gone.

———

Ram saw her first. He was huddled in the booth with the Sylvanias, just as he had been when she saw him earlier. It was like time had not passed. Could she have made it up, a kind of reverse amnesia?

Ram saw her and saw her tears and did not change his expression. "What's the matter, babe," he said, "didn't win anything?" His friends snickered.

"Where's Joey?" she said, ignoring them. "I need the phone. Now." She hoped she looked as fierce as she felt.

"I'm right here," Joey called from under the counter. "What's the problem?"

Crystal peered over and there was Joey kneeling on the floor, his Nice n Easy ball cap sitting lopsided on his head. And there was Harry on his back, waving a disposable diaper in his hand like a flag of peace, a double-toothed grin on his broad, untroubled face.

"I just changed him," Joey said casually, as if changing diapers was part of his job description, like filling the ketchup pumps and running credit-card authorizations.

"What the hell for?" she said. She was livid, full of a furious rage that she couldn't contain and didn't want to.

"He was wet," Joey said. "He was crying."

"How did you know?"

"I heard him when I went to get the trash," he said, "and I didn't know where you were."

That was a lie, she was sure of it. Everyone knew where she was. And if they didn't then, they did once Ram slipped back inside when her back was turned.

"Well, give him back," Crystal said, as if Joey might not.

Joey hoisted the baby off the floor and handed him to Crystal. The diaper was still in Harry's hands. He put it on top of her head like a hat.

Back in her truck, she let the tears flow. She held Harry tight and cried and sniffled and said that she was sorry. To stanch the tears, she closed her eyes a long time and let herself enjoy her baby's smell and his small, damp hands ringing her neck, and his head resting on her breast. When she leaned down to adjust his snowsuit, Harry stretched upward at the same time, and his full red lips grazed her cheek. She didn't know if it was intentional, but she didn't know that it wasn't. She looked at her watch. 11:28 A.M.: what seemed to be his first on-purpose kiss.

She picked him up and sat him on the steering wheel and looked him over proudly. No doubt about it, and she wasn't bragging, not even to herself, Harry was a handsome little boy. He had her wavy blond hair and Cuzzy's big brown doe eyes and someone else's cheekbones. She loved those cheeks; she loved thinking about where they came from. Which ancestor, which side, which century?

"What is this glitter?" she asked Harry gaily, wiping at a constellation of silver specks around his mouth. "Did Uncle Joey sprinkle fairy dust on you?" She giggled at her joke. Harry laughed, too, a big belly laugh, and that was when Crystal saw there was something on his tongue.

"Open," she told him. "Spit." A large wad of chewed red cardboard rolled into her palm. "Now, that's more like my kind of luck," she told him, flicking what had been three hundred dollars out the window.

GRAVEL

Colton's Applied Materials Science says gravel is made of sand. But sand is soft. Sand is inconsequential. (Unless you are a crab!) People expect things of consequence to be big, don't they? Even so, gravel hurts when you walk on it.

C uzzy had stayed. It was Tracy's idea, but he went along with it. He had woken up that first morning and made his way to the kitchen, plotting his escape: he would tell Tracy he was leaving, and then he would. Maybe Tracy would give him a ride, maybe he wouldn't, but either way, he was out of there.

"I guess you have to go," Tracy said, beating Cuzzy to the punch. Tracy was eating oatmeal. He pushed a bowl toward Cuzzy, then a spoon. "Breakfast gets the day's work done," he said. "When you're done, I'll drive you there."

"Where?" Cuzzy asked, his voice still heavy with sleep.

"To work," Tracy said. "The driveway is clear. It rained. Gus didn't even have to plow."

Cuzzy grunted. "I don't really have a job right now," he admitted.

Tracy feigned surprise, but he'd known. Reverend Trimble had already told him. "This guy is going nowhere fast" was how the minister put it. They were in his office in the church, after the ten o'clock service. The Scripture had been from Luke 10, where Jesus, trying to explain what it means to "love your neighbor as yourself," tells the story of a man who was beaten and left for dead on the side of the road, and whose cries for help are ignored by a priest and a Levite, both of whom cross to the other side of the road and hurry away. Then a Samaritan—a man from Samaria, also a Jew, but a different kind, one the other Jews despise—sees the man and ministers to him with oil and wine, brings him to an inn, tends to his wounds, and pays the innkeeper to look after the man until he is well. Hence the term "Good Samaritan."

Trimble's sermon was based on the story, too. It was called "Who Is a Neighbor?" and the minister's point, as Tracy heard it, was how, in the face of someone who is not like you, you should not lose your humanity to your fear.

"People think that being a Good Samaritan means helping someone who is sick or in trouble," Reverend Trimble said. Tracy was only half listening. The church was shabby. Someone needed to clean the carpet and pull down the spiderwebs in the rafters. He fixed his eyes on these, how the light from the stained glass beaded up on the threads of the web, how it looked like dew in the morning, when the sun made prisms of each drop of water. This was the first time Tracy had been in a church since Algie died, and he wasn't sure what he was doing there. He knew it had something to do with his friend, who had turned to the church—to the Catholic church, of all things—near the end, as if the rituals and the building, as much as the people inside, were going to cross to his side of the street and save him.

"Jesus meant more than that," the minister went on. "He meant that, yes, yes, of course he did—*by all means* help one another—but he meant more than that, too." The minister paused. He looked at Tracy, whom he had never seen before. "'Who is a stranger, and who is a neighbor?' This is the question Jesus is asked. And to answer the question, he tells a story of four men, three of whom, strictly speaking, are neighbors, members of the same tribe—the man who is wounded, the priest, and the Levite. Yet which man, Jesus says, was neighborly to the man who fell victim to the robbers? Was it the priest, was it the Levite, both of whom were Jews, like the man who lay bleeding? No, it was not!" The minister, who had been picking up steam, fairly hissed these last four words. Tracy hadn't been looking, but heard it as a dog hears a high-pitched whistle: his eyes went directly to Jason Trimble.

"*This* is the question Jesus puts to the man whom Luke calls the legal expert, perhaps ironically. The man who says, basically, 'Come on, Jesus, how am I supposed to love my neighbor as I love myself if I don't even know who my neighbor is?' So Jesus tells him the story of the bleeding man and asks him, 'Tell me, who was the neighbor?' And that man answers the truth. The real neighbor, the 'legal expert' says, is 'the one who had mercy on the man.' *That* is the answer. The *only* answer. And so I urge you. Have mercy on the man. And the woman, too," he added, smiling.

But then his smile left him, and he searched the pews with his eyes, making contact with each person, if only for an instant. It wasn't a scan so much as a troll, Tracy thought, as if he was looking for something in each of them. There were only twenty worshipers—the congregation had been declining for years—and they all looked up, each in his or her own way, and surrendered to the search.

"And that is good," Reverend Trimble continued, but quieter. "And that is fine." His voice gained volume again. "And the world would be a better place if that were what we did." He paused again. Tracy half expected him to shout, but he didn't. Instead, he dropped his voice to a whisper, and they all had to move forward in their seats to hear him: "But Jesus is saying we must do more. We must be *like* the Samaritan. And like the Samaritan, we must reach out to people who are *different* from us. Black people. Asian people.

Jews themselves. The infirm. The elderly. The disabled. We must be willing to risk our comfort, our sense of security. Jesus is saying that we must expand the boundaries of our neighborhood. He is saying that we should have no boundaries, just our humanness. That is what a Good Samaritan does—he breaks through the walls that separate us and, by his example, shows us what a neighbor is. Amen."

After the service, Tracy hung back, realizing he would have to go through the door and shake the hand of the man who had brought tears to his eyes. Besides, the elderly and the infirm went first, and by the time they had made their way along the ragged carpet, Tracy was the last person left in the sanctuary.

"It is good to see you," Reverend Trimble said to him, as if they had met before.

I am the man who was left bleeding on the side of the road, Tracy wanted to say, only he was not that dramatic. He just nodded. "Michael Edwards," he said. "Or Tracy. It doesn't matter."

"Oh, you're the one Gus and Molly Meacham told me about. The teacher. You're up at the Larches." And then, in a different tone of voice. "I'm sorry about your friend."

"Thanks," Tracy said, though he thought it sounded stupid, thanking the man for Algie's death. Like a lot of things, it made no sense.

"How are you coping?" Reverend Trimble said. His voice was full of concern. It was the voice of what Algie always referred to as "a caring *professional*." Tracy smiled to himself. It was good, sometimes, to hear Algie's voice.

"Oh, you know," Tracy said. The caring professional always knew.

Reverend Trimble put his hand on Tracy's shoulder. "I wish I did," he said. Then he went on, "Would you mind helping me pick up the programs? I always ask people to put them in the recycling box on their way out, and some of them always forget. They're old—and ornery." He laughed. He clearly liked these people; Tracy saw that.

"How could I say no after that sermon?" Tracy said playfully. He was feeling better. It had been days since he'd had a conversation.

"Actually," Reverend Trimble said, "if you don't mind, I have another favor to ask."

They moved into his office. It was big and drafty, with a long desk on one wall and a coffee table and a couple of padded chairs in the middle. Reverend Trimble's diploma hung near the door in a black plastic frame that was made to look like wood, the kind sold in packages of three at discount stores. Sure enough, there were two other frames hanging nearby. In one was a picture of Mother Teresa shaking hands with President Carter, and in the other, a picture of Mother Teresa shaking hands with a leper.

"Sometimes I think it's pretentious to have them up there," Reverend Trimble said when he saw Tracy looking at them. "But it must be like a painter having a Monet or a Matisse in his studio: it's inspirational, and it's humbling."

"If you like Monet or Matisse," Tracy said. He was thinking of Algie, who warmed to Impressionism only when his sight began to falter.

"Yes, of course," Reverend Trimble said, and Tracy felt embarrassed. He had not meant to be rude. He had meant to be judicious and full of goodwill.

"So how do you like our little hamlet?" the minister asked, and though Tracy sensed this was not exactly small talk, that Reverend Trimble did want to know, he chose to answer as if it were.

"It's very beautiful," he said.

Reverend Trimble smiled at him and said nothing. It was,

Tracy thought, a practiced psychiatric silence. What choice did he have but to keep talking?"

"I haven't seen much of it since I got here. I've mostly been holed up at the Larches, working," he added.

"So I've heard," Reverend Trimble said. And then, sensing Tracy's discomfort: "Things get around in a place like this."

Trimble removed his stole, and then his robe, draping them both over the back of a chair, absently flattening the wrinkles with the edge of his hand. When he turned, Tracy was surprised to see that, instead of a sweater over his shirt and tie, he was wearing an old Red Sox sweatshirt, gray with red writing.

"It's my wife's idea," Trimble said helplessly, grinning. "She has this thing for the Red Sox. She says that if I wear this sweatshirt to church long enough, maybe God will intervene on their behalf. In some places they call that magical thinking, but in this place we call it faith."

The phone rang, and Tracy heard Trimble say, "In a little while" and "ham," and then it rang again, and he said, "Which hospital?"

"Gus says you're a teacher," the minister said when he hung up the phone.

"Yes," Tracy said. Hadn't they established that?

"That's why I thought of you," Reverend Trimble said, and then did not say for what. Instead, he asked Tracy about himself again, *how* he was doing, and though Tracy could feel pressure on the inside of the bridge of his nose—a sure sign of tears to come— he said, "Fine, fine, I'm doing fine," and the minister did not challenge him.

"Let me tell you about a young man in town who could use some help," Reverend Trimble began. He was standing, his arms crossed over his chest so that only the letters "ED S" were showing. Who is Ed S? Tracy wondered. Somewhere in the world there existed an Ed S. If Algie were here, he'd probably be looking him up in the phone book.

"He's sleeping in the woods," Jason Trimble said. "Lord knows how he feeds himself. No job. He's not in school. He's had some tough breaks, both the mother and the father. I've tried to cross to his side of the street for years, but he keeps sending me away. It's got to be a stranger. Someone who doesn't know him."

Tracy listened to the story with a racing heart. Reverend Trimble was asking him to seek the boy out, to take him under his wing, as if Tracy still had a wing under which someone could huddle or hide or seek shelter. That was the fallacy. His wings had been clipped when Algie died. No, his wings had been torn off. He was emotionally disfigured now. He couldn't fly to anyone so of course no one could fly to him. That was the math of it. It was an equation.

"He could help you, too," Trimble suggested.

Tracy looked at him doubtfully.

"No, I'm serious. Remember the beginning of the Scripture, when the man Luke calls 'the legal expert' asks Jesus, 'What must I do to inherit eternal life?' That question causes Jesus to lead him through the colloquy that ends with the question 'Well, what is a neighbor, anyway?' According to the Gospels, you get eternal life if you love your neighbor as yourself—that's what Jesus says."

Tracy laughed bitterly to himself. Eternal life? What good would that do?

But he said he would consider it—no promises. And then it so happened that he ran into Cuzzy Gage. And then it so happened that it snowed. And there Cuzzy was, sitting in his kitchen—in Algie's family's servants' kitchen, technically—spooning brown sugar onto a bowl of oatmeal. Cuzzy's hair was in his eyes, his expression was dull. So different, Tracy thought, from what we were like at his age.

Algie had wanted to kiss him. He put his mittened hand on the nape of Tracy's neck, and each finger conveyed that intention. He didn't close his eyes. Tracy remembered this, the way Algie seemed to be reading him.

And then he stepped out of Algie's grip and they kept walking, down Thompson, across Sullivan, over to Waverly, up Sixth Avenue, talking in fits and starts, and it was those sounds that carried the message, not the words themselves, and the message was about fracture, about what was now broken.

Tracy had thought the friendship they were making was pure, that it was uncorrupted by sex, the way no friendship with girls could ever be. Wasn't that what gave it its power—its chasteness? They were supposed to be brothers. Their minds were supposed to have met. So how come he didn't know, how come he had missed this essential thing about his friend?

"I thought that's what you wanted," Algie said evenly as they crossed over Forty-first Street. If he was disappointed by Tracy's reaction, he didn't show it, and this, strangely, infuriated Tracy, too.

Cuzzy looked over at Tracy, who seemed very faraway. "In China," as his father would say: *"How's the weather in China?"*

"I was hauling stone for my cousin Hank," Cuzzy offered. And then, defensively: "I'll get something."

Tracy sighed. He was a cautious person, about to do an incautious thing. He took a deep breath and thought of a bumper sticker he'd seen on the turnpike, driving up north, that said BREATHE. Only that, as if there was a choice.

"You could work for me," Tracy said. The words came out quickly, tumbling over one another like dice being rolled. But they were out. He had made the effort. He could tell Jason Trimble.

"What?" Cuzzy asked.

"I've got this odd job," Tracy said. "Emphasis on 'odd.'" He told Cuzzy about Algie's tree house, a wooden model of the Larches that, over the years, had gotten lost somewhere on the property.

"Lost?" Cuzzy said with real interest. "How do you lose a tree house?" He looked expectantly at Tracy.

"I said it was odd," Tracy said. "According to Algie, it's in an ash tree somewhere, which may or may not rule out some of the five hundred and eighty-seven acres of land you have to work with, if you take the job. The problem is that Algie didn't say which ash tree. He only said I should go to the tree house. He made me swear I would. This was right before he died. He was pretty out of it. But he was insistent.

"I looked when I got here, but I couldn't find it. Jason Trimble says you really know the woods—"

"Trimble—" Cuzzy bridled, but let it go.

"I can't pay you much," Tracy continued, "but you can stay here, and I'll feed you"—as he listened to himself, he decided it didn't sound like much of an offer at all—"and you can drive the car sometimes," he added. "Someone with your skill, it will probably take a day or two at most."

There, he had done it. Like it or not, he was working his way toward eternal life.

R A I N

How can it be hard, if it is drops of water? Is it a paradox of science or of perception? What about emotions? We assume that the experience of feelings is universal. We recognize one another as ourselves. In my storybook, Narcissus falls into the water and drowns.

Cuzzy walked through the woods with his head angled back till it stiffened there like a frozen hinge, but the tree house stayed lost. At first he was methodical, walking a hundred paces east, turning, walking twenty paces south, turning, walking a hundred paces west, turning. He had seen the rescue squad do something similar when they were searching for lost hikers or dead bodies (Ram Pullen's very own half sister, for one, killed by her brother-in-law and left for the coyotes on Fry Hill; the Lee girl for another, who was never found). But it didn't work. There was too much understory—it kept tripping him up—and no way to walk in a straight line, so after a while he followed his feet, which were following his eyes, which were fixed overhead. When a chipmunk tightroped from spruce to pine, Cuzzy went in that direction. When a nuthatch called from the trunk of a hemlock, Cuzzy responded with his feet. From somewhere deep in the forest, he heard warblers predicting the weather: "Sleet, sleet, sleet," they declared, and though it was damp and chilly, Cuzzy thought no, they were wrong, it would be another month, maybe two, till ice fell from the sky.

"'If a tree falls in the forest and nobody hears it, can you say for sure that it has fallen?'" Crystal had asked one day, reading the question off a quiz she'd torn out of a *Psychology Today* that had been lying around the health center ("for *years*," she said, to justify her theft). The quiz was called "Know Your Philosophical IQ," and Crystal told Cuzzy that it was important they both take it—"for the baby's sake." She had just found out she was pregnant, and was still talking to Cuzzy, and making him talk into her belly button as if it were a microphone, because a study she had seen in *Ladies' Home Journal* (boring, but Therese sometimes picked it up) said you could raise your baby's intelligence at least five points that way.

"What kind of question is that?" Cuzzy said. "If I slip on the ice in, I don't know, the middle of the night when no one is around, and I break my leg, because no one sees me do it, is my leg still broken?"

"Well, it *is* your leg. *You* would know," Crystal said thoughtfully, chewing on the end of her pen. It was full of little holes, as if she were teething, he thought. "I'm going to write down yes, for you. You think yes, the tree has still fallen."

"Don't you?" he demanded.

Crystal didn't answer. She was busy counting up yeses and nos. "Okay," she said finally. "According to this assessment"—he remembered that she used that word, not "quiz" or even "test"— "you are a logical positivist with something called 'heuristic leanings.'" She looked at him seriously, impassively, as if she herself had made the diagnosis.

Logical positivist. It didn't sound too bad, but you never knew with Crystal. It could be the kiss of death, as in: "My boyfriend had logical positivism with heuristic leanings, so I had to dump him." Which, of course, she did two months later.

"What is it?" Cuzzy asked cautiously. He wasn't sure he wanted to know. "What does it mean?"

Crystal read the definition to herself, frowned, and read it again. She was making Cuzzy very nervous.

"What?" he asked.

"I don't know," she said slowly. "I don't really get this. It says, 'People who are logical positivists believe that scientific knowledge is the only kind of factual knowledge, and all traditional metaphysical doctrines are to be rejected as meaningless.' The heuristic thing is pretty good, though. It means you're basically good to go."

"Oh," Cuzzy said. It didn't sound too bad after all. At least it didn't say he was going to grow up to be a serial killer, or insane. "What about you? What are you?"

Crystal smiled at him sweetly. He knew that smile. It meant she knew something he didn't know, something that, if he did, he might be envious of. "I took the test when I was waiting for my pre-nate"—that's what she called it; he thought it sounded like Crystal and pre-nate were old friends—"I got the super-skinny nurse this time. The one who feels like she's petting my uterus. It's really gross.

"Okay. It said that I was a 'mystical meliorist' and a 'latent pragmatic optimist.'"

"What the hell is that?" he said. At least it didn't sound any better than his.

"Watch your language around the baby," Crystal said sharply. "She can hear you, you know." And then, reading: "'A mystical meliorist is a person who believes in the existence of human cognitive power above reason; a pragmatic optimist is someone who believes that she can make things better.'" She looked up from the page. "From what I'm getting, 'latent' means that I'm someone who believes that this hasn't happened yet but will."

There were lots of trees down in the forest. Cuzzy had to climb up and over root balls and wrestle with tree limbs that still had enough fight in them to pop up and scratch his forearms and face if he wasn't careful. Even trees that were standing became enemies that had taken his bounty as their prisoner and were hiding it in full view. They were watching him. What was in that tree house, anyway? Tracy hadn't said. It was probably something big, something valuable. Why else would Algie insist that Tracy find it? It had to be big. Cuzzy smiled to himself. He thought, I'm starting to think the way she thinks.

Cuzzy came back at dusk to a vague light circling the cottage like mist around the moon on a cloudy night. He imagined Tracy inside, making dinner. But this was wishful; he was starved. Tracy had promised steaks for dinner, "big slabs of juicy meat," he said in the morning as Cuzzy stepped off the porch to begin his second day of "reconnaissance" (also Tracy's word), and now Cuzzy could hear the sizzle and pop of the fat on the griddle—though, being a logical positivist, he knew that it was really the sound of pinecones breaking under his boots. Music was coming out of the house—or what Tracy called music: loud, energetic tambourines being slapped and shaken, and women wailing while waggling their tongues.

"It's in your honor," Tracy said when Cuzzy came through the door. "Gypsy music."

Cuzzy looked at him dumbly. It was weird.

The steaks *were* on the stove. Tracy was salting a bowl of mashed potatoes—shaking out little bits of salt, then stirring, then tasting. Cuzzy wanted to grab the spoon.

"Any luck?" Tracy asked.

Cuzzy shook his head. He felt like a jerk. He should have found it.

Tracy pulled the steaks off the flame and put one on each plate, then gave the potatoes one last beat and doled them out. "It's got to be there, right?" he said. And then, when he saw Cuzzy smiling at him: "What?"

"Nothing," Cuzzy said.

"Nothing what?" Tracy insisted. Cuzzy could see that he was about to hold the food hostage.

"I'm starved," he tried.

"Tell."

"All right," Cuzzy said. "I was thinking that you may be a meliorist-pragmatist. Something like that. I read it in a magazine once."

Tracy handed him his plate. "Reverend Trimble didn't tell me you were a philosopher," he said.

"Reverend Trimble doesn't know me."

"Well, who does?" Tracy asked.

What he meant was: who knows anyone? Really knows them. When Tracy was around Cuzzy's age, he thought he knew Algie. They talked on the phone. They *corresponded.* They gave each other books as if they were sharing food; it was what nourished them. One would say, "You have to read Vonnegut." The other would say, *"Four Quartets."* And there was music, always music—Ives and Copeland, Bach, Satie. Wasn't that how people knew each other, by what took their breath away? Hadn't he heard Algie gasp when he listened to *The Unanswered Question?* He had heard. So why didn't he *know?* And why, when he sought assistance from his dictionary (he was his father's son, after all), did it mock him: "Know(v.): to perceive directly; to apprehend immediately; to recognize as valid or as fact on the basis of information possessed or of one's understanding or intelligence; to have sexual intercourse with."

When he was younger, he remembered laughing about this. How could knowing mean having sex? How could they possibly be the same thing?

The warbler almost had it right. No sleet, but sometime around nine, rain began to fall and continued through the night. Ten hours later it was still falling, not as hard, but with the same steady insistence. Cuzzy saw it from bed, hitting the window in round drops, then lengthening into lines, like upside-down exclamation points. In the other room Tracy was playing his strange music again, something high-pitched and twangy that reminded Cuzzy of the time he and Crystal went to the Chinese takeout place in Halcyon Falls, an hour in the truck because she was pregnant and had a craving for shrimp fried rice. When she got there, she decided that shrimp fried rice was disgusting—the shrimp, tiny, pink, and curled, reminded her of dead fetuses—and she threw the box in the trash because she couldn't bear to have Cuzzy chewing "those poor babies" any more than she could eat them herself. Instead, she ordered a quart of egg-drop soup with extra noodles. While they were waiting—Cuzzy remembered this clearly, *Jeopardy!* was on the overhead TV, and the category was "Birthstones for $200," and Crystal got every one except "opal" right—the old man who worked in the kitchen came out, caught sight of Crystal's belly, and, gesturing in her direction, said, "Donkey, donkey, donkey." He said it again and again, smiling a big, excited smile, until Crystal, furious, stood up and walked over to him and said, "Just who are you calling an ass?" The other customers were looking at her, and the old man was smiling and pointing at her belly, which was especially prominent when Crystal had her hands on her hips. Cuzzy had stood up, too, though he didn't know what to do. Deck the guy? The man was old and not much over five feet.

"This February birthstone was once thought to be a cure for drunkenness," Alex Trebek said. Crystal turned away from the man and addressed the television: "What is amethyst?" In that moment a young Chinese girl who had been sitting behind the counter, writing in a workbook, put down her pencil and stood up.

"He means your baby will be born in the year of the donkey," she said, as if answering a question in school, and sat down.

"Oh," Crystal said. "Why didn't he say so?"

The old man nodded. "Donkey," he said.

"Is that good or bad?" Crystal demanded.

They gave her the soup for free.

Tracy heard the rain, too, and put on the music so he wouldn't have to think about sending Cuzzy out into it. But if Cuzzy stayed inside, what would he do all day? Tracy guessed that he wasn't exactly a reader. Strictly speaking, Tracy had done what Reverend Trimble had asked him to do: he had crossed the road for Cuzzy Gage. But if Trimble asked him directly, he'd have to say no, it hadn't been hard. Cuzzy was a nice enough kid—not much company, but not bad company, either.

Tracy caught a glimpse of Cuzzy on the way to the bathroom. He was wearing a T-shirt and a pair of navy boxers; his hair was in his face. Tracy imagined him in there, leaning over the sink, brushing his teeth. It was such a simple, everyday thing, toothbrushing, a moment when people were guileless. No, he wouldn't send Cuzzy into the rain.

"How are you with the alphabet?" Tracy asked Cuzzy a little while later, handing him a cup of coffee.

"You mean, A, B, C, D, E, F, G?" Cuzzy asked. Tracy could be very—as Joey might say—unusual.

"Exactly," Tracy said.

"Okay, I guess. I never thought about it." Cuzzy still had not called Crystal. He thought he wanted to, and then he didn't. It was sort of the opposite of having sex with her: he'd think he wanted to, then he did want to, and then they did it, and then he'd want to some more.

"I'm thinking I could use some help," Tracy continued, "if you're interested." He looked at Cuzzy's face, hoping it would give him an answer, but it was blank, completely. Tracy was disappointed. He wanted something from Cuzzy, some gesture. He looked at him harder. Maybe that would do it.

"What?" Cuzzy said.

Tracy sighed. "I just thought maybe you'd show more enthusiasm."

"For what?" Cuzzy was pissed. This guy was an odd duck.

"For the job."

"*What* job?" It was like they were having a fight, but Cuzzy couldn't figure out what it was about. Crystal did the same thing. They'd be having what he thought was a regular conversation, like when he told her once he was going fishing with Hank, and then she'd get all chilly, or huffy, and he'd say, "Why are you pissed?" and she'd say she wasn't, and then they'd get in a fight about that, and finally, in the middle of that argument, she'd narrow her eyes and wag her finger and shout, "I know you'd rather go fishing with Hank than help me pick out the layette. And you're not even going to keep the fish, if you even catch one."

"The job of alphabetizing and organizing Algie's letters and papers," Tracy said. Maybe he wasn't angry after all, Cuzzy decided. He seemed almost nervous.

"I've been so busy going through Algie's notebooks, I haven't had time to sort out the boxes." Tracy waved in the direction of a stack of cartons pushed against the wall opposite the wood-stove. Most of them said BUDWEISER; a couple said RED RIVER VAL-

LEY PINOT NOIR. Cuzzy had wondered about them, what Tracy was doing with all that alcohol, never guessing they were filled with paper.

"What about the tree house?" Cuzzy asked, feeling suddenly protective, worried that Tracy might be abandoning it.

"You can look for that, too," Tracy said, "only not in the rain."

"I don't mind," Cuzzy said, but this was just talk. He was glad to have an excuse to stay dry.

The papers had been tossed in the boxes in no particular order. Letters and postcards were sandwiched amid xeroxed articles and journals and musical scores and maps. Cuzzy knelt in front of the first box and pulled out what was on top. It was an article called "Initiation for Beginners." The first line began, "Everyone only gets initiated for the first time, once."

"What should I do with this?" Cuzzy said, waving it in Tracy's direction.

"What year was it published?"

Cuzzy had no idea. Tracy got up from his desk and came over and took the article from Cuzzy. "It's right here," he said, pointing to the fine print at the top of the page. "Start a pile for 1963. Put all the papers from that year in the same pile."

Cuzzy took out the next item, a monograph between light blue covers entitled "The Case for a Gendered Music," by someone named Bettina Mudlich. This one was easy. The year, 1981, was printed right on the cover. Cuzzy made another pile, as far from 1963 as he could get. It was as if he could span eighteen years, as many years as he'd been alive, between his left hand and his right. He wondered about Bettina Mudlich: had she been teased when she was a kid? Mudlicker?

Tracy watched Cuzzy work for a while on his knees, starting

piles, adding to piles, pausing to comment on titles ("A Celebration of Ululation in the Makeebo Piercing Ceremony"; "Ontology and Chanson: A Disquisition on the Monkees").

"Your friend read some pretty weird shit," Cuzzy said.

"I'm not sure if he read them or if he thought they were worth saving because the titles were so funny," Tracy said.

Cuzzy held up a letter. "Here's one from you," he said. Tracy came over and took the envelope. He looked at it a moment, then slipped it into the top drawer of his desk. Tracy knew that letter. He'd read it so many times before finally sealing the envelope that it felt as if it was written directly onto his brain.

Algie had written as soon as Tracy left their hotel room. This was the morning after the kiss that hadn't happened. Algie had offered breakfast—"my treat"—and Tracy said he had to catch a train, which was a bald-faced lie, which they both knew, which gave Tracy some satisfaction. The letterhead bore the Waterston Hotel coat of arms, a shield emblazoned with a phoenix, next to which Algie had drawn a small arrow with the thinnest of strokes; it could have been an eyelash.

"My dear friend," it began,

I should probably write you a simple apology and be done with it (and you with me), but nothing I want to write right now is simple. Certainly we love each other. Certainly Aristotle would elect us to the pantheon of friendship! It is my nature to get carried away, to want everything. You, above all, know this.

Since you gave me Letters to a Young Poet *last summer, it's been in my backpack. I have read it, and reread it, and have always cast myself in the role of the young poet. I imagine that*

when you read it, you do the same thing. Here's what Rilke tells
him/me/you:

". . . the point is to live everything. Live the questions now.
Perhaps, then, someday far in the future, you will gradually,
without even noticing it, live your way into the answer. Perhaps
you do carry within you the possibility of creating and forming,
as an especially blessed and pure way of living; train yourself for
that—but take whatever comes; with great trust, and as long as
it comes out of your will, out of some need of your innermost
self, then take it upon yourself and don't hate anything. Sex is
difficult, yes. *But those tasks that have been entrusted to us are*
difficult, almost everything serious is difficult, and everything is
serious. If you just recognize this and manage, out of yourself,
out of your own talent and nature, out of your own
experience and childhood and strength, to achieve a wholly
individual relation to sex (one that is not influenced
by convention and custom*), then you no longer have to be*
afraid of losing yourself and becoming unworthy of your dearest
possession."

I want to believe this is possible, Tracy. I do believe it's
possible. I am sending the book back to you. Please read it again.
                    My best love, from your dear friend.

Tracy did read the book again. It seemed always on the cusp of
telling him something important, something he needed to know,
and then trailing off to a whisper that he could not make out. Algie wrote another letter: "Of your silence, this: 'Better be a nettle
in the side of your friend than his echo. The condition which high
friendship demands is the ability to do without' (Ralph Waldo)."

It was all so cerebral. Tracy had liked that. Theirs was a friendship of the mind. Bodies did not enter into it. Bodies were incon-

stant. They were messy. Still, the question had been raised: why not "know" Algie in every sense of the word—why know him only part of the way? What cowardice, what fundamental need for ignorance, held him back? *"Achieve a wholly individual relation to sex (one that is not influenced by convention and custom)."* But when he tried to imagine himself doing that, tried to imagine what it would have been like to lean in and meet Algie's kiss on its own terms, as if that one gesture represented their love and expressed their love and made that love more complete, he couldn't. His imagination failed him, and secretly, he was relieved.

"It looks like you're making a good start," Tracy said, feeding a log—ash, Cuzzy noticed, looking up—into the woodstove.

"Listen to the title of this one," Cuzzy said. He was becoming more animated. Tracy saw it in his eyes. "'Mandible and Mandolin, Corpus and Construction,' by Geoffrey Farthington, Clifford House, and Claudia House-White. Do you think Clifford and Claudia were married?"

"No, then it would have been Claudia White-House. As in Pennsylvania Avenue. They're siblings. Twins. Friends of Algie's from graduate school."

"Oh," Cuzzy said, scanning the paper for a publication date.

"Let me guess," Tracy said. "1987."

"Close," Cuzzy said, tossing it on one of the piles farthest from where Tracy stood. "Eighty-eight."

Tracy smiled to himself. It was in 1987, a year after Claudia House's marriage to Erik White, that her twin proclaimed his undying affection for Algie Black, an affection that Algie returned, though not before accusing Cliff of liking the symmetry of it: Clifford House-Black and his sister, Claudia House-White.

"Of course, to me he is now Clifford House-Guest," Algie wrote to Tracy, explaining that he and Cliff were "cohabitating." They were friends again, Tracy and Algie, and not by accident. Tracy had gone to college with Cliff House's sister. For a short time, they were lovers. That was the real symmetry of it.

DIAMOND

Why is what is clearest often hardest?

S he was going through one of those "I hate my body" jags
that would come over her periodically, like PMS, which she
didn't get anymore, ever since she started to drink raspberry
nettle tea four times a day, which was a pain, but not as much of a
pain as PMS. Four times a day was twice as much as the health ad-
viser in *Allure* recommended, but she figured if it helped when you
drank it two times a day, it would help twice as much if you increased it to four. She considered what might happen if she took it
six times, or eight—she wouldn't notice she was bleeding at all—
but the stuff was vile, and four cups was about all she could toler-
ate without feeling sorry for herself and for the whole unfortunate
condition of women everywhere.

But there was nothing to take that would shut up the voice
telling her she was too skinny. Not as skinny as Amber-Rose—that
truly would be a nightmare—but skinny enough to see the con-
tours of her breastbone and each individual rib, even the floating
ones, when she looked in the mirror. It was like she was halfway to
being dead. God, she didn't understand people who wanted to be
cremated. It sounded awful: they stuck you in an oven, and you
went up in smoke. That was what thinking about her skinny body
did. It made her think things like that.

It was obvious to her what body type Cuzzy Gage preferred, and she guessed if she was a guy, she might, too, if the alternative was fat girls, which a special on *60 Minutes* said there were more and more of. (It didn't say there were guys who got off on girls like that, who confused "smothering" with "mothering," as if they were sexual dyslexics. She had seen a show about that on *Montel*.) So Cuzzy liked skinny, but she, Crystal, was plain sick of it.

Her breasts were all right. Guys liked them, so she guessed she liked them, too. They were *substantial*. They just poured out of her hardscrabble chest like water from a most productive well. Thirty gallons a minute of soft flesh. Guys could be very thirsty.

Cuzzy, though—Cuzzy was a drought. She hadn't seen him in weeks, since before he met the rich guy. She heard about him; people stopped her and said they'd seen him in this place or that: the Laundromat, walking in with a big green comforter (king-size?) and stuffing it into the dryer (what was that about? where had he washed it?), and at the Grand Union, buying a rotisserie chicken (he never bought a rotisserie chicken with her). She couldn't decide if he was more like a celebrity or more like a ghost, the way people reported sightings. A ghost to her, anyway. But when he and the rich guy showed up at the Poverty General Store, all the kids gathered around the car and wanted to touch it.

Shirley LaValle, who had been in her class at school, was the one who told her this. Shirley was subbing for her sister, Lucky, who was down at the hospital in Halcyon Falls with her husband, Chuck, who had accidentally gotten shot in the rear end with a nail from a roofing gun. Shirley called up Crystal and said, "You are not going to believe who was just in here," and sounded a little hurt when Crystal was not more surprised. But that was what everyone said when they called her up: "You are not going to believe who I just saw."

"They asked for *The New York Times*," Shirley reported.

"They?"

"Well, the guy."

"Oh," said Crystal. She was thinking that maybe some of that New York stuff was rubbing off on Cuzzy, though which part, she'd rather not think about. But the problem with Cuzzy Gage, the real problem from the "do I want to wear his ring" perspective, aside from his having a crazy father (whose genes were already mingled with hers, in any case), was that he was too *local*. Ask him where he was born, and he'd say, "Poverty." Ask him where he was going to be in five years or ten, and he'd say, "Poverty." If his ambition was to live in Poverty, he had already achieved it. That was why she had fudged that *Psychology Today* test, adding the heuristic thing. Being a pragmatist herself, Crystal believed that sometimes, if you told a person he was a certain way (kind or smart or thoughtful or generous), he would rise to the occasion and become it.

Cuzzy was still on his knees, pushing papers from one side of the cottage to the other. Crystal should see me now, Cuzzy thought. It wasn't quite a desk job, but it was kind of similar—a floor job. But he'd rather think of himself as a farmer, making the piles grow higher, like crops in rich loam. Seventy-nine was a good year for drum initiation in Mali; 1985 it was female (!) circumcision.

As he worked, Cuzzy stole glances at Tracy, who was bent over his desk, pen behind his ear, concentrating, or thinking hard, *in China*. Cuzzy was looking for evidence, any little thing, that could tell him for sure: was Tracy or wasn't he? There was that letter from Tracy to Algie, which would probably tell him something, but it was in Tracy's desk, and Cuzzy couldn't think how to get at it—not yet, anyhow. There was Tracy's denial ("not lovers"), but people were always denying it. You could never be certain. People had hidden lives. Those married guys who got off on wearing garters and stockings under their three-piece suits: you never knew. *Your friend the fag.* Who your friends were had to count for something, didn't it? And the poetry. Tracy was so into it. On the other hand, he was an English teacher, and teachers were supposed to like that sort of thing, or at least say they did. Cuzzy could tell that Tracy liked it though. He wasn't making it up.

Tracy knew Cuzzy was looking without even raising his head. He could feel it, a momentary stillness and a breathing that was aware of itself, and he was pleased. For weeks the two of them had been sitting in close quarters, nudging another man's life into a shape it didn't have on its own, at first without meaning to, and then with more vigor. Tracy found himself doing the same with Cuzzy Gage. Maybe it was the Good Samaritan thing, maybe it was being a teacher; Tracy did not stop to analyze his intentions. "Just do it," the sneaker ads admonished, and Lord knew, he was trying. So when Cuzzy paused, and looked up, and regarded him, Tracy understood that the boy's curiosity, long dormant, was beginning to wake up. "The beginning of curiosity is the beginning of the world." Tracy could not remember where he'd read that. A poem, an essay, it didn't matter. It was true. Cuzzy was beginning to wake up to the world. His wariness, that of the fox prowling the margins, was still there, but his diffidence lifted now and then like a curtain, parting to show what might have been—if his father hadn't been taken away; if his father wasn't sick; if his mother hadn't died—and what might be there yet.

After lunch they walked, looking for the tree house, up a corridor of beech and down a corridor of birch, through the white pines and along a rocky draw, accompanied as much by each other as by the sound of the frozen earth pushing back against the weight of their feet. Once they were outside, Cuzzy was at ease in his body, which got looser and longer-limbed as he glided between the trees like there was a road there, pointing out bear sign and moose scat, taking note of a chickadee nest hidden behind the bark of a blue spruce, calling out, "Red-breasted nuthatch. Cardinal. Evening grosbeak. Jay," unbidden. Every sound had a name.

"You should make a life list," Tracy said.

Cuzzy didn't answer. The only ambition you should have in the woods is to be in the woods. "Junco," he said.

Inside—he didn't know what ambition should be inside. He listened at breakfast as Tracy folded and refolded the newspaper. That world was far away. Once Tracy said, "What matters?" which Cuzzy heard as "What's the matter?" and even so, his answer was the same. "Nothing," he said.

What Cuzzy liked best were the evenings, lying near the wood-stove, the cottage lit yellow like the pages of an old book. He rolled himself into a blanket and soaked up the warmth of the fire as if he were at the beach, and Tracy sat in the rocking chair with a book in his lap, looking like the teacher he had been. Tracy did this the summers he was a camp counselor and when he was a dorm parent, reading aloud at night, as though the boys at his feet were six and seven, not twelve or sixteen. They arrayed themselves around him like spokes, many of them facing away so no one could see their pleasure and mistake it for need, or see their need and think that they were weak. Cuzzy, too. He lay with his head tucked into his arms, eyes closed, listening to the sound of Tracy's voice as if it were the tide. Or his father reading from the Book of Psalms. With Tracy it was poetry, always. One night Emily Dickinson, another night W. H. Auden—names of people who could be his neighbors. Wallace Stevens once ("one must have a mind of winter"); and often—because, Tracy said, he was getting used to the sound of the wind and hearing no misery in it—he read Robert Frost: "I dwell with a strangely aching heart / In that vanished abode there far apart / On that disused and forgotten road / That has no dust-bath now for the toad." The poems were tones to Cuzzy, syllables independent of meaning, like the Maori chants Algie had collected. Cuzzy lay there, and they washed up and over him and, in the same way his father's words had, coaxed him to give up the pretensions of his body, to slip out of it like clothes.

"This is weird," Cuzzy said. He was sitting cross-legged in front of one of the Budweiser boxes, holding a blue tissue-paper envelope that said "Par Avion" across the front.

"What is?" Tracy said, though not right away. He was like that sometimes. Distracted.

"This letter has never been opened." Cuzzy studied the return address and the canceled stamp. "It's not that old," he reported. "It looks like it was sent after Algie . . ."

"Who's it from?" Tracy said, hardly looking up.

"No name," Cuzzy said. "Just an address. Seventy-third Street. In New York."

Tracy jerked to full attention. "Oh my God," he said. "That must be from Brennan Perkins."

"Who is Brennan Perkins?" Cuzzy asked, but Tracy didn't answer. He took the envelope from Cuzzy's outstretched hand, looked it over, and then, with a practiced motion, slid his index finger under the flap and opened it along the glue line. Cuzzy was impressed. He would have torn it himself. Tracy fished out the letter, which was written on matching blue tissue paper. The person who wrote it had typed.

"It *is* from Perkins," Tracy said. "Damn."

Cuzzy sat there like a dog waiting for a piece of meat, and at last Tracy seemed to notice and threw it.

"Brennan Perkins is this really old expatriate Tasmanian land surveyor and explorer Algie knew. He lives at the Voyagers' Club in New York. Algie was convinced that he had the only recordings in the world of certain Australian aboriginal initiation ceremonies, and he wanted to get ahold of them."

"To keep?"

"Well, at least to listen to. All the anthropologists said they didn't exist, and Algie believed they did, and he wanted to beat them at their own game. Here, wait a minute." Tracy homed in on a notebook on his desk and flipped through the pages. "Okay, here it is. This is from an article in *American Anthropologist* from 1936: 'As with the Yahgan, so likewise with the Southeast Australians: the initiation ceremonies include pantomimes and dances in which the behavior and cries of (totem) birds and animals are realistically imitated. Unfortunately, no phonographic records were made of Southeast Australian (and Tasmanian) songs before the curtain dropped forever on the history of these natives.'"

"But it says there were no known recordings," Cuzzy said. He was confused.

Tracy shook his head. "I'm not explaining it right. Apparently the anthropologists had been wrong in the past about stuff like this, and Algie thought they were wrong again. There were recordings made at the turn of the century of other native groups who lived nearby, and no one knew about them for decades. Algie thought the same thing might have been true with this group, mainly because he had by accident seen an unpublished letter to the editor of *American Anthropologist* that Perkins wrote, hinting that the scholars—most of whom he hated because they considered him a bush-league amateur—had given up too soon. Algie used to visit him, but Perkins never did anything but bitch and moan about bloodless academics. Algie loved that. He would sometimes refer to himself that way, although when he was dying, he'd say, 'Tell Perkins he was wrong. Turns out I've got a lot of blood, if he'd care to see it.' He had a shunt then, right in the wall of his chest. It looked like a hose bib, you know, on the outside of a building. The thing you hook a sprinkler up to.

"The thing was, Algie didn't need those recordings for anything. He wanted them, yes, but he didn't need them. He mainly collected instruments. His recording collection was pretty haphazard. But this thing sort of became an obsession. He said he knew that Perkins was going to unload his tapes one day, and he wanted to be the one on whom they were unloaded. Algie was like that. He made things into quests. I never thought of it before, but maybe that's why he studied what he studied."

For the longest time—twenty-four months, to be precise—Tracy had been the object of one of Algie's quests. He knew how dogged (stubborn? unrealistic?) Algie could be. The letters started after their night in New York, one a week, always written at ten o'clock on Sunday, week after week for two years. Algie continued to send poems and articles he'd clipped from magazines, and short reviews of movies and plays he'd found interesting. His own words were brief: "Thought you'd find this interesting" or "Check this out" or "This is *amazing*." And Tracy did check it out, and he did find it interesting and amazing, but he never told Algie; he wrote back only that first time. One year in, and Algie wrote a different sort of letter on "the anniversary of the breach in our friendship." Someday it would be restored, Algie said, and the letters "will be a bridge on which we will stand and reflect on the past and look to the future." At the time Tracy thought it was pretentious and stupid, but a couple of years later it turned out to be true.

"I want you to come to a party Cliff and I are having for some of our friends," Claudia House had said on the phone. She was up-town at Columbia, Tracy was across the river in Englewood, teach-ing at the Strand School, and they still got together sometimes. He went, with a cellophane-wrapped bouquet of flowers that he had gotten at the Korean grocery next door to the subway, and a bottle of wine someone had brought to his apartment once for dinner.

The party was on 119th Street, on the roof of a walk-up build-ing. WEST SIDE BEACH, a hand-drawn sign said. People were sitting around on blankets and towels and playing old Bob Dylan songs on a guitar and roasting hot dogs and marshmallows over a hibachi grill. It was one of those unlikely New York scenes that Tracy loved.

"Hello, Tracy," said a voice from behind him as he took it all in. Algie's voice, only deeper. Tracy turned around and there he was, taller, with longer hair, the same deep blue eyes. Tracy searched around for Claudia—he could use some help here—but her back was to him, and he couldn't exactly shout.

"She knew I'd be here," Algie said, watching his eyes. "It was her idea. She thought it had been long enough."

"I've got to go to New York," Tracy said, putting the letter back in the envelope. "I think he wants to give us the recordings."

Cuzzy blanched. "Us." Tracy had said "us," and he hadn't even noticed. What did that mean?

Tracy was writing something down. He was putting on his coat. He was moving around the cottage urgently. "You want to go to town, Cuzzy?" he called from the bedroom. "I've got to send Perkins an overnight letter. To tell him I'm coming. He never an-swers his phone."

"You go. I'll stay here." Cuzzy didn't like going to town anymore. He was sure people were looking at him funny, like they hadn't known him all his life.

"You sure?"

"Yeah." Cuzzy went back to sorting. He listened carefully for the recessional of stones hitting the underbelly of the Porsche, waited till they were faint and then fainter. He stood up, stretched, and looked out the window, waiting till the image bored him, before walking over to Tracy's desk. Cuzzy opened the top drawer and saw what he was looking for, just lying there, unguarded.

"Algie," it began,

The answer is no. No, "that" is not what I wanted. I'm not sure why you didn't know this, or that I didn't know it about you, but it suggests the ultimate failure of our friendship then, and now, and for all time.

— Tracy

Cuzzy slipped the envelope back into the desk. He supposed he had his answer, too.

There was a single vehicle in the post-office parking lot, and when Tracy walked by it, someone called out his name. Tracy looked up. It was Ram Pullen, Cuzzy's friend, sitting in his truck with a gaunt, brown-haired girl who was wearing a down jacket with the hood pulled up.

"Hey," Ram said. "You guys sure have been strangers."

"Yeah, we've been working hard," Tracy said.

"This is Amber," Ram said. The girl drew further into the soft carapace. "She used to know Cuzzy, too."

Tracy looked at his watch. "I hate to be rude, but I really have to get in there before it closes." He nodded in the direction of the post office.

"Well, tell Cuzzy that there are, quote, certain, unquote, people in town who have been asking about him."

Tracy nodded. "Will do," he said.

"Hey," Ram called as Tracy walked away, "everyone's been wondering when you're going to ask for the ransom money."

Tracy turned. "What?" he said.

"For holding him hostage."

"Very funny," Tracy said. "He can leave whenever he wants."

"Sure," Ram said. "Just tell our Cuz that we miss him. And Joey really misses him."

There was something genuine in the way he said this. Tracy heard it, and he wondered momentarily if Cuzzy missed his friends, too. It was a thought that had never occurred to him before.

Ram was still idling there with Amber when Tracy came out. The letter was on its way. Perkins would get it in the morning. Two days later Tracy would go see him.

"Do you have a piece of paper?" Tracy said, leaning in Ram's window.

"Not unless you mean the kind you roll."

"Here," Tracy said, tearing off the envelope flap of Brennan Perkins's letter. "I have to go to New York for a couple of days." He wrote down a phone number. "Why don't you and Joey visit Cuzzy when I'm gone. Give him a call and tell him you're coming. He'd like that."

IVORY

"The hard creamy-white modified dentine that composes the tusks of a tusked mammal," says Routledge, Biology 10; *Ivory as composition, composition as the prelude to music. We are so concerned with first principles. How about this: solace before all!*

There were flying squirrels in the attic. Cuzzy was almost sure that was what they were. He heard them especially in the afternoon, when the sun dropped below the Notch and they began shimmying in between the vents under the eaves. Their little feet pattering, and the seesaw of air as they moved from one side of the house to the other and back again. He had a trap, an old steel one that Tracy had rescued from the basement, the kind that snapped off their heads as they sailed in, loudly and without a doubt. "Can't do it myself," Tracy said, assuming that Cuzzy, who used to set lines for mink and pine marten, could.

"Use this when I'm in the city," Tracy said, pointing to the dusty metal cage, and now he was gone, and the trap was still on the floor near the broom closet, and the squirrels remained camped overhead. Cuzzy was not unhappy to have them there. The regularity of their arrival every day, like shift workers, pleased him.

Tracy had been gone for two days. The time felt endless to Cuzzy, yet it had gone fast. Hours were lost under the covers, listening to peculiar-sounding Senegalese, Inuit, and Bulgarian music full blast through the headphones, and to longish hikes around the property looking for the tree house, filling the bird feeders. Cuzzy didn't believe in this—the birds could fend for themselves—but Tracy insisted. Otherwise, he didn't ask for much. Not even the mail to be collected or the house to be cleaned, just handed Cuzzy the keys to the car, said, "See you," and got on the Trailways bus, waving once from the window before unrolling his *Times*. Cuzzy was determined to keep those squirrels alive as long as possible.

It felt odd, almost wrong, to be by himself again. Cuzzy had been at the Larches for weeks, each day following the one before it like a paving stone, as if together they made a path from one place to another.

That Wednesday Cuzzy discovered the notes. Not Algie's notebooks, which Tracy spent whole days poring over. These he'd seen before. Each (there were thirty) looked like a standard composition book, the marbleized kind with black tape binding and the words "This Book Belongs To" and "Date" on the front cover. In those spaces, in a linear, architectural hand, was "Algernon S. Black," and the dates the book spanned, and the places it was composed: Harrare, Fortaleza, Montevideo, Jakarta. Places that sounded to Cuzzy like frozen foods.

But that was nothing compared to what was on the inside. Each page was a collage of images and words and textures—maps of a mobile, inconstant, and aching mind. Letters cut from magazines and strung, like ransom notes, into words, the words into sentences; and canceled stamps and puzzle pieces jigged from postcards; and lines excised by razor from letters. Tracy had shown Cuzzy a phrase from one of his, "boys in their beds," written when he was a camp counselor. "That was his vision," Tracy said. "That he could lift four words out of context and drop them into a new context, even one that seemed to have nothing to do with them, and they took on a whole new significance. They became freighted, if you see what I mean." He paused, breathless, then inhaled deeply, as if he had been running.

"'Boys in their beds.' It sounds sinister and seductive all at once, innocent and dangerous. And it's only a tiny part of a single page. See the bus ticket to Iguacu Falls? See the inky imprint of a sugarcane? Which I know is sugarcane only because I sent a copy of it to a tropical-plant guy at the Museum of Natural History in New York. Talk about natural history. This is Algie's natural history. Not of the world but of himself in the world."

Cuzzy had thought Tracy was going to stop talking and turn the page—he was anticipating it—and Tracy did stop talking out loud but didn't make a move. He just stared at that page and ran his fingers over it as if it were an arm or a shoulder or possibly—the stroke was so delicate—a cheek.

"Every page in these books tells a story. No—they tell a bunch of stories," Tracy went on. "They show what's happening at the time. See this headline from the *International Herald Tribune*? And this one from *La Razon*. They both date the page to some money-laundering scheme in Argentina involving aging Nazis. But also what was going on with Algie. He seemed to be lonely, for instance. Everything he did, he did alone. But here's the receipt for a sleeping hammock. *Para dos.* A double. He was always an optimist. Even when he was sick."

This was Tracy's main work, deciphering the notebooks page by page to tell the story more conventionally. He wrote things like "On January 26, Black took a bus to Recife, a poor coastal town known for its international lobster trade. There he struck up a friendship with Hector de Sousa, a cannery worker and sometime street musician who introduced him to the Forro (cf. snapshot of de Sousa dancing, #25). From all accounts, Black spent a month in

Recife and Fortaleza, studying that form, then left in late February, the height of summer in Brazil, for Iguacu Falls. It was near the falls the he first encountered the Argentine ocarina . . ."

"Algie would hate this," Tracy told Cuzzy. "It's so straight. But he would be flattered by it, too."

Tracy said this, but did he believe it? Some days he did, and some days he was sure that it was as pointless as Algie's death. On those days he wondered if the fact of death, its very certainty, made every life pointless.

His old girlfriend after Claudia House, a buoyant music teacher at his school named Chloe Murray, told him no. "Who has time for doubt," she'd say, rushing off to glee club or shushing him playfully when he'd begin a sentence with the words "But what if." It was so unconflicted, her vision of the future: a girl, two boys, a golden retriever—the whole map of their lives laid out like a AAA TripTik, a single red line running across the center. But Tracy wasn't sure: what if that line was an arrow lodged in the heart?

Algie was failing. Tracy would write, "Chloe and I went to hear Kodo at the Japanese Cultural Center," and it was code for "I am thinking of you. I am remembering when you were in Kyoto, and your stories about the men who hefted drums as tall as cars are wide." He knew now that Algie had gotten it. Why else was that line pasted in one of his notebooks?

Then Algie died, and Tracy couldn't look at Chloe anymore. Could not look at her and had to quit his job, because it occurred to him that the person he had loved most in the world had left it, and that even so, he loved the idea of this man more than anything or anyone on earth. It was algebra, plain and simple—even in death, his love for his friend was greater than his love for Chloe, who breathed next to him at night. He left a poem on her pillow by William Carlos Williams that began, "The whole process is a lie, unless, crowned by excess," and shut the door.

Those were the months of regret, when he wondered why he had not claimed Algie and his love for him, why he hadn't put a stake in that ground and a shovel, too, till there was a hole on one side and a mound on the other and they could climb that hill together. "That's what death is *about,* regret," his father told him, which was the kindest thing he ever said, even if it was about something else altogether (Omaha Beach? A dog he had to put to sleep? Tracy couldn't remember).

Why did his love feel like a haiku missing a single syllable? What was sex, anyway? And why, when it was offered (almost, that kiss), had he shied away? Because, he told himself, he could not conceive of doing it. Flesh to flesh. It was Algie, of the two of them, who had the imagination after all.

So it wasn't the notebooks, it was the notes. Cuzzy saw them Wednesday morning when he sat down at the piano in the big house and picked out a tune, a Christmas carol, he realized, "God Rest Ye Merry Gentlemen." First the melody, then an improvised bottom line, a series of heavy triads that made the song sound like a funeral march, which caused Cuzzy to smile. For a year, when he was eight, his father had taught him piano, and he felt the muscle memory awakening as his fingers touched the keys, which were polished and unbroken, unlike those on his parents' ancient Jacob Brothers upright.

When he tired of playing, Cuzzy stood up and stretched, yawning with his eyes closed, so he didn't see that he was about to send piles of music to the floor as his hands dropped to his sides. The music rushed to the ground, called suddenly by the whistle of gravity. It woke him with a start, and so did his hand where he'd smacked it on the instrument. It was red across the back, with a welt already rising, and when Cuzzy finished examining it, he no-

ticed that only one book of music remained on the stand, blue im-
printed with a gold lyre. Even if he didn't see the title, he knew
what it was. *The Sacred Harp.* At one time in his life, like it or not,
he knew it well.

Cuzzy picked it up. The edges had worn through to the cardboard. This book had been in his own house when he was a boy—
twenty-two copies of it, picked out of the trash and people's attics
or bought from churches where they had been mildewing in their
boxes. Sometimes at night, after the family hymn ("How Great
Thou Art" or "Go Tell It on the Mountain") and the bedtime
prayer, the three of them on their knees, his father would crowd
the end of Cuzzy's mattress and tell the story of Willard Randles,
the itinerant singing master who swept through Stover once every
year or so over a hundred years before, preaching the Gospel
through song. First he'd sell them the book, then he'd teach them
the songs, then they'd give a concert, and two months after he came
in with the harvest wind, he'd be gone. The singing would go on
without a master, Cuzzy's father said, but with the one and true
Master, as if Randles's departure and the music he left behind were
proof.

The notes. Cuzzy didn't even have to look. A triangle was "fa,"
a circle was "sol," a square was "la," and a diamond was "mi." Just
four tones, but quite sufficient, his father would say, to praise Jesus.

Cuzzy opened the book and let the pages fall at will. This, he
recognized, was what his father did, too. He'd call on a worshiper
to "allow the hand of God to lead them to the water of song," and
she'd let her *Sacred Harp* fall open to a page, and they would sing
what was written there. Which was why "Done with the World"
was repeated three times one Sunday, a turn of events that left everyone but his father, who was ecstatic, giggling. "The hand of Christ
Jesus indeed!" he bellowed.

This hymn was "Wondrous Love." Cuzzy shut his eyes. It was a test. How much did he remember? "'What wondrous love is this!'" he started. "'Oh my soul, oh my soul!'" and had to peek. "'That caused the Lord of Bliss / To bear the dreadful curse / For my soul.'" It was not perfect, but it was close. Cuzzy guessed his father, the father he had known, would be pleased with him. He was even a little pleased with himself.

Cuzzy closed his eyes and tried again. He heard the squirrels skittering overhead—they were in this house, too—and then the beat of wings, which reminded him of Leo Gage, standing in the gap between the three sides of singers, with his elbows out and shoulders raised, conducting. The first words came into Cuzzy's mouth: "'What wondrous love is this!'" and this time he got all the way to the last verse before he had to look. "'And when from death I'm free / I'll sing on, I'll sing on / I'll sing and joyful be / Throughout eternity / I'll sing on.'"

And he did, he sang it, tentatively at first and then louder, hearing his father's charcoal baritone in his own, and it startled him. With his eyes closed, he could be listening to his father. Cuzzy opened them, though, to make certain he was not.

His father drew them into an incomplete rectangle, three sides of people facing one another like the walls of an unfinished building. "This is the house of God," he said, pointing to the space between them. Which always made Cuzzy wonder: why is the house of God empty?

But the music filled it. An invisible filling, like God Himself. First the sopranos, singing "What wondrous love," then the altos and tenors, "What wondrous love," then the baritones, "What wondrous love," and the basses, "What wondrous love." The sound was like a skein of yarn wrapping around them. It was the Tilt-A-Wheel in the school playground. What, what, what, what, wondrous, wondrous, wondrous, wondrous, love, love, love, love. It made Cuzzy dizzy. When he was a child, he thought this dizziness was God. But then his father went away, and it was just Cuzzy and his mother, and they never went to church again—not that church—and before Cuzzy even noticed, the feeling of God had gone away, too.

The phone was ringing. Cuzzy heard it through the distance of memory, thinking briefly that it was ringing in his mother's house, not in the cottage, and that she would get it—that he was eight and she would get it and it was not for him. And then it stopped, and the stopping roused him to where he was, in the house of a dead person, and he knew at once that he was all alone in a way that he hadn't been before.

The phone rang again, and this time Cuzzy picked it up.

"Yo, asshole." It was Joey. "Unlock the gate, we're coming to see you," and before Cuzzy could reply, Joey hung up.

Joey was standing over Cuzzy grinning wickedly, as if he could not decide whether to goose him, like he did sometimes when they were kids. "Oh, cousin Thomas," he said gently, but with an edge of mockery.

Cuzzy opened his eyes. The last time anyone had called him Thomas was after Harry was born and the nurse was filling out the insurance forms. He smiled lazily at Joey and sat up slowly, yawning and raising his arms above his head in a languid stretch.

"Jeez," he said. "How long have you been here?"

"A little while. We let ourselves in. Tell your friend thanks for the ham-and-cheese sandwiches. And the chips."

"He's not here," Cuzzy said. "He's in New York."

"We know," Joey said. "He told us. We're here by invitation." He held out the envelope flap on which Tracy had written the phone number.

They both heard Ram in the kitchen, and then he, too, appeared, wiping his mouth with the back of his hand. "Your friend has fancy taste in beer," he said, and Cuzzy could not tell if he was stating a fact or leering. That was the thing about Ram. You could never tell. "So why don't you show us around?" Ram said, and again Cuzzy found the tone confusing. Ram was a loaded gun.

"There's not much to see," Cuzzy said, standing up defensively. "This is the carriage house for the main house, which," he lied, "is closed up for the winter. Tracy calls this the dollhouse because it's so small."

"Or because there are dolls here?" Ram said, raising an eyebrow in Joey's direction.

"What's in there?" Ram asked, pointing to Tracy's rolltop desk.

"Just paper," Cuzzy said. He was remembering his father showing him pictures of the Dead Sea Scrolls. That was the image in his head. Something that might, if fingered, turn to dust.

"Money is just paper, too," Joey piped up.

"Yeah," said Ram, moving closer to the desk. "How does this fucking thing work?"

Cuzzy didn't answer.

Ram pushed on the slats, which didn't budge.

"So what's really in there, Cuzzy?" Ram lowered his voice to a whisper, then added an exaggerated, insinuating wink.

Cuzzy exhaled, sending notes of indifference and weariness through his voice. "I just told you. Papers," he said, shrugging. "No big deal."

He was lying, he hoped, well. In his mind he saw one of Algie's notebooks, in which paragraphs of an article from *The Lancet*— about a parasitic worm that burrowed under the cornea, so the only thing its victims saw out of that eye was an image of the worm, which, when both eyes were functioning, was superimposed like a watermark on everything that person ever saw again—alternated with lines from a human-rights report on rape in Argentina during the Dirty War ("Seven-year-old-girl, by multiple soldiers, in view of her parents; thirty-three-year-old woman, by son with gun to his head, shot at climax").

"What was that!" Ram shouted, spooked, like someone was coming to get him. "That was really weird. What was it?" The Sylvania brothers wandered in from the kitchen, where they had been eating Mint Milanos, obviously. All of them listened. There were footsteps behind the wall, and fierce gnawing. Cuzzy recognized his companions, the squirrels.

"Eastern boreal tree rats," he said solemnly. "They've been coming inside since it got cold out. For some reason they really like this corner of the room. I've tried to get rid of them"—he gestured toward the metal trap in the kitchen—"because of hantavirus. Where your lungs fill up with blood."

"Fuck that," Ram said, walking back to the kitchen.

"Yeah," said Squint, "fuck it."

"Yeah," his brother said. "Fuck rats."

"Go fuck yourself then, you rats." Ram said, smiling at his clever wordplay.

Cuzzy wanted them out of there. He wanted Ram gone, and the Sylvanias and even his cousin Joey. He wanted the silence restored so he could get under the covers and hear that singular voice singing, "He comes! He comes! The Judge severe, / Roll, Jordan, roll," as a lullaby. And then he had an idea. "Let's take the Porsche for a ride," he said, meaning he and Ram, since it was a two-seater. But he knew the others would go along with that, since that's what they did.

The funny thing was, he didn't like the Porsche after all. He thought he would, but then it turned out to be like driving a corpse. The whole time Tracy was gone, it sat in the driveway, gathering fallen leaves till it could have been raked. The wind was blowing them off in all directions. Cuzzy was doing fifty-two, the car was in fifth gear, cruising the county road. Slung low in the seat, Cuzzy concentrated on the road. There was a car ahead, and when he got up behind it, Ram reached over and flashed the lights.

"Pass him, pussy," Ram said. Cuzzy knew better than to point out the double yellow line. He accelerated. The speedometer said sixty-four, then jumped to seventy-five, and the force of the speed pushed Cuzzy back in his seat. Ram, too.

The straightaway ended, and the car began to melt into a series of turns like a skater on new ice. Cuzzy dropped back to the high sixties. The yellow speed sign on the side of the road said twenty-five miles per hour. "Fuck that," Ram said, and let out a war whoop. "This is fine," he shouted. "Want some blow?"

Cuzzy shook his head. "The only thing I blow when I'm driving is the horn," he said, and leaned on the steering wheel.

"What about your new . . . oh fuck!"

The Porsche flew by the county sheriff's car coming in the opposite direction. The police car grew smaller in the mirror, and with it, the danger. "We were going so fast that the fucker didn't even see us," Ram gloated. He glanced in the mirror. "Oh shit. He's coming back."

The sheriff was the same officer, Napoleon James, who had stopped Cuzzy once before, the night he was pushing ninety in Joey's brother's Firebird. Nap James, he was called, and Cuzzy couldn't remember whether he'd come to the county with that name or it had come with the sheriff's well-observed tendency to use his patrol car to catch up on sleep. But the thing was, like the other Napoleon, Sheriff James was short, and it made him mean. Even his fingers were short and round, like a child's. It made his gun look all the more awesome. Cuzzy thought.

"Where'd you boys get such a nice car?" the sheriff wanted to know, when he had pulled them over. He said it in a friendly, almost neighborly way. Something in his glasses caught Cuzzy's attention. It was Ram, pointing at Cuzzy.

"It's his friend's car," Ram said.

"Your friend know you're driving it this afternoon, Gage?" Apparently he remembered Cuzzy, too, since he hadn't even looked at his license.

"Basically," Cuzzy said.

The sheriff frowned.

"Is that against the law, Sheriff?" Ram asked, feigning innocence.

Sheriff James pointed one of his stubby fingers in Ram's direction. "When I want to hear from you, Pullen, I'll let you know," he said.

Ram made a small gesture with a finger held between his knees. Cuzzy caught it in the sheriff's glasses.

"What was that?" Sheriff James said.

Ram didn't answer right away. "Oh, are you talking to me?" he said lazily.

"Open the door and get out of the car," the sheriff said. "I want to show you something."

"There's the road," he said when Ram got out. "Use it."

It was six cold miles back to Stover. Ram began to shuffle down the road, weaving this way and that, like a drunk. It was a pathetic little show; in the face of the law, mockery was the only thing left to him, but even as slowly and circuitously as he went, he had soon rounded his first corner and was gone from sight.

Sheriff James turned to Cuzzy. "So, here we are again, Gage," he said. "You know, I could really do some damage this time. Which I will if you don't show up at my office tomorrow at nine to talk about your, um, behavior. Understand? And if I find out that you picked up your buddy from this little hike he's on, that's two points on your license, no questions asked. Get it?"

Cuzzy nodded.

"Thursday," Nap James repeated, "or you'd better start saving your money to get yourself a bicycle, if you see what I mean."

CONCRETE

"A mass formed by the coalescence of individual particles of matter into a single body," Colton's; *Is there a better explanation for the Church and its fallibility at the same time? Colton says that concrete fails when there is too much grit, or not enough. So where do we fit in?*

For the second time that week Cuzzy found himself driving Tracy's car toward town. Only he didn't think of it as Tracy's car, he thought of it as Algie's, and of Algie as the guy in cutoffs and a T-shirt from the photograph. It was like that with his mother. Most of the time she was no more than a single image: morning, coming off the night shift, unnetting her hair. Her waterfall of hair tumbling over itself.

Twenty minutes till he was due at the sheriff's office—enough time for a Coke and a doughnut. He had cash in his pocket, since Tracy was paying him. It didn't occur to him to ask where Tracy's money came from. In Cuzzy's experience, that was what rich people had: money from nothing.

He was thinking that maybe Crystal would be at the Nice n Easy. He wasn't sure he wanted to see her, but he wasn't sure he didn't want to, either, though he wanted her to see him at the wheel of the Porsche. He liked Crystal with his feet on the gas and the brake at the same time—which, he was coming to see, got him nowhere *and* cost him. But Crystal's truck wasn't in the parking lot,

Ram's was, and he wanted to see Ram less than just about anybody, so he kept on going, then made the next left, down Seymour Street, to kill time.

Three long streets down, two up, two over, and he would be at Crystal's house, anyway. Cuzzy slowed and took his hands off the wheel. "You decide," he told the car, which kept going in a straight line. "Nice alignment," he said, then executed a flawless three-point turn and got out of that skein of streets. He backtracked to the county road and decided to go to town, to the Grand Union, and wander the aisles, certain he'd find something he didn't know he needed yet.

She was in the parking lot, Crystal was, pushing empties into the bottle return. He could see her from the road well before the entrance, and her truck, its engine running, was unwinding a spool of exhaust parallel to the curb. Cuzzy assumed Harry was in there, asleep, curled up with that pink dog he always seemed to be clutching. But he didn't want to see Harry, either. Not just then. He was sick of goggling at him through the truck window like a zoo animal. So Cuzzy kept on going, past Crystal and the truck, past Harry. The timing wasn't right, he told himself. He'd catch them some other time.

"You're early, Gage," Sheriff James growled when Cuzzy came through the door. No one else was in the office; morning speed traps were especially lucrative. The sheriff was sitting behind a metal desk, filling out paperwork. He was wearing glasses—regular ones, not his *In the Heat of the Night* knockoffs—halfway between the bridge of his nose and the end of it. "Sit down," he barked, but didn't indicate where, so Cuzzy kept standing while the sheriff went back to his pen and papers, mumbling now and then but never looking up.

It wasn't a particularly congenial room: a cinder-block box with three gray desks, a wall of dented filing cabinets, one of which was topped with a coffeemaker, another with a police scanner. A thirsty ficus tree stood next to the one window, a brown lawn of dropped leaves leading up to it, and next to the tree, propped in the corner, was a furled American flag. Cuzzy studied the old Thomas wall clock opposite him, the way each second jerked as if it were palsied; it was hypnotic, but not enough. His eyes drifted to the unwanted relief map that covered the top of Nap James's bald head, an archipelago of angry red skin stretching from one ear to the other, some of it sloughing off. Cuzzy was embarrassed. The failing body. He looked away, back to the clock on the wall, where every second, each tick and each tock, existed independent of the others yet wasn't. They called to Cuzzy's mind a page from Algie's notebooks called "Stop Time," which was filled with a series of frame-by-frame pictures of a gray whale. Put them together in succession, and they would make a movie of the whale breaching the ocean, a movie only hinted at by the individual shots.

Cuzzy's eyes took in the sheriff's short fingers, wrapped tightly around a ballpoint pen, and his own boots, which needed oiling the way his baseball glove had when he was a boy. The glove his mother said she "found," not adding the words "at the Goodwill," where she often "shopped." School clothes, winter jackets, even underwear. Cuzzy didn't like to think about those briefs cradling the skin of another boy, but how could he not?

"Gage! What are you eyeballing?" the sheriff shouted. "Didn't I tell you to sit down?" But again he did not say where, and Cuzzy didn't ask, he just leaned on the desk next to the sheriff's.

The office was a small-time operation. The county had three police officers who spent most of their time sweeping up after the inevitable Friday- and Saturday-night telephone-pole wraparounds and administering Breathalyzer tests if there was a mouth left to administer to. The rest of the week they wrote speeding tickets, which paid the bills. A chambermaid from the Driveon Inn used to come Mondays and Thursdays but quit when an out-of-state waste hauler—in Stover jail for three days while the matter of his expired hazardous-materials license was sorted out—went back to Scranton, towing her Le Car behind his rig like a dinghy. That was around the time of the budget cuts, so the officers took turns cleaning up after themselves, but not too often, it looked like.

The jail itself was in an annex in the back, three cells in a row, prefabricated in Ohio and shipped to Stover on the back of a flatbed. The whole thing had been dropped into the shell of the building and cemented there like an inlaid crown. Cuzzy had seen it before, when Joey was in for that thing with his sister or with the dog, before he was sentenced to time at Laslow Village; and the weird thing, Cuzzy thought then, was that Joey's cell looked like a kennel. There was even a hole in the center of the sloping concrete floor where he was supposed to do his "business."

When Joey was there, the cell to his right was occupied by a friendly man with a slight limp who was wearing a torn Wayne Gretzky Edmonton Oilers jersey who, apparently, sent his wife to the hospital with a concussion. ("Body check, slap shot, wham," the man said about once an hour.) A woman with a fierce buzz cut was in the cell to Joey's right. "Did you mean to stab Vance in the thigh?" she said in a pretend lawyer's voice. "Of course not," she answered herself sweetly. "I meant to get him where it would have done some good."

"Fuck you, cunt," the man on Joey's right shouted.

"You wish, pig," she said.

"You wish I wish," he yelled.

It was like being on the playground in a dream, Joey said. "Come on, guys," he coaxed, trying to make it okay.

"Who the fuck are you to tell us to come on?" the woman said, turning on him. "What do you mean, 'come on'? You're a fucking pervert, that's what. You should have your dick sawed off with a pocketknife and pickled in brine. And you should have to look at it every goddamn single day."

One cell over, her husband started to laugh. "What's so funny?" she demanded angrily, like maybe she wasn't being taken seriously.

"You know that TV show with the stupid pet tricks?" He was laughing silently, holding on to the bars of his cell as if he might otherwise tip over.

The woman started laughing, too. "Oh, honey," she said, clapping her hands. "You are so funny."

"So, Gage," Sheriff James said, shuffling the papers, then knocking them on the desk to straighten the edges, "what do you have to say for yourself?"

"I don't know," Cuzzy said.

"You don't know?"

"No," Cuzzy ventured. The sheriff looked at him, and he looked at the sheriff. It was a standoff, though Cuzzy knew who had to win. He dropped his eyes. There was a dark brown stain on the beige linoleum. He stared at that.

"How about I give you the opportunity to find out?" Nap James said brightly, as if he had just thought of it.

"Whatever," Cuzzy said.

The sheriff leaned back and rested his head in the sling he'd made of his two hands. "Glad to see that you didn't exactly dress for the occasion," he said, smiling, which caused Cuzzy to reflexively finger his sweater. Tracy's sweater, actually, a coarse gray crewneck with a torn elbow.

"It's a good day here, Gage," Sheriff James said. "No one is in the tank. Which means that no one will get in your way when you're scrubbing it down. Maybe by the time you're done, you will have figured out what you'd like to say to me. There's a sponge and some Ajax in there." He pointed to a closet.

Cuzzy walked over to it without a word. He would not give James the satisfaction of seeing how angry he was.

"By the way, Gage," the sheriff added, "I'm really sorry we don't have a mop. Some lowlife stole it, if you can believe it."

Well, Cuzzy didn't. He imagined that if he looked hard enough, he'd find the mop stashed away, hidden for this very moment. But did he care? Not really. Mop or not, how hard could this be? Concrete floors, concrete bed, metal drain, metal sink. He retrieved a plastic bucket, cleaner, and a sponge from the closet and walked through the back door of the office to the annex. The three cells were there, exactly as he remembered, identical and all in a row, like three genetically modified peas in a pod. Cuzzy walked into the one in the middle, Joey's cell, and stood on the other side of the open grated door. Two steps and he was at the cell's back end, where the sink was. He filled the bucket with water and soap, sloshed the mixture, then dumped it on the floor, using his boot to circulate it before it went down the hole in the floor. The only problem, Cuzzy saw too late, was that there was Larches mud lodged in the soles of his boots. The floor, which had been pretty clean, was now brown around the drain, like a child's mouth after a draught of chocolate milk.

"Doesn't pay to be lazy," Nap James said, coming up behind him. Cuzzy jumped and turned to face the sheriff, who was holding out a can of WD-40. "Do me a favor, Gage," Sheriff James said. "The door's got a dry bearing. Get some of this crap up there and work it into the metal. But finish the floor first."

This time Cuzzy took off his boots. He took off his socks, too, and pushed them under the boots' tongues, then put both neatly on the other side of the door, like people did in Spain at Christmas. (A picture from Algie's notebook: a row of doors with a row of shoes at the thresholds, filled with candy, and the eyes of a child peeking out from one, and a quote from the Gospels, John 13, verses 14–16: "If I then, your Lord and Master, have washed your feet; ye also ought to wash one another's feet. For I have given you an example, that ye should do as I have done to you. Verily, verily, I say unto you, The servant is not greater than his lord; neither he that is sent greater than he that sent him.")

The floor was cold and grainy. Whoever poured the concrete had used a lot of sand to stipple it. Braille, Cuzzy thought. It was like walking on Braille, back and forth, side to side, though no message was forthcoming. What would it be? "You're a loser"?

The simultaneous insistence of the first-responder alarm and the phone ringing in the other room reminded Cuzzy exactly where he was: the Stover jail. He could hear Nap James's voice blending with the voices on the scanner, each of them short and coded, as if numbers were a spoken language, and then the sheriff's voice thrown in Cuzzy's direction: "When I get back, we'll have our little chat, Gage," and the front door opening and closing. It had a dry hinge, too. A minute later the siren on Sheriff James's cruiser started up, loud at first, then fading, and Cuzzy wondered if the reason real police behaved like police on TV was because TV cops had learned their cues from guys on the beat, or if people like Napoleon James peeled away from the curb, siren wailing, because they had taken instruction from Don Johnson and the guys from *Hill Street Blues*. Crystal could debate this question for hours, Cuzzy thought.

The floor was done. It wasn't hard or bad work, really, except that Cuzzy's feet were cold, and he was hungry. Lately he'd been getting this way two hours after breakfast—famished, craving something sweet. Growth spurt, his mother had said when he was a boy and finishing meals before, it seemed, she was finished serving them. He could still hear the ambivalence in her voice. "Growth spurt" meant new clothes, more money, no money. But Cuzzy had done all his growing. He was never going to be taller than (a respectable, Tracy said) five foot nine.

More likely, his hunger was a force of habit. Every morning around eleven Tracy popped up from his desk like a piece of bread ejected from the toaster, calling, "Elevenses, elevenses!" and went to the kitchen for a cup of coffee and a snack, and Cuzzy would follow like a faithful, unquestioning retriever. Elevenses, Tracy explained, was snacktime in England. Not that Cuzzy cared what it was called. He had a bottom-line approach to food: food was food. He liked it. But he didn't have any at the moment, and wished he did.

A clanking water pipe, the intermittent buzz of the scanner, and nothing. Cuzzy had no idea that a jail could be so much like a church. The fluorescence gave the place an anxious look, as if the light itself were staring. It made Cuzzy feel anxious, too. As in church, where he remembered feeling guilty even though he wasn't precisely, this place made him feel like confessing to something he hadn't even done.

The hinge wasn't rusty. Cuzzy saw that right off. When he pushed on the door, though, it was sticky. He aimed the nozzle of the spray can and pressed hard. It hissed, then spit on the metal. "Let the lubricant penetrate the joint," Cuzzy read on the back of the can, "then reapply." He waited and sprayed again, pulling on the door as he did, and before he could react, before he even saw it happen, the door slid easily along its track like a runaway train. The sound was definitive. Not only had it shut, it had locked. Cuzzy gave it a halfhearted tug, though he knew it wouldn't open. Guilty or not, he was a prisoner of the Stover jail.

"How fucked up is that?" Cuzzy asked himself, hanging on the door, but of course there was no answer. And no clock, either, he noticed. The clock was in the other room, and so were the windows. "This is how they mess with your head," he said, and noticed that his words bounced off the walls with more spin than he'd applied. The best acoustics in town were in the jail, it seemed.

Cuzzy paced the cell, counting to sixty, then starting again. A minute passed, and then another, and the phone rang and the answering machine clicked and clacked and five minutes went by, then twelve. Cuzzy walked in circles, reversed direction, walked in circles, turned. There used to be a one-legged veteran in Halcyon Falls who would plant a crutch in the ground and go round and round till he fell over dizzy. "Cheaper than Thunderbird," he'd say to anyone who stopped to put coins in his surprisingly clean air force dress hat, and to those who didn't, too.

Cuzzy lay down on the cell's bottom bunk, and made a pillow of his hands. Above him, on the underside of the top bunk, were the words "You are one sick ———," and then a word that looked like "Lewis" that was crossed out with heavy looping marks. "You are one sick Lewis?" he said, wondering what it meant and who Lewis was. Last name or first? He saw the words, yellow, on the back of his eyelids. They faded to brown, and he was asleep.

———

If he dreamed, Cuzzy didn't remember. He was awake, and the phone was not ringing. Cuzzy called out to Sheriff James, but his voice went unmet. If he hadn't known the time before he dozed off, he knew it less now. There was no reason to stand up, so he lay there and wondered about Tracy, where he was right that very second, not that he could picture the Voyagers' Club or the Broadway local or the main reading room of the New York Public Library, the twenty-foot polished desks Tracy described, the brass lamps with green glass shades, and the black screen the size of a billboard on which numbers lit up when your books arrived from the stacks. The last, at least, Cuzzy could make sense of: how much firewood had he corded in his life already, and how much was to come? Once he'd helped Crystal and Marcel. Cuzzy smiled. That was an understatement. They were so strong, both of them. Crystal, where was she? Feeding Harry? Feeding Harry what? What was in those little jars? Steak, he hoped. Not just peas and carrots and corn but glazed ham. Pork chops. He could imagine Crystal trying to make Harry into a vegetarian, like Frank Zappa's kids or that guy from *Cheers*. "Guys like that, after a while, their dicks look like asparagus," Joey had said, but he didn't say how he knew. "Girl ones smell like cauliflower," he added.

"You'd better get her a burger," Ram had said to Cuzzy, who was with Crystal. This was a Sunday afternoon at the Nice n Easy. Joey was coming off his shift.

"Nothing like fresh asparagus," Crystal had said, and licked her lips.

The front door of the sheriff's office opened and shut pneumatically. Cuzzy was sure he heard it groan on the uptake, then ease back to close.

"Hey!" he called. "Hey. I accidentally locked myself in." He was talking at a pair of footsteps walking in the other room.

The footsteps stopped, taking time with them. Cuzzy listened. "Hey!" he called again. "Sheriff James!" The footsteps receded. It was like the story Tracy had told him about a hiker who got lost in the woods, and days went by, and when the search-and-rescue helicopter finally found him, the hiker frantically waved his red shirt, not knowing he was giving the pilot the all-clear signal, so the pilot banked and flew away and never came back. The guy nearly died.

"Help!" Cuzzy yelled louder. His voice in that empty place sounded like a little boy's. He tried lowering it a register. "Goddamnit, help!" he yelled again. He hoped he was hearing the scrape of shoes turning around. He hoped those were footsteps he was hearing, coming closer.

A tight, careful smile held up the corners of Reverend Trimble's mouth like clothespins. His hands were clasped together, waist-high, and preceded him as if they held a leash attached to his middle. Cuzzy caught sight of Trimble's wedding ring, a simple gold band, and wondered who would marry *him*. But he had met Nora Trimble, and she was all right.

Was Jason Trimble surprised to see him? Cuzzy wondered and couldn't tell. The minister seemed momentarily stunned, and Cuzzy guessed it was because he was deciding whether he should chide Cuzzy for taking the Lord's name in vain. You couldn't live in Stover and not know that Jason Trimble was big on the Ten Commandments. If the Bible had begun and ended with them, that would have been enough for him.

"If the guy didn't like himself so much, maybe he'd leave the rest of us alone," Joey once told Cuzzy on the phone from Laslow Village. "You know, the whole 'love your neighbor as yourself' thing." But did Joey turn the other cheek when the minister came calling with Ring Dings and comic books? Christian comic books, with Jesus as a superhero named Chris, a poor, self-doubting carpenter who was never thought to be good enough to do finish work and was miraculously transformed into a master builder, able to create whole worlds in under seven days, when called by prayer.

"Hello, Cuzzy," Reverend Trimble said in his gravest voice. "I have to say that I am disappointed to see you here."

Cuzzy picked up the can of WD-40 and walked toward the door. Trimble took a step backward. The nozzle was pointed at him. "It's a mistake," Cuzzy said, waving the can. "I was fixing the door, and it closed on me."

Reverend Trimble looked at Cuzzy with practiced compassion. "Oh, son," he began in a preacherly way. "If you only knew how many times I've heard—"

"But it's true," Cuzzy broke in. "Ask Nappy James."

"Ask *Sheriff* James what?" boomed Nap James's voice from the other room, but moving toward him.

How long, Cuzzy wondered, had he been there. "I accidentally got locked in here," he said.

Sheriff James flashed him a patronizing smile. "Did you, now?"

"Obviously," Cuzzy said, rolling his eyes.

"Now, Gage, don't get smart with me," Sheriff James said. "I'm the one with the keys."

Cuzzy felt the anger rise in his chest with nowhere to go. It was big in there, and it hurt. There were tears behind his eyes. He vowed not to give them the satisfaction. He pulled on the bars. Saliva flooded his mouth. He would spit.

"Ever hear of disorderly conduct, Gage?" the sheriff said.

"Fuck you," Cuzzy said.

Reverend Trimble held up his hands. "Gentlemen. *Gentle-men!*"

Cuzzy sat back down on the bed, defeated.

The minister turned to Sheriff James. "I would like to propose that you release Cuzzy to me," he said.

"I don't need to be released to anybody," Cuzzy growled. "I didn't do anything."

"But you do need to be released, Cuzzy," Reverend Trimble said in his brightest "Joys and Concerns" tone of voice.

Sheriff James stepped forward and flipped a lever on his side of the door, and it popped open. No key. "He's all yours," he said to Reverend Trimble.

"You only thought it was locked, Gage," he said to Cuzzy.

GRANITE

"A very hard natural igneous rock formation of visibly crystalline tex-
ture formed essentially of quartz and orthoclase or microcline" (Youngblood*); not just "hard" but "very hard," suggesting that degrees of*
hardness can be felt, not only measured; the Mohs' Scale rates the hard-
ness of minerals by their "scratchability" or resistance to abrasion.

J ason Trimble walked one step ahead of Cuzzy, who lagged behind on purpose. When the minister slowed, Cuzzy slowed or
stopped altogether, and so they stuttered along Main Street.
Anyone watching would have guessed that the two men, one not
yet twenty, the other over twice that, were playing a game. And
Cuzzy *was* playing a game with him, Jason Trimble knew. The
minister was not always the most emotionally nimble man ("Delib-
erateness can be its own virtue," his pastoral counselor assured
him), but this was hard to miss—the sullenness, the petulance, the
deliberate way Cuzzy was making him work the two blocks from
the sheriff's office to the Gotham.

The pastor swallowed his annoyance, but it didn't go down easily. This was why he chose the ministry, he told himself, for fight-
ers like Cuzzy Gage, though in the beginning it had confused him,
why *he* was choosing *it* and not the other way around. He was under the impression that it was supposed to call his name or tap him
on the shoulder or knock him down. Yes, knock him down.

"Don't be so damned sentimental," his father, a Presbyterian minister, had told him. "What are you expecting, choirs of heavenly angels? It's a damn good outfit, and if you do half the job I do, you'll be doing just fine." Jason had stood in the doorway to his father's study, looking down at his own two feet. He wondered if his father had been absent from seminary the day they taught about hubris. They were so different, the two of them, even physically. His father was big; his aura was big; his bigness made people feel safe and protected. Even Jason felt it sometimes, though not now. Now he felt his own smallness tucked into a corner of his father's shadow.

"This capital campaign is a bear," the first Reverend Trimble said, not looking up from the spreadsheet that stretched from one end of his desk to the other. And then, so abstractly that Jason didn't know if he was talking to him or to himself, "What more do you need to know?"

"It's like that whole John F. Kennedy thing," Jason told his roommate, Bob Becker, when he got back to school. Becker was a lanky forward on the basketball team, with aspirations to play pro ball. "I look at ministry and say, 'Why?' My father looks at it and says, 'Why not?'"

"Do you still get to get laid if you're a minister?" Becker asked. He shot an invisible ball through an invisible hoop. "Score!" he said loudly.

"Cripes almighty," Jason said. "I'm being serious."

"I'm all too aware of that," Bob Becker said, rebounding his invisible ball and dribbling it three bounces beside his right hip, crossing over and dribbling three bounces beside his left. "Have you considered getting a life before you try to figure out what you're going to do for a living?"

People were useless, Jason decided. At the library he picked up a copy of *Follow Your Rainbow* and read it cover to cover, then went to the bookstore and bought a used copy of the *Follow Your Rainbow* workbook, which had once belonged to someone named Shauna Vaughn. He thought it was good luck to possess a copy that someone—Shauna—no longer needed. He imagined her sitting cross-legged on the floor of a pleasant old house, cradling her particular pot of gold.

"Assignment One," he read. "Interview five different people in five different professions and ask them why they love what they do." Jason started with his Greek and Roman history professor, Allen Jackson, who extolled the life of a college teacher so passionately that Jason worried he had missed his calling before it had even called his name. But later, when he went over his notes, he realized that what Professor Jackson liked most about his job was all the time he didn't have to teach—the summers, the sabbaticals, the semesters with only a single course and no advisees.

Jason moved on to professional number two. This was Nora Kline, the physical therapist at the student health center who spent hours each week working on Jason's inflamed left rotator cuff, injured playing one-on-one with his roommate.

"Why did you become a physical therapist?" he asked Nora as she loosened his shoulder with the ends of her fingers, kneading it as if she wasn't sure it would rise.

"It's a good way to take out my aggressions," she said, squeezing him so hard he winced.

"No, really," Jason said.

"Oh, I don't know." She paused and loosened her grip. "I guess because it's portable. I can take it anywhere. You know, travel the world alleviating people's pain."

"And have you?"

Nora jammed her fingers between his shoulder blades so suddenly that he gasped. "Sorry," she said. "No. Not yet. But I'm still young, aren't I?"

"Oh yes," Jason assured her. The interview was going better than he could have predicted. He was thoroughly, unexpectedly smitten with this woman he had visited twice a week for a month and never quite seen before. Her teeth were so white! Her gums were so pink! Her hands were so strong! Her hair was so short! If last week he thought it mannish and unattractive—if he thought of it at all—this week he found the tonsured look challenging and appealing and sophisticated and, he had to admit, sexy.

"How old are you, anyway?" he asked boldly. Anything under thirty, he decided, and he was in the running.

"Twenty-seven," she said. "Christ, that sounds elderly, doesn't it? Three more years and forget it."

"Forget what?" Jason took a quick deep breath.

"Shoot, did I hurt you?"

"Not yet," he said, smiling. He was feeling giddy and reckless and so not like himself that he asked her out to dinner before he had a chance to think about it.

Nora shook her head. "Can't," she said solemnly. "The good old doctor-patient relationship."

"But you're not a doctor," Jason protested.

"No, I'm not, as my mother and father, who both are, like to remind me. But I still can't."

Jason sat up and slid off the table. His blue examining gown hung off his good shoulder. He was in his socks. "Then I quit," he said. "You're fired!" He had never been more spontaneous or bold in his life.

Nora laughed. He liked the way lines rose on her forehead when she did so. Waves of happiness, he decided. "Call me in a couple of weeks," she said, "but only if you do your shoulder exercises religiously, every day."

He took her at her word. He did his exercises, and in two weeks to the day, he called her.

"I don't really go on dates," she said. She sounded tired.

"Me, neither," he said.

"No, I mean it," she said. She sounded petulant.

"So do I."

"Stop making fun of me," she said angrily.

"I'm not," he said. "Really."

They settled on dinner at her place, as long as he understood it wasn't a date. Bob Becker told him to bring a bottle of chardonnay—"women love men who bring them white wine"—and to stop along the side of the road and pick her a bouquet of flowers.

"What if there aren't any left?" Jason asked anxiously. "Shouldn't I just go to the supermarket? They sell flowers there."

"Cliché," Bob said. "Plus, how hard is that? What does that tell her about you?"

By the time Jason reached her apartment, he had burdocks on his socks and berry stains on his chinos, and his best blue shirt was dusted with a sticky pollen that made him sneeze.

"Here," he said, practically shoving a little bundle of asters and ferns and black-eyed Susans into her hands before rushing off to blow his nose. Nora fussed over them, just as Bob Becker had said she would. As for the wine, she said thanks and poured them each a beer. Wine, she said, gave her a headache. Plus there was that whole migrant-worker grape thing.

"You know what I said about not really going out on dates," she said when they were cleaning up. It had been a lovely evening, and Jason was basking in the sunny prospects ahead: other dinners, walks through the college arboretum, trips to the beach, running his fingers through what was left of her hair. But now her voice was heavy, like a raincloud. He looked up. She was frowning. No, she was grimacing.

"I can't," Nora said.

"You can't what?"

"Do this."

"Do what?" Jason asked.

"Pretend that I can do this."

He could see that this was going to be one of those circular chase-your-own-tail conversations. He reached down and picked a burdock from his sock.

"I guess I should be going," Jason said, and Nora didn't stop him.

Bob Becker was waiting for him when he got home.

"I can't believe it," Bob said. "You did the flowers and the wine and she didn't go for it?"

"I don't think she liked the wine," Jason said. "I mean, she thanked me and all, but she said it gave her a headache. And there's that whole migrant-worker grape thing."

"She is giving *me* a headache," Bob Becker said, and indeed, he was sitting on the edge of his bed with his head in his hands. "I just don't get it. Let me think about this." And then he was quiet for so long that Jason thought he might be sleeping.

"It's not you," Becker said suddenly. "Oh shit. It's her husband."

"Her husband?"

"Her name is Nora Kline, right?" Bob Becker said. "Don't you remember that guy, Chris Kline, the ice climber? I think it happened our freshman year."

Jason shook his head. "What happened?"

"He's walking down College Street, right, talking to his wife, and he trips on a crack in the sidewalk and falls and hits his head and boom, he's gone. No one could believe it. This was a guy who had free-climbed in Antarctica!"

Jason took a job as a reporter on a small weekly newspaper, where he was responsible for court news, the weather roundup, the school board. He went to meetings, worked the phones, took good notes. It was straightforward and well defined, and it suited him to be a participant without being an actor. But there was a problem: after he took the notes, he had to write them up. It wasn't the blank page—he had always loved to write. It was the long notebooks with the wide spaces that were brimming with detail and conflict and other people's passions. How to tell the truth? Listening to different people talk about the same event, and he wasn't sure what the truth was. He got reassigned to sports, but it was the same thing. Yes, one team won and the other team lost, or they tied, but how to tell that story fairly? How to honor all the players? What about the ones who never came off the bench? What about the food vendors and the kids under the bleachers drinking beer? And the hockey coach's wife, who attended every home game with her head buried in *Madame Bovary*? He tried obituaries next, but it was no use. How to do justice to any person's life?

His father told him that the only way to do justice to another person's life was to try to do justice to another person's life. Then he sent Jason down the street to talk to the new Catholic priest, Father Octavio, from Mexico, who told Jason the reason the universe was expanding was that God's love—which, confusingly, was made manifest by the actions of people on earth—was growing and could not be contained by present boundaries. For Jason, who had never been an especially curious science student, this image was satisfying. His physics professor, after all, had been able to say only that the universe *was* expanding, not why. On the back of the priest's Pinto was a bumper sticker that said IF YOU WANT PEACE, WORK FOR JUSTICE. Jason loved that. It was so clear. It reminded him of the chore wheel at Vacation Bible Camp. He had always loved that, too.

Divinity school was two years, and then he'd be set. The Methodists would give him a job, a place to live, a community, standing. And he'd be ahead of his classmates who were in medical school, like, of all people, Bob Becker, or the ones who had signed on for doctorates. Not that it was a competition. He simply liked knowing he was going to have the answers to the whos-whats-whens-hows-wheres of his life, which themselves, he prayed, would eventually answer the whys.

Of course, it was not quite that simple. There was first the matter of Nora Kline. She was still at the student health center. She was still single. (Still widowed.) And she remembered him.

"I think you should marry me," he said when he called her.

She laughed. "I don't even know you," she said. Still, there was something in her voice that suggested it wasn't out of the question, something intrigued by the impetuousness of it, like daring yourself to jump into the ocean from a high place.

"Over half the world's marriages are arranged," he said. "Nobody knows anybody." He was making this up. He had no idea.

"Over half the world's marriages end in divorce," she countered.

"No, over half of American marriages end in divorce," Jason corrected her. "So what does that say about the benefits of getting to know your partner before marriage?"

Nora laughed again. She agreed to go out with him, but only if she could tease him about his earnestness, which, over time, and much to her own cynical surprise, she came to love.

What he loved, aside from her, was having a book with the answers to questions that hadn't been asked yet, and to questions that rose as reliably as heat. At first it bothered him; if the Bible had the answers to age-old questions, why were they still being asked? Why hadn't people gotten past them? Then it dawned on him—he remembered exactly where he was at the time, balling socks in the

Laundromat—that he was conceiving of those questions as if they were math problems, done once and solved. Human beings are distinguished from other animals by their ability to reason, he thought to himself, digging through the pockets of his jeans for the last quarter needed to restart the dryer, but *that does not mean they are rational.* History repeats itself, he thought, but consciousness is ahistorical. He found the quarter, stuck it in, and watched his clothes circumnavigate their equatorial world. He thought: questions of good and evil will always perplex us, because conscience is not inheritable. Jason enjoyed the Laundromat, its warm drafts and percussive industry, and was sorry when he got married and they moved into a house of their own that an unspoken understanding said going to the Laundromat had been a phase in their lives, and in this next phase, the phase that everyone, including him, had always called real life, they would have their own washer-dryer set, which they did.

So Jason found himself married and living in a house and working in a church. Not his own church. Youth ministry was like being an associate at a law firm, he told his college friends, to give them a point of reference. Someone else told him where to be and what to do and how to do it. Jason took careful notes. Little came naturally to him. Not the gimmicky children's sermons, for which he dressed up as Lucifer or Moses, or projected hand puppets on the sanctuary wall; not the youth groups, with their implied sexuality. His wife, sensing his uneasiness, suggested it was because he didn't have a church of his own and wasn't his own boss. "My boss is a Jewish carpenter," he told her, quoting a bumper sticker that was popular in the church parking lot, but she rolled her eyes. That was often the way she dealt with him. "Everybody likes to run their own show," she told him, making it clear that she was stating the obvious. Between his wife and the Gospels, he consoled himself, he should just get by.

But when the job in Stover was offered, Nora didn't want to go. "*Up there?*" she asked, as if the miles between where they were and where they'd be going were vertical, not linear. As if the air was too thin. "There's no one there," Nora said once they had visited and met the congregation, meaning there was no one like her. "I don't have anything against poor white people," she told him, which was probably untrue, since Nora couldn't see any reason for white people to be poor in the first place. But that was before she tried to put in a garden when the growing season started in June and ended in August, and before they taped sheets of plastic over the storm windows and still had to wear hats to bed. To remind her that poverty was a spiritual condition would be sanctimonious— even Jason knew that. And the truth was, once they got there, Nora did fine. She was a furnace of radiant goodwill; people warmed to her immediately.

As for the new minister, he was respected. That came with the collar. Nobody expected to be his friend. That was not why he was there. Nobody was going to stay out late with the pastor, polishing off Jell-O shots. No one was going to take him to bet on the ponies. He was there to rein them in. He was there to remind them there was a bit in their mouths by pulling on it once a week, and because of it, he was lonely.

His college friends fell away—they were in cities, making money—and his seminary friends were overworked and faraway, and his wife had never seemed happier. Nothing in Stover reminded her that she had ever lived anywhere else, with anyone else, and she loved the forest, how big it was, and how the wind drew patterns on one part of the lake while becalming another. She adored snow. She was from the desert, so how would she have known? And that was a good thing, because there was so much of it. "So goddamned much of it" was how she liked to say it to the road-crew guys when they'd come off plowing into the Health

Center, crooked with unbending backs and tender glutes. They loved that she swore, the minister's wife. She worked their muscles and talked like them, and it was exactly the evidence they needed to reaffirm their belief in the existence of God in the world.

Did it surprise anyone, even Jason Trimble, when Nora left the first time to serve on a medical mission to Mali? No, not at all, though it surprised them (even Jason, when he was being honest) that she returned. She did it twice a year now, picked up and went away with a band of gypsy doctors, to Guatemala and Biafra and Timbuktu, and returned brown, with circles under her eyes, as if she had tried to sleep in the sand but couldn't get used to it.

Jason went down with her once to Guatemala City, but since he was not a medical man, there was little for him to do. Religion, unlike eyeglasses or tetracycline, was something these people had already. He came home chastened, recommitted in his heart (he told himself) to do more for the people of Stover. And not only his congregants but everyone. The preferential treatment of the poor, he decided, was nothing more than loving your neighbor as your-self—which was to say, it was everything.

"We are all impoverished in some way," he preached one Sun-day, trying out his new idea. "Even the man who works on Wall Street and has a sizable bank account is poor in some way." He looked at his parishioners hopefully and saw in their faces that, to a person, they'd rather be poor the way that man was poor than the way they were, with towels stuffed under the doors to slow the cold. Oh, he hated himself then and lost his resolve. Anything more than preaching the Ten Commandments was reductive, he told himself. Who else was there to tell this to? Nora was still away, and his district supervisor would use the call as an opportunity to harangue Jason about his congregation's financial obligation to the regional conference and how they were in arrears and how much more they'd owe by year's end. Jason knew if he listened hard enough, he'd hear the cha-ching of the adding machine in the background.

He decided that his next sermon was going to be about loneliness. It was going to be a colloquy between head and heart—a little play. If Nora was around, he could recruit her to take one of the parts. Heart, most likely, since he would be a more believable head. Without Nora, he'd have to ask Janine Morrow, the irascible choir director, which was a joke, since she was an even less credible heart than he.

On a Tuesday, two days after his humiliating self-sacrifice at what he called—to himself, of course—"the altar of liberation theology," he sat down to write "The Trial of Loneliness." Jason always began writing his sermons on Tuesdays, a holdover from his years in elementary school, when they'd hand out the week's homework on Monday and he'd wait a day, then rush to get it done by Wednesday in case something else came up. Not that it ever did. What looked like responsibility, and was praised as such, was in fact anxiety. His dirty secret.

On Tuesday Jason sat at the kitchen table (another holdover from grade school), clutching a fat pen that had caught his attention one day in the gift shop of the rehab hospital in Halcyon Falls. He was in there because the amputee he was visiting had been rushed to radiology for a CAT scan to explain what appeared to be her sudden aphasia. Not more than three minutes after the minister arrived, she seemed to lose her words as surely as she had lost her leg, and the doctors, suspecting a brain bleed, ran her out of there so fast that Jason didn't have time to say good-bye. So he stuck around, pacing the waiting room, bored and nervous about time, then he wandered into the gift shop to amuse himself. That was when he saw the pen. Along a wall of oversize can openers and silverware was a rack of similarly bloated ballpoint pens. "Get a Grip," each one said along the shaft. That appealed to him. Get a

Grip. He got five. Five had always been a good number for him. (As for the amputee, false alarm. "Just didn't feel like blabbing to the priest," she told the technician as he aimed to take a picture of her head.)

That Tuesday, the Tuesday of the sermon on loneliness, he sat at the kitchen table click-clicking his pen. Then he wrote "The Trial of Loneliness" at the very top. More clicking. Clicking was the second best feature of the pen, after its constant "Get a Grip" message. Should he name the two main (and only) characters Mr. Sad and Mrs. Happy, or something less obvious, like George and Martha, and let people figure it out for themselves? Or should he spell the whole thing out for them, leaving nothing to surprise: Mr. Head and Ms. Heart? "Nothing wrong with didactic if it gets the job done," he told himself. Jason moved the ballpoint against the pink left margin. "Mr. Head," he wrote. Underneath it, he added, "Ms. Heart." He went back to Mr. Head and added a colon after the "D." He dropped down a line and did the same after the "T."

The phone rang. Sometimes he was so grateful for the phone, which could ring just when he needed it to ring. Everything is an instrument of God. He believed that.

The person on the other end of the line began by clearing his throat. Like he had already said something and was waiting for Reverend Trimble to comment.

"Can I help you?" Jason asked. He hated those preachers who picked up the phone and said "Blessings" in a blandly cheery voice. Lord, did he hate that. (He'd have to work on not hating.)

The man on the other end laughed. "No one else has been able to," he said.

"Who is this?" the minister demanded. He got his share of crank calls, teenagers who wanted to know if he had Prince Albert in a can, boys who asked if his refrigerator was running, and if it was, why didn't he go catch it. But this voice belonged to an adult.

Even so, there was something creepy about the caller, as if at any second he was going to hang up or resort to deep breathing. Jason had half a mind to hang up himself and get back to "The Trial of Loneliness."

"You don't know me," the man said. He spoke slowly, as if he'd had a stroke. "My name is Leo Gage."

Leo Gage was only half right. Though Jason had never met him, he knew of him. The story was famous. How many times had he heard about Gage standing naked in hot asphalt in the middle of the road. How many people greeted him in his first two months by saying, "Last preacher in Stover said he was Pontius Pilate." It was like moving into the house of a suicide, he complained to Nora. "Don't be dramatic," she said, "that guy was a Baptist." As if that proved something. "I went to a Baptist seminary," he sulked, "even if I didn't come out one." "*He* didn't even go to seminary. He was a lay minister," she countered. "People loved him," Jason said, to which she had no quick reply.

Jason was doodling on his pad. Above "Mr. Head," he careted the word "Potato." Above "Ms. Heart," he wrote, "Lonely." He drew a plus sign between them and framed the whole thing in a valentine: "Mr. Potato Head + Ms. Lonely Heart." "4 Ever," he added, shading the number so it looked three-dimensional. Leo Gage continued talking. That was one of the best tricks Jason had learned in divinity school: if you were quiet, the other person would fill in the silence with what he wanted to say. ("Needed to say" was what the professor said, but it was Jason's experience that a person's sense of entitlement extended even to language. Most people *needed* to say very little.)

"When were you planning on visiting me?" Leo Gage said in his slow, almost courtly way. Though Jason made weekly hospital rounds in Halcyon Falls, the "hospital" at Newkirk, forty minutes west, was not on his roster. It always seemed futile, all those extra miles to talk to people who already thought they were God or something close to God. It was a failing on his part, he knew, one of many, and a perfect example of the calculus of personal comfort he sometimes preached against on Sundays: "If you enumerate your sins, does that lessen their venality?" he'd ask. "If you say, 'I know I should not do such and such,' does that mitigate the sin of doing it? No," he explained. "No, no, no. It only makes *you* feel better." He should know.

There were ways of answering Leo's question, ways they taught in school that seemed cold then, and unchristian, but had served Jason Trimble well over the years, and, by extension, he believed, his parishioners. He could lob the question back, sending it softly into Leo Gage's court. He could say, "When were you expecting me?," though this would leave Jason wide-open and vulnerable, like a dog rolled over on his back, feet in the air. It also wouldn't exempt him from the harangue he expected was coming (or was that guilt speaking?): why hadn't Reverend Trimble come before this, why hadn't he called, why had Leo Gage been forgotten, left to fester? (Okay, he calmed himself, the last was overly dramatic. But still.) No, the lob was out.

Maybe he could spin it, say, "I've been waiting to hear from you. It's wonderful to hear your voice." No, not the last sentence. That would be a downright lie. So would the first, but a little less so. Leo Gage was long gone by the time Jason Trimble came to Stover. Jason had heard the stories, *he had been warned*, but stories and warnings were nothing compared to a living voice, even a disembodied living voice. No, the spin was out, too. "I don't know," Jason told Leo Gage, who let out a laugh like a sputter of steam.

"What's so funny?" Jason asked, his voice betraying the hurt he was surprised to feel.

"It's not what I was expecting, that's all," Leo said. "The last person I asked that, some female Unitarian, says something like

'Oh, Mr. Gage, it's so good to hear from you, when would you like me to visit?' As if she had been waiting to hear from me all these years. Like she actually cared. So I said, 'Never, you daughter of Judas Iscariot,' and hung up on her and got my phone privileges taken away for three months because she called the director and said I was harassing her. I'm harassing her? *She* was harassing *me*."

So he really is crazy, Jason thought. All those years and all that medicine, and Leo Gage was still a raving lunatic. And now he was going to be Jason Trimble's own personal raving lunatic, because they were making a date to get together.

"Is there anything you want?" Jason asked before they said goodbye. His regular parishioners knew to ask for books or photographs or clock radios from home; sometimes he felt like a courier service.

"God's love," Leo Gage said, and hung up.

The hospital at Newkirk looked benign enough. Once Jason got past the guardhouse and a ring of concertina wire, it looked like an august, if moldering, college. The buildings were dark brick and ivy-covered. The lawn was expansive and neat. Normal-enough-looking people strolled the paths. If they had been playing Frisbee, if there had been a dog on the grass, a black Lab with a red bandana knotted around her neck, Jason would not have been surprised.

He found Cottage B with no problem—it was next to Cottage A. It must be wishful, he thought, calling them cottages, as if they were small and windswept and on Nantucket. Jason pushed on the door and felt himself being sucked inside. Or maybe he was feeling his own resistance. He looked around. The plaster walls, painted muted shades of beige, closed in on him. The door shut decisively; he saw then that it had no knob. The windows were double-paned, with what looked like chicken wire in between. Electrified, he decided. A bored guard was in the lobby, which had three worn chairs and a coffee table, no magazines. Jason gave his name, stated his business, and let himself be patted down. The guard picked up a black telephone, mumbled into it, waited, then nodded in the direction of a set of double doors. Jason pushed, but they were locked, so he waited there, aware of a small TV camera pointed in his direction. He wondered who was watching and what they saw.

A woman was coming. Jason heard her heels striking the linoleum. It took a while, and there she was, a tall black woman in a blue dress that flared from the waist like a bell. A handsome woman, carefully made up. Her lipstick, he noticed, had been recently freshened.

"Good morning, Father," she said carefully. Jason reflexively felt for his collar, which he had put on in the car for safety, so they would know he'd be leaving.

"Reverend," he corrected her gently. "Jason Trimble. I'm here to see Leo Gage."

"Yes," she said demurely. "I was sent." She smiled broadly, a smile he couldn't read.

Leo Gage was in the sunroom—so named, Jason decided, for the shade of orange it was painted rather than for its natural light, which sneaked in dimly through two small windows. Leo was seated at a long metal folding table, facing an open book with his head bowed slightly. A pencil was lying beside it, on top of a notebook. His hands were round and ill-defined. Leo wasn't fat, exactly, but he was puffy, as if there were an inner tube of air between his der-, mis and epidermis. He had black hair gone to gray, and his skin was the color of goose eggs. He was wearing a faded blue pajama top and a pair of stiff jeans. He wasn't much to look at. Or maybe he was too much. Jason Trimble focused on the open book, a Webster's dictionary.

When Jason got closer, he saw another, smaller book nested in the first. It was a children's book about rocks and minerals. "Some rocks are basic, like milk or eggs," Jason read. "These rocks are called minerals. Other rocks are mixed, like cake. Cake is made of milk and eggs. Granite is like cake." Jason glanced at the notebook. The same words were copied there, along with the dictionary meaning of "granite." Leo Gage breathed in deeply. He was asleep.

"It's the meds," the woman said confidentially, touching Leo gently on his shoulder.

"Oh, Larry!" he said, jerking awake.

The woman scowled and pursed her lips, pivoting on the balls of her feet so the dress spun out like a centrifuge. "Nice meeting you, Father," she called over her shoulder to Jason.

"Larry?" Jason said.

Leo Gage blinked and looked around the room. "She is a he," he said matter-of-factly. "She would prefer to be called Lucia, but we're not allowed. I'd like to, but it's possible she's miked. Or you are, for that matter."

"I don't think so," Jason said. "I mean, I know I'm not." But he patted down his flank as if he weren't sure.

"How do you know?" Leo said. He had nervous eyes. "Really know? How do you know this is not all a dream? Have you ever read Heidegger?"

"Heidegger?"

Leo dropped his voice. "I'm not really crazy," he told Jason, "I only act crazy."

"Oh," Jason said.

"No, I mean it," Leo whispered.

Jason was uneasy.

"So they leave me alone," Leo Gage said. He was almost mouthing the words.

"So who leaves you alone?" Jason whispered.

"Them. You. Everybody." He extended his arms like an orchestra conductor inviting the audience to applaud the whole ensemble.

"Oh," Jason said.

"You don't believe me," Leo said flatly.

Jason ignored this. "Why do you want everybody to leave you alone?"

"Because I remain here under false pretenses," Leo said. "If they found out I wasn't crazy, they'd send me home. Then what would I do? I don't have a home. Where would I go?"

"Certainly someone could help you with that," Jason said. "There are agencies—"

Leo Gage cut him off. "Then I'd have to get a job. I don't want a job. Who would hire me?"

"I don't know," Jason said honestly.

Leo Gage smiled. "I knew I'd like you."

Jason hadn't known he would like Leo Gage, but he did. The man's mind was wild and stormy, but it was insightful, too. He was offended by the twelve-tone scale in particular and disharmony in general and considered John Cage no more talented than a three-year-old; he was a selective student of philosophy ("John Stuart Mill went crazy, too, you know"); he thought Preston Sturges should make a movie of the Book of Job.

"What's all this?" Jason asked before he left, pointing to Leo's books and papers.

"I wondered when you'd ask," Leo said. "It's notes. For a book. 'The Book of Hard Things.'"

"And the hard things are rocks? Is that why you're reading that kids' field guide?"

"Don't be so literal-minded," Leo said. "Why are so many ministers so literal-minded?" For the first time that day, he looked directly at Jason. It was a penetrating look, and Jason felt it go through him, head to feet.

"Here's the thing about the book," Leo said in his slow, even way. "Everyone thinks that the problem with God is the problem of evil, right? You know, how can there be a God if there is so much pure horror and pure evil in the world? I think"—he leaned close to Jason—"that this is *wrong*. I think it's beside the point. Evil, real evil, like the Nazis or something on that scale, which gets everyone's attention, is unusual. It's intermittent. It doesn't happen very often. That's why it gets people's attention. From my perspective," he said, forgetting, Jason thought, that his perspective was that of a man who looked out on the world through an electrified fence and razor wire, "evil is not the main theological question."

"What is?" Jason asked. He was curious.

"The main dilemma of theology," Leo went on, "is hardness."

"Hardness?" Jason asked.

"Yes," said Leo. "Why is everyday life so *goddamned* hard?" He leaned back and took a breath.

"Do you understand?" he said after a while.

"I don't know," said Jason. "I guess I'll understand more when I read your book."

"I'm not writing a book," Leo Gage said.

Jason's head started to hurt. "But you just said—"

"All I said was that I was making notes," Leo Gage said.

Jason was getting impatient. The problem with crazy people,

he decided, was that they made you feel crazy. The domino *affect*. He smiled at his own joke.

"You don't believe me."

"I believe you," Jason said.

"That's good," Leo said, "because I am not going to write 'The Book of Hard Things.' You are."

Jason laughed nervously. "I am?"

"You think I'm out of my mind," Leo said, "But you'll see."

"I guess so," Jason said, standing up to leave.

Unbidden, Jason showed up at Newkirk the next week, and the week after that, and the week after that, and then two things happened. First: if, in the beginning, he thought of the man in the thin blue pajama top as his Habitat for Humanity, he gave that up three weeks into the snowiest winter on record, when the roads were closed and he was unable to get to Newkirk. Alone, at home, he found himself poring over an Audubon guide to rocks and minerals that he had bought in the mall bookstore in Halcyon Falls. "It's for a friend," Jason told the clerk there, as if she cared. But it was true, and that was the second thing: Leo Gage was becoming a friend. They could talk. Yes, Gage could be crazy, but couldn't everybody?

Reverend Trimble stopped in front of the diner and waited for Cuzzy to catch up. "We're going in here," the minister told him.

Cuzzy scowled but followed doggishly to a booth in the back. The lunch crowd was just beginning to arrive, but the place was still pretty empty.

"Look, Cuzzy," Jason said as soon as they sat down, though

Cuzzy was decidedly not looking, not at him. His face was angled toward the window; he blew on it and wrote a word: "Lewis," it looked like.

"I want to ask you one thing."

Cuzzy looked up despite himself. What one thing did Trimble want?

"I want you to visit your father," Jason said.

BEDROCK

"The solid rock underlying loose deposits (i.e. soil)," (Colton). Any wonder that Simon is Peter and Peter means "rock"? But even though the disciples are the foundation, do not be lulled into thinking the design is intelligent, even if it is.

"I want you to visit your father," Jason said again, when Cuzzy did not respond. The boy was playing with the sugar packets, stacking them higher and higher till they toppled, then starting over. Cuzzy didn't look up, and if the minister's words had registered, there was no outward sign. Jason was encouraged. Silence was better than "no." That was another thing he had learned in his line of work: to claim victories wherever you find them.

On the other hand, Cuzzy was stonewalling. He was pretending not to hear, and his intentional muteness was daring Jason to repeat himself once more, and to lose patience and call Cuzzy names—"obstinate" and "selfish" were the ones that came to mind—and knock down the sugar tower with the back of his hand, sending the pink and white envelopes skittering across the Formica and onto the floor. Jason saw himself doing this, then saw every head turn and look at him with reproach. It might not be the worst thing—they would see that he, too, struggled with his weaknesses. But that was not how he needed the people of Stover to know him. Which of the Commandments said it was all right to ha-

171

rangue a sullen teenager? Jason sighed. Cuzzy looked up. Their eyes locked, as if the click of the latch had been audible, but only for the shortest of seconds. Then Cuzzy shook his head and broke free, frowning contemptuously. Pushing the sugar packets in a heap toward Trimble, he stood up to go.

"What's up with him?" the waitress asked, delivering two cups of coffee to the table as Cuzzy rushed by her. "You know what you want, or do you want me to come back?"

"Yes," Jason said.

"Yes what?"

"I need more time," he said.

He really did. He hadn't made any promises to Leo Gage; the fact was, Leo hadn't asked to see Cuzzy. His questions were less direct.

Jason looked out through the unlit (for how many years?) red "H T" of THE GOTHAM and saw a faint approximation of his own face in the glass. I look defeated, he thought, and watched his frown deepen. But even that, he knew, was not quite true: he *was* defeated.

Someone was touching his shoulder. Jason glanced up and saw the waitress staring down at him.

"Oh, sorry," he said sheepishly, picking up the unopened menu.

"The sheriff is here to see you," she said. She nodded in the direction of the cash register.

Jason looked over to see Napoleon James buying a pack of gum.

"I noticed he was outside and you weren't," the sheriff said as Jason approached. He was pointing a silver gum wrapper at the window. There was Cuzzy on the other side, leaning against the Porsche. "You finished with him?"

Jason hesitated. He did not want to get Cuzzy into any more trouble than he was in already. "Well," he began.

Napoleon James cut him off. "Here." He reached into his shirt pocket and drew something out. "Hold on to this till you're done," he said, handing over Cuzzy's license. "I'll send him back in."

"I know your father," Jason said when they were seated again. He waited for Cuzzy to take this in; then he continued. "I'm his friend. And he's mine."

His father's *friend*. It had been years since anyone described himself that way. It had stopped seeming possible that his father had friends, even before Cuzzy stopped believing he had a father. His father was easy to forget. He could forget him for whole days. And when he remembered, he wished to forget him and assumed everyone else did, too.

"It's been a few years," Jason continued. "At first I just felt it was my obligation to visit him, especially after he asked me to. But at some point I found myself looking forward to our Wednesday afternoons. He's got an interesting brain, your father. It's always in gear. He thinks about things, and he's not afraid to say what's on his mind. 'Jesus Christ was not Jesus Christ,' he likes to say, meaning that Jesus was only a man, the same way we are only men, living the best life that he could. 'Where were *his* collar and stole?'"

Cuzzy did not know what to say. It was as if he was learning that his father, long presumed to be dead, was in fact alive and living a whole other life without him. A wave of jealousy, followed by a wave of resentment, washed over him. He felt wet and realized, to his embarrassment, that there were tears in his eyes, and on his cheeks, and in the folds of his hands, which were cradling his chin. "If he's such a genius," he said angrily, "then how come he's locked up *there*?"

Startled by the boy's raw anger, and by his tears, Jason looked hard at Cuzzy, at his narrowed eyes, the eyes of a child who recognizes that he's in the presence of the arbitrariness of adults. Jason smiled weakly. He was not unaware that Cuzzy had raised himself. Who wouldn't be angry under those circumstances? What had the minister told his congregation? "Anger is a heat-seeking missile that finds and explodes at the warmest body." It wasn't an elegant metaphor, and he should have been able to anticipate the note scribbled on the empty collection-plate envelope: "Don't we have enough violent images on TV without getting more when we come to church?" (Leo had been particularly amused by that one. "Haven't they been reading the Bible?" he said.) So Jason was Cuzzy's target, and that was okay. At least the boy was feeling something. At least Jason would have something to tell his friend: I've been with your son. But how to answer the son's question?

"Well, Cuzzy," he began in his preacher's best, most compassionate baritone. (Oh Lord, Jason thought. I sound like Billy Graham). "It's complicated. Your father is complicated. No one is saying that he is not a sick man. Even he says that sometimes. Not always. There are times when he says he's fine and ready to get out and wants me to have him released, but I can't do that. He's liable to hurt himself, especially if he forgets to take his medications. That's one of the problems with what he has. When he's feeling good, he gets it into his head that he's cured and doesn't need the lithium, and he resists taking it. Thankfully, that's not up to him as long as he's in Newkirk. It's very typical in cases like his."

"So he's crazy," Cuzzy said dismissively.

Jason's spirits plunged—like an elevator that's snapped its cable, he thought. He felt the rapid descent and the darkness. He thought he had been getting through to Cuzzy, and he was, but to the wrong part of him. "Look," Jason said. "If he wasn't sick, he wouldn't be in there. Most of the time, though, he's okay. Like I said, it's complicated. But the thing is—the thing is, it's not clear how long he's going to be able to stay there."

Cuzzy looked at him, perplexed.

Now that he had the boy's attention, the minister waited a moment. It was like fishing: you let the fish itself drive the hook in deeper. "There's been some talk in the state legislature of phasing out places like Newkirk," Jason said neutrally. "Too expensive. Not enough staff. Endless lawsuits."

"Where will he go?"

"That's the question," Jason said.

"Hey!" Both Cuzzy and Jason turned in the direction of the word, and there was Tracy, coming toward them. "I saw the car," he said. "On the street." Tracy's face was bright, as if it were in bloom. He was wearing a watch cap of the same blue as his eyes, and a pea jacket two shades darker. He could have been a sailor home on leave.

"New York was great," he ventured. "What are you two up to?"

"I was just leaving," Jason said, standing up. He leaned over the table. "Think about it," he said to Cuzzy, putting the boy's license down on the table.

"Think about what?" Tracy asked, taking Cuzzy's license and giving it a long hard look as he took Jason Trimble's place. "Hey, it's almost your birthday," he said absently, handing it back to Cuzzy. The waitress arrived then like an ambulance chaser on the heels of an accident, and Tracy was ordering waffles and bacon and home fries and grapefruit juice and scrambled eggs for himself, and onion rings for Cuzzy, and the question was forgotten.

"You would have liked New York," Tracy said.

Cuzzy frowned. Of course he would not have liked New York. That would be someone else. He'd read somewhere that New York was an island built on rock. Bedrock. As if you'd want to sleep on it.

"You are not going to believe this story," Tracy went on, oblivious to Cuzzy's pleated brow, or ignoring it. "I went to the Voyagers' Club, and there was Brennan Perkins in the library, just like Algie said he would be. He was reading an account of three female missionaries in the Congo who ended up as concubines in a rubber plantation, out loud to these two blushing women librarians, and he was loving it. Afterward we had tea in the parlor, and I got to meet the man who swam the Nile. He was huge. He must have weighed two-seventy. By the time he finished his swim, all the hair on his body had turned white. Not gray but pure white. He looked like a polar bear."

Cuzzy smiled, imagining it. A guy who looked like a polar bear. A guy who looked like a polar bear hanging out on an iceberg with a bunch of polar bears who looked liked the guy. But not in the Nile. In the Arctic, maybe.

Tracy went on. "After breakfast Perkins said he had to take a nap, so when he went up to his room, I went back to the library and talked to the librarians about Algie's archives. They don't know for sure, but they deal with the archivists from the University of Indiana all the time. Well, maybe not all the time, but when someone comes back from an expedition with transcriptions or instruments and wants to sell them. Indiana has a really big ethnic-instrument collection. Anyhow, they said that they would probably want it.

"By the time Perkins woke up, I was feeling flush, so I asked if I could take him out to lunch. He doesn't own a coat anymore, that's how rarely he goes out, so he had to borrow one. I took him to a steak house on Eighteenth Street—older men seem to love thick slabs of meat—and he walked in and ordered a double Oban, neat, which he swallowed like lemonade. He then proceeded to tell me and everyone within earshot about how he sailed solo to Tierra del Fuego when he was in his early twenties in a boat called—get this—*The Pup of the Bitch,* after *The Beagle,* Darwin's boat, and how at one time he lived among the Maori and traded didgeridoos.

"Which turns out to be completely appropriate for me," Tracy said, taking a deep breath and smiling proudly, "because I got the Fulbright."

"You mean he gave you the recordings?" Cuzzy asked.

"No," Tracy said. "The Fulbright. To teach in New Zealand. It starts in January—their summer. Didn't I tell you I had applied? I can't believe I got it. They pick almost no one. I'll be at a high school in Wellington that's right on the water."

Cuzzy glanced through the unlit neon to the street. Only the postman was walking outside. Otherwise, Main Street was gray and still. The little silver Porsche was there, and even it looked gray and overcast.

"That's cool," Cuzzy said, but flatly, sounding purposefully bored. Tracy didn't notice. He was still as animated as a small child who has been asked to tell what happened in a movie he's just watched. He was in the story, and nothing outside of it could touch him.

"I know," Tracy said triumphantly. "It's really amazing." He leaned toward the floor, unzipped his duffel bag, and rifled through it. Cuzzy could see only Tracy's left elbow above the Formica table. It was like he was gone already.

Tracy put something on his lap and something on the table. Cuzzy saw a paper wrapper with the words "Edison Records," written on it.

"Do you know what they were?"

Cuzzy shook his head.

"Edison Records," Tracy said. "The first records. They were made of wax. Perkins gave it to me. And this, too." He passed a piece of paper across the table to Cuzzy.

"London, 1893," he read. "Australia was the asylum for the Fauna and Flora of past ages. Here the animal and vegetable world had remained stationary, here even human life had remained as it was in earlier times and thus affords us an immediate example of what we once were. In Australia a similar history may be recorded of the music which, because of its original character, gives us a welcome picture of the simplest art form. *Primitive Music.* Richard Wallaschek."

Cuzzy handed the page back to Tracy. "Let's see it," he said.

"See what?"

"The wax record."

"I don't have it yet. Perkins said he'd send it." Tracy dug through his bag again. "Here," he said, "I brought you this. A present. It's a book." He navigated it around the empty plates, the coffee cups, the pitcher of maple syrup, the napkins. "It was mine. I got it years ago at a used bookstore in Wales. I wanted you to have it."

Cuzzy looked at the book lying there but did not open it. The book was browned at the edges. *The Collected Poems of Wallace Stevens.*

"I wrote something inside," Tracy said, but Cuzzy still made no move to touch the book. Touching would be claiming. Claiming would be accepting. Accepting would be forgiving. This train barreled through Cuzzy's head. He nodded slightly, as if any extra effort would give something away. Part of himself. *Even more* of himself.

"Hey, cut that out," he said suddenly as Tracy reached across and parted the hair that was hiding Cuzzy's eyes. The trace of his fingers lingered, like breath. He didn't want Tracy touching him.

"Should I read it to you?" Tracy asked, ignoring Cuzzy. He took back the book.

We make ourselves a place apart
Behind light words that tease and flout,

But oh, the agitated heart
Till someone really find us out.

"Robert Frost," he said, shutting the book with a soft clap. "And I guess if we're lucky," he went on wistfully, "someone will."

What was that supposed to mean? Cuzzy hated the teacher thing, the riddle thing, that Tracy did sometimes. He made things confusing on purpose, and then they'd worm their way into Cuzzy's brain, and like it or not, he'd have to think about them.

Tracy handed the book to Cuzzy, who put it on the seat next to him.

"Aren't you even going to look at it?" Tracy said. "It's a really great book."

Cuzzy picked it up and shuffled the pages like a deck of cards, but weakly, as if he could hardly be bothered. "'That's what misery is, / Nothing to have at heart. It is to have or nothing,'" he read aloud. "'It is equal to living in a tragic land. / To live in a tragic time.'"

"Nice," he said. He looked up, expecting to see Tracy's hurt face, but Tracy was smiling, looking amused.

"Very funny," he said. "Give me that." He turned to "The Snow Man" and passed the book back to Cuzzy. "I wanted you to have your own copy of this."

The waitress passed by with her coffeepot, stopped, and regarded the two of them curiously. "I went on break, and you're still here," she said to Cuzzy. It wasn't judgmental—she was just reporting. "You boys want refills?" She leaned over the table to put more coffee in Cuzzy's cup, and he could see the tops of her breasts gathered there like a bouquet, and he didn't care. Nothing was the way it was. Tracy was going; his father was coming, maybe. The time he and Joey rode a bobsled, gravity had delaminated his skin from his bones: that was what he felt like now.

"What's this?" the waitress said, putting down the coffeepot and picking up the book. "Poetry? I love poetry. You know Carl Sandburg?" she asked. "You know the one about fog coming in on little cat feet? We had to memorize that in school."

She moved away like a fly, landing at the next table, chatting with the two women there about the weather and the Stover Summits football team, which was having its typically mediocre season despite the efforts of the two women's husbands, and Cuzzy and Tracy were by themselves again, each with his hand around his coffee mug and the book between them.

"You want me to read you the poem?" Tracy offered quietly. His enthusiasm was spent; it had slipped away like gambling money, but he was willing to try again.

"No," Cuzzy said. He didn't need anyone reading him a poem in the Gotham.

"Well, read it yourself, then," Tracy said, annoyed, pushing the book over to Cuzzy, who was so unused to Tracy telling him what to do that he picked it up and read it.

"You've been cold a long time," Tracy said. "Like me," he added.

A S H

"Tough elastic wood from ash tree"; Leslie, **Common Trees of North America;** *baseball bats are made from this. A bunch of us spent summers working in the bat factory north of town, breathing that sawdust; seconds were sold for a dollar each, so we'd always make sure we made a few mistakes. One day I realized something important, that the words "ashes to ashes" were a reference to life itself, not death or unbeing. I tried to explain this to my boss. I said, "Life is the line." I said, "The first ash is the point at which you didn't exist, and the second ash is the point at which you exist no longer, and the thing that connects them, that line, is your life." My boss said he didn't know what the hell I was talking about.*

B ack at the Larches, Cuzzy slipped into the woods, taking off through the tamarack even before Tracy slammed the trunk and saw that he was gone. Cuzzy was angry—kick-the-dog angry—and found himself pawing a hemlock root that was frozen above the ground till his toes hurt. He didn't care. He was glad. He hated Tracy. He hated Jason Trimble. He hated Napoleon James. He hated his father. He hated having been born. Yes, that was what he hated most.

A ruffed grouse took off, sounding like a two-stroke engine, startling him. Cuzzy looked up and saw it lift slowly through the air and vanish. What he wanted to do, too. Jason Trimble wanted him to visit his father. No, it was worse than that. Cuzzy kicked harder at the root. He imagined his socks red and bloody. Warm blood turning to ice. He hoped so. He kicked harder. Nothing hurt enough.

"O wondrous fucking love!" Cuzzy said out loud, sending a clod of frozen dirt into the trunk of the tree.

A gray jay flew overhead, then a grackle. He didn't like grackles, thought of them as trash birds, though the jays were not much better. Camp robbers, everyone called them. Cuzzy looked up. The sky was the color of smoke.

Tracy was leaving. Of course Tracy was leaving, and he'd go back to his own stupid life. Who stayed in Poverty who didn't have to?

Their conversation in the car replayed in Cuzzy's head. A history of Edison Records and how researchers would haul big gramophones into the bush, one for each copy, and how the wax would melt or crumble. All the while Cuzzy looked out the window, straight ahead, until Tracy noticed the silence and the unturned head and said curiously, "I thought you hated Jason Trimble."

"So," Cuzzy said, and stopped there.

"Then what were you doing with him at the Gotham?" Tracy pressed, and Cuzzy, who had been waiting all along to be asked, though he hadn't realized it, told the story. He told about Ram and the car, and about Sheriff James and getting shut in the cell (he didn't say it hadn't been locked), and about getting released to Trimble, then walking away from him right into the stubby body of Nap James, and getting released to Trimble again, leaving out the part about his father.

It was Tracy who said it. "Did Jason talk to you about your dad?" was how he put it, as if Leo Gage were his *dad*. The word shivered up Cuzzy's back. Or maybe the snake was the possessive, the "your." As if his father was something to own up to. But the car was at the end of the driveway, and Cuzzy didn't.

He was deep in the woods now, walking among the trees, trees that had sprouted on cut-over land a hundred years before and grown to look like they'd been there all along. It was a mixed forest of conifers and hardwoods, dense with undergrowth. Cuzzy never came this way; it was too much work. But he pushed on incautiously, punching through the understory. Snow covered the ground thinly, a crusty snow that broadcast each footstep and then recorded it. Cuzzy was insensible. He wanted to think, and he didn't. Branches snapped back and stung him, but barely. What caught his eye? He wasn't sure. Some movement over the snow. A chickadee or a mouse, maybe. He glimpsed it, and then it disappeared. Still, he had a feeling it was out in the open, staring at him, camouflaged, but by what? He stared and stared, then he saw it. Not the animal but his blind. It was the earth itself, the bare earth, no snow, a whole swath of it, big enough not to seem random. Cuzzy instinctively looked up the straight gray trunk of a mountain ash and, squinting, saw what made that space: a ceiling of plywood, or something like it, high in the tree. No, it was not random at all. It was Algie's tree house. He was sure of it.

But how to get up there? Cuzzy could make out a set of rungs nailed into the towering tree trunk, fifteen feet overhead. He stepped back and studied the other trees. If he could only climb one of these, then drop down on the decking. But those branches started too high, also. A rope might do it. Cuzzy circumnavigated from below. Toss a rope over the railing, secure it, shinny up. But he didn't have a rope, and who knew if the wood would hold him.

"Jesus, Cuzzy." Cuzzy turned. There was Tracy, three yards back, panting, the cuffs of his pants muddy and his city shoes soaked and stained. He held his watch cap in his hand, which was on his hip. He leaned over to catch his breath. "Jesus," he said when he had. "Didn't you hear me calling? At least I could follow your footsteps."

Cuzzy's arms were folded, and his face bore the slightest trace of amusement.

"I just don't see what's so funny, taking off through the woods like that," Tracy said.

Cuzzy's smile deepened.

"Could you please tell me what's so hilarious?" Tracy asked. "I'd really like to know."

Cuzzy pointed. "Look up," he said.

Tracy tilted his head. "What's that—" he started. And then, "Oh my God, you found it."

In the house, by the fire, they plotted how to get up there. Gus's bucket loader wouldn't be able to get near it. Heavy machinery was out. A ladder might work, they decided, if they could level the ground around the tree.

"Pitons," Tracy said, circling round Cuzzy, who lay on the floor. "You know. What rock climbers use. We'll put in pitons and work our way up to the old ladder. That should work. Though we'll probably have to wait until spring, when the tree's not frozen."

Cuzzy sat up. "What? When the tree's not frozen? Trees hold the heat. They're like the warmest thing in the forest."

Tracy grinned sheepishly. "Flatlander," he accused himself.

"And anyhow, you're not going to be here in the spring," Cuzzy said.

Cuzzy stayed by the fire—he couldn't get warm enough—while Tracy went to unpack. In his duffel bag were ten slender volumes of poetry, lifted randomly from his shelves in New York, and his winter boots and parka. He felt like he was unpacking his own ambivalence. At the bottom of the bag, under his long johns, was a copy of the letter Perkins had written years ago to the Royal Anthropological Society, suggesting that the historical record was wrong about aboriginal vocalizations. A souvenir. He wondered which Algie would have cared about more: that the recordings existed or that people said they didn't. Not that it mattered. They did, and Algie didn't, and pretty soon the recordings would be gone again, too, packed away in a library like a body in a morgue. Pull it out, identify it, call the pathologist.

People die over and over again, Tracy thought. Their physical death is just the beginning. Why hadn't he seen this before: the death of someone you loved was your own involuntary initiation into the kiva of loss, an initiation that ended with your own death. It was the perfect initiation ceremony, and it was universal; he wished he could tell his friend.

They had become friends again, slowly. There were wounds, and there was wariness. But the two of them were older, and if they had not yet achieved a wholly individual relationship to sex, they were, each in his own way without trying to, living their way to the answer. "Rilke was really just talking about growing up," Algie told him.

"Why did you stop writing?" Tracy asked the night they stood on West Side Beach under the discreet but watchful eyes of Claudia House and her brother, Clifford.

Algie smiled. "A better question is why did I keep writing for so long?"

"Okay," Tracy said, "answer that, then."

"Penance," he said.

How was it possible to miss someone, miss him as much as it was possible to miss him, and then miss him *more*? Until Algie died, Tracy always thought of missing someone as a condition—you either missed him or you didn't. Then Algie was gone, and Tracy felt the absence of his body on earth, and felt that absence grow as if it were a number, negative in value but an integer nonetheless—expandable, manipulable, real. Tracy moved to the doorway and looked out on Cuzzy, now balled up in the chair, connected by a black umbilicus to the stereo. The boy was still there, but for how long? Soon enough he'd get a job hauling gravel or pushing snow or laying pipe—good solid work, but hard. It would be a dog's life: seven years for every one, and he'd get old fast.

The poem is incomplete, Tracy said to himself: it's not just the death of any man that diminishes me, it's the life, too.

"The phone's dead," Tracy said when Cuzzy came and stood in the doorway later. Tracy was sitting on the floor, fiddling with the phone jack, though Cuzzy knew it was no use. The squirrels must have chewed through the wires in the attic. They used the insulation for their nests.

Cuzzy turned and went to the refrigerator and pulled out a quart of milk, which he drank directly from the bottle. He could feel Tracy's eyes on his back. He took another swallow.

"It wasn't like I was going to stay here forever," Tracy began.

"You can do whatever you want to do," Cuzzy said. "That's what makes you different. From us," he added, though he meant "from me."

"You could come, too, you know," Tracy said, as if he hadn't thought of it right then.

"Fuck you," Cuzzy said, turning. Tracy was holding the green wire in one hand and the red one in the other, as if at any moment he might complete the circuit. It was easy to be generous when you were offering something the other person could not accept. "Fuck you, Tracy," Cuzzy repeated, and went into the other room.

Tracy dropped the wires and followed him. "Why not?"

"Why not?"

"Yeah. Why not?"

"Because it doesn't happen that way, and you know it, that's why not," Cuzzy said, and walked back into the kitchen and out the door and onto the porch.

"You're the only one who says you can't," Tracy said, right behind.

"According to you, I have a fucking mind full of fucking snow," Cuzzy said, turning yet again and walking inside, heading straight to the stereo, and pulling on the headphones. "Once a woodchuck, always a woodchuck." He turned up the volume and stared vacantly at Tracy. Music seeped out like a cool draft. Brazilian Forro, it sounded like. Dance music. "Forro" was what the Brazilians thought the British railway workers were saying when they held their going-away dances, but in fact it had been "farewell."

"Forro," Tracy said, and walked away, leaving Cuzzy to it. He wasn't going to beg. It was a crazy idea, he admitted that, but not outrageous. He could help Cuzzy, give him opportunities he'd never have in Poverty. This would not be like plucking the natives off Tierra del Fuego and bringing them to England to civilize them. It would be more like Karl Malone leaving high school to play for the Utah Jazz. The image appealed to him. A level playing field, Tracy thought, that's what I can provide. He really thought he could.

They ate spaghetti for dinner, Tracy in the kitchen, Cuzzy in the other room. Tracy left him alone. This would not be impossible, he thought.

Cuzzy brought his bowl into the kitchen and rinsed it out in the sink. Tracy's was there, too, and he rinsed that one as well, which Tracy took as a sign of rapprochement.

"I brought back this film about distance running in Kenya, want to watch?" he asked Cuzzy, and didn't stand around in the kitchen long enough to hear "I don't care." Tracy slid the cassette into the VCR and sat on the couch, and before long Cuzzy sat down beside him.

On the screen two boys with dark skin kicked a rock, wrapped in a rag, around a dusty field. They were barefoot. The announcer, who had a British accent, said, "Though it may not look like it, these boys are playing football." Cuzzy smirked.

"It's supposed to be a good film," Tracy said. "Just wait."

"They do not wear shoes," the announcer said.

"Really good so far," Cuzzy said as the boys ran up and down the field. They looked happy, Cuzzy thought. Happier than anyone in Poverty.

"I guess this stuff about your father is hard," Tracy said, trying to sound as if they had been talking about it all along. On the screen the boy with the "ball" tripped over a rotting yucca plant—the soccer pitch was a picked-over farm field—and fell, and another boy took over and drove toward the end zone. The boy on the ground got up slowly and limped away, blood running down his leg. Close-up of flies on his wound.

"How would you know?" Cuzzy said.

"Three days later he was dead. Sepsis," the announcer said.

"I guess I wouldn't, really," Tracy said.

"I'm getting out of here," Cuzzy said. "As soon as I get a place to stay."

"If people in the Malki tribe live past thirteen, they tend to have longer-than-average life expectancies," the announcer said. "But most of them don't."

In the morning neither of them said anything about it. Not about Tracy's leaving, not about Cuzzy's moving out. They resumed their life in the cottage as if it were sufficient, like a good meal. Tracy had been up for hours, listening to the radio and catching up on mail. There was a note from the Shorehams' housekeeper in California, saying that a contingent of Shorehams would be arriving "in anticipation of Christmas"; and five requests for the "current resident" to transfer the balance of his credit bill to another company and cash in on lower interest rates. There were endless solicitations for money, including one addressed to "Black Al." If Algie were here, Tracy thought, he'd cut that out and put it in one of his notebooks. Tracy tossed it in the trash and picked up the *Times*.

"IBM soared yesterday," Tracy said, looking up from the paper when Cuzzy wandered in.

Yesterday had happened after all, Cuzzy thought. The jail part, the Trimble part, the father part, the Tracy part, and through it all, IBM soared. As a child he'd been fascinated by the idea of parallel universes—that there could be another planet out there somewhere with another Cuzzy doing exactly what he was doing (imagining a parallel universe with another Cuzzy). By now he knew that there were indeed two universes, and in one of them people like him existed only in shadow, as reflections of people looking in. So he had listened to music from Burkina Faso. So he had absorbed those rhythms. So he had read "The Snow Man." So he had read "Dry Loaf." So he had absorbed those rhythms, too. He was going to get a job moving earth. He was going to get a job hauling logs. Some night he was going to be pushing snow from one side of the road to the other, three A.M., with the river catching the moon and carrying the light downstream, and the words "Regard now the sloping, mountainous rocks and the river that batters its way over stones" would come into his head like the fortune on a Magic 8-ball. Here was the poem itself, laid out before him. And he would be able to hold it in contempt.

"Phone working yet?" Cuzzy asked.

Tracy lowered the business section. "Tomorrow. They promised to come out here in the morning."

"Great," Cuzzy said. "I need to get in touch with Joey." Joey would have to let him stay over for a while, sleep on the floor. Grand Union was looking for a meat cutter. How hard could that be?

"I've already been in touch with him," Tracy said. "He'll be here tonight."

Cuzzy started. A quick buzz of annoyance, fear, hatred. Tracy was one step ahead of him. Tracy was ready for him to leave. Fuck him.

"He'll be here at six," Tracy said.

Cuzzy stepped onto the porch. The thermometer said thirty-one, but it was raining, so he retreated to his place in front of the woodstove, where, when he shut his eyes, he could imagine being in equatorial Africa wearing nothing but a loincloth, kicking up dust clouds with his bare feet, which were, in his imagination, like smoke signals advertising his availability. Sex would be so simple. Like breathing. No one would think anything of it. Mindless fucking. It was never that way with Crystal. Amber-Rose—that was more like it; and Charlotte. He'd be seeing them all soon enough, slicing their bologna at the Grand Union. Fuck Tracy.

At four o'clock Tracy quit work and went into the kitchen. Cuzzy was watching a video he'd found in one of Algie's boxes about the Are'are people of the Solomon Islands. The men wore crowns of leaves on their heads and tennis shorts, except for the elder, who wore nothing and looked sad. "The Are'are number between seven and nine thousand," the narrator said. "They raise pigs and tubers." Cuzzy was bored and restless. He could pack, but having come with nothing, he was leaving with little more. His father had told him once about monks in India who walked from town to town relying on the kindness of strangers, owning nothing but the clothing on their backs. Leo had said he'd be tempted to do something similar if it weren't so cold in Poverty.

Tracy was banging away in the kitchen; his cooking always sounded industrial, Cuzzy thought, like he was operating heavy machinery. And then there was the strange food he'd come up with, the fried squid, the underdone tuna, leaving Cuzzy's tongue in a panic. He enjoyed the "afters," as Tracy liked to call them, the crème brûlées and caramels, the Linzer tortes and ginger cheesecakes, which he sometimes ate while Tracy read. "Listening is hard work," Tracy would say, which irked him. Milling wood was hard work. Pushing snow was hard work. But Tracy had a point, Cuzzy thought. Taking things in was its own kind of work. So much of listening was forgetting.

"The problem of transcribing music," Algie had written in one of his notebooks, "is that we (I) have European ears. We (I) can hear only what we've been raised to hear." Then, cut from a textbook: "Exact measurement of tempo, rhythm, and pitch can be more easily approached if the transcriber can cast aside the concept of the articulated note as the main point of order." On the same page, up the left margin, across the top, down the right, and across the bottom, Algie had copied sentences from deaf people about "hearing" vibrations, and then the words "I feel to know," and then, in a small, parenthetical hand, "Possible book idea: 'Notes on a Sensuous Epistemology.'"

The video ran its course, then rewound itself. In the kitchen Tracy was singing "Oklahoma" aggressively. On the other side of the window rain had darkened the sky, bringing on Cuzzy's last night at the Larches even sooner than time would. You don't have to be so happy, Cuzzy wanted to shout, but didn't.

At five he did get up to pack, so he would be ready. Five minutes later he was at loose ends. "Do not think of coming in here,"

Tracy warned, stepping through the doorway to shake a wooden spoon in Cuzzy's direction. He was wearing a yellow apron, and there was an ellipsis of sweat across his forehead. "What's that?" he said, pointing to the black trash bag on the couch beside Cuzzy.

"My stuff," Cuzzy said. "So I'm ready. When Joey comes for me."

"When Joey comes for you?"

"Didn't you say Joey was coming at six?" Cuzzy said. Tracy's bewilderment bewildered him.

"Oh, right," Tracy said. "But you don't have to leave. There's no reason to leave."

"You're leaving," Cuzzy said.

"But not tomorrow. We've still got lots of work to do."

"I'm getting a job," Cuzzy announced.

"You have a job."

Cuzzy smirked.

"Is it money?" Tracy asked. "Because if it's money, we can work it out."

"I don't need more money," Cuzzy said. An out-and-out lie. He could hear Crystal: "Who doesn't need more money?"

Tracy wiped his brow with a corner of his apron. "There is no reason for you to go, Cuzzy," he said again, but stiffly and remotely, as if Cuzzy already had.

When the doorbell rang at five till six, Cuzzy jumped off the couch. He'd been watching the second part of the Are'are video.

"Yoo-hoo," Ram called before Cuzzy got to the door. The Sylvania twins were on his heels, with Joey and a bottle of vodka bringing up the rear.

"Surprise!" Tracy said, coming up behind Cuzzy.

Surprise what? Why were they having a going-away party when Tracy had just asked him to stay?

"Happy birthday, Cuz," Joey said, presenting the bottle. "Aren't you going to ask us in?"

Cuzzy stood aside, and they all crowded into the kitchen, talking at once.

"I know it's not till tomorrow," Tracy explained, "but Joey has to work. Are you surprised?" He smiled proudly at Cuzzy—the smile of a man who had pulled something off.

Cuzzy nodded shyly and thought back: Tracy in the Gotham, looking at his license. The unexplained call to Joey. All that commotion in the kitchen.

"Nice apron," Ram said to Tracy. "I like the little peppers."

Dinner was alphabet soup—in Cuzzy's honor, Tracy said, for the great work he'd done—lamb chops with new potatoes, and gingered string beans, which they ate crowded around the kitchen table, all elbows and knees. Two candles lit the room, sending a vague, inconstant light across their faces like a rumor.

"Very fancy," Ram said, but even he was rendered quiet by the simple elegance—the delicate wineglasses and cloth napkins, especially.

"Do *not* put these around your necks, or I'll strangle you," Ram said to the Sylvanias when they were sitting down to eat, but in an avuncular, almost kindly way that Tracy, who had taken care with the table, appreciated.

The cake was chocolate, three layers separated by mocha butter cream.

"Do we get to sing the monkey part?" Larry asked, and then they did.

These are my friends, Cuzzy thought. Tracy will leave, and they will still be my friends. And he felt strangely peaceful, like he was there and watching himself there, and he could see how it was going and how it would go. The food, Tracy's food, the food that Tracy made for him, sat warmly in his stomach. Tracy would go away, and maybe he would come back sometime, but maybe not, maybe he would turn out to be one of those tourists who stopped for a view of the river and of the mountains, charged a tankful of gas, and moved on. And the truth was, the thing Cuzzy saw for the first time, was that it didn't matter. It didn't matter if Tracy left or if he stayed, because Cuzzy's real friends were the ones who had always been there and were always going to be there. He felt like a person who had secretly believed he was adopted and found out he wasn't. He wasn't making this up. Crystal had shown him an article from *Women's Life* called "The Inauthenticity Syndrome," which he only remembered because he thought that name was so strange, and because Crystal had to read the five stages to him three times before he got it: belief—that your biological parents actually adopted you. ("Why would your real parents have to adopt you?" he asked Crystal more than once.) Confusion—about where you came from and to whom you belong. Annoyance—at your parents' constant and, to your mind, phony assurances. Doubt—of their truthfulness. And finally acceptance—that they are who they say they are, and so are you. At the time it struck Cuzzy as ridiculous, the leap from doubt to acceptance, but not anymore. That was precisely what had just happened to him. These were his friends. This was his place. Tracy was right after all: he did have a mind of winter.

"Shoot, I almost forgot these," Joey said, pulling out a package of Scooby-Doo party hats from the inside pocket of his jacket. "I grabbed these this morning," he said, winking.

"You mean you stole them?" Tracy asked.

"Yeah," said Joey. "They were real cheap."

"I guess so," Tracy said. "But what if you got caught?"

"Who's going to catch me?" Joey asked. "Me?"

Tracy tapped his fork gently on his wineglass, and they all stopped talking and looked at him. "I'd like to propose a toast,"

Tracy said, raising his glass. "To Cuzzy Gage, who has taught this teacher a lot."

"Whoa," Ram said, raising his eyebrows.

"No, I mean it," Tracy said earnestly. "If it weren't for Cuzzy, this would have been a miserable time for me. And how would I know that porcupines scream and tamaracks shed and raccoons love turtle eggs."

"Everyone knows that," Squint said.

"Well, I didn't," Tracy said. "Just as I didn't know I'd become friends with"—he looked at Cuzzy—"a woodchuck."

"You did?" Larry said. "I didn't know woodchucks did that. What do they eat?"

"Birthday cake, moron," Ram said.

"Wow," Larry said.

"Happy birthday to Cuzzy," Tracy said, raising his glass even higher, then taking a drink. He set his wineglass down carefully and put his hand in his shirt pocket. "I know this won't seem like much," he said, extracting a gray felt ring box, "but it means a lot to me, and I want you to have it." He handed the box to Cuzzy. "Go ahead, open it," he said, sensing Cuzzy's hesitation.

Inside, on a bed of satin, sat a single blue agate. Cuzzy looked at it a moment, then closed the box. He knew what it was, and where it was from, and he knew how hard it must have been for Tracy to part with it. But he couldn't say anything, not even thanks.

"It's a marble," Larry said.

"Yeah, it's a marble," Squint said. "I thought it was going to be a ring."

"Well, it wasn't," Larry said.

"Well, it could have been," Squint said.

"How could it have been a ring if it was a marble?" Larry asked.

"I don't have a toast or anything," Ram said, rising, "but I do have a present. I made it myself." He reached into his boot and pulled out a small plastic bag and put it on the table. "Crystal," he said to Cuzzy, "and I don't mean the mother of your child. It's in-fucking-credible."

"Yeah," said Larry.

"Yeah," said Squint.

"Who says I brought any for you?" Ram said, turning on them. "This is Cuzzy's big day." From his other boot he retrieved a metal pipe.

Cuzzy glanced at Tracy, who looked stricken. "Look," Tracy began, "would you please not do that here—"

"Not to be rude or anything, Trace," Ram said, "but it is raining outside." He held the pipe out to Cuzzy. "Does the birthday boy want his present?"

"I don't know." Cuzzy hesitated.

"Just take a hit," Ram said, lighting it, "and then we'll play a game. This is a party, isn't it?"

QUOIT

The New Oxford Dictionary *gives two meanings: "1. A ring of iron thrown in a game to encircle or land as near as possible to an upright peg; 2. The first covering stone of a dolmen." A dolmen, remember, is a megalithic tomb, like Stonehenge.*

"Okay," Ram said, leaning back in his chair till it rested on two legs, "the game is called Truth or Dare. Ever heard of it?"

Cuzzy was not sure. Maybe. Maybe he had heard of it. But who cared? His left thigh was talking to him. Well, not speaking to him, not using words, but it was glowing at him in an intense kind of way, as if it were gold, and when he looked down, he expected it to be gold, matte gold, but wasn't that a story his father told, about wanting too much, and his leg wasn't gold, he was relieved to see that, though his jeans had a hole in them, as if a hole punch made it, black around the edges, and alive, it was moving, he loved that, like it was an insect, molting, getting bigger and—

"What's on fire?" Larry asked. He was taking short, quick dog breaths.

"Me," said Squint lazily. "I'm on fire."

Ram took another hit off the pipe. "There's the door. Go put yourself out," he said. And everyone laughed except Tracy, and the sound roused Cuzzy enough to encourage him to lick his thumb and press it over the hole in his pants. His leg was burned. He knew it was, but he couldn't feel it.

Cuzzy looked over and saw how uneasily Tracy's skin hung on his bones—saw it more surely than he felt where his own body ended and the air began, or where his mind resided. A runny egg. It felt like a runny egg. His father's brain. Cuzzy shuddered and closed his eyes. Except his eyes were already shut.

"Do they play Truth or Dare in the big city?" Ram asked, passing the pipe to his left. He folded his arms over his chest, boardroom-style, and looked down the table. Ram was in charge now; Tracy's party had become his before anyone knew it was contested. Cuzzy studied the two of them for what seemed to be a long time. Ram was ruddy and thick around the shoulders, and though he moved gracelessly, his carelessness spoke its own power. Tracy, by contrast, was pale and thin. His heavy sweater was subterfuge—it couldn't hide his essential boniness, or the unbending rigor of his muscles. He looked unhealthy, Cuzzy thought, like he was fading in direct proportion to Ram's glow. Wasn't there something like that in nature? Weren't there wasp larvae that were laid under another animal's skin, eating the animal from the inside out in order for the wasp to grow?

Oh God, did he feel good. Like he was having sex without actually having to have it. No muss, no fuss, he thought, and laughed out loud, which got everyone's attention, as if he had burped. He felt great, really terrific. He was an Are'are guy wearing nothing but leaves in his hair, blowing on a panpipe. He was—

"I wouldn't know," Tracy said slowly, blinking, answering Ram but looking at Cuzzy, no one else, which reminded Cuzzy of those prisoners of war who were made to speak propaganda but tried to communicate to the free world using Morse code with their eyelids. But then Tracy was walking out of the room; Cuzzy could see only his back; no eyes there, he didn't think.

Tracy stepped out of the house, onto the porch. He hoped Cuzzy would follow, and he stood there waiting, listening to the trees brush against the cottage and to the voices inside the house. When Cuzzy didn't come, when his voice was indistinguishable from the others', Tracy wondered if he shouldn't drive away and leave Cuzzy Gage to the life that he was determined to have. That is the fallacy of the Good Samaritan, he said to himself, and to the trees that were dripping rain. It wasn't about the bleeding man *getting better*, it was only about his neighbor crossing the street.

Chastened, Tracy went back inside and nearly collided with Joey, who was wandering around the room, fingering whatever caught his eye. He ran his hand up and down a stack of books as if it were a keyboard. He lifted an eighteenth-century quoit off the wall and peered through it. Tracy was about to tell him to stop, Cuzzy knew he was, because for some reason he knew exactly what Tracy was going to do before he even did it. But then Ram said, "Sit down, Joey," and Joey sat down and Cuzzy sighed and the pipe was passed to him.

"Okay," Ram said. "Does everyone get that? You say 'truth' or you say 'dare,' and then the person has to do that."

"What person?" asked Larry.

"Shut up," Ram said.

"What person?" Larry growled, agitated. "You didn't say what person."

"You, asshole," Ram said. "Okay? You go first. You and Squint. Be our role models."

Larry considered this. "What if he says no?"

"Then he gets punished," Ram said. "Understand?"

Squint rested his chin on his knuckles to think. "This is going to be good," he said. He stayed quiet for a minute, and then a delighted smile catapulted across his face. "This is a dare," he said, looking at his brother. "I dare you to dress up as a girl and go trick-

or-treating!" He said this triumphantly, as if he had just solved a difficult problem.

"But it's not Halloween," Larry complained.

Squint giggled. "I know."

"And there aren't any houses up here," Larry continued. "You want me to knock on Gus Meacham's door and say, 'Trick or treat'?"

"It's only a game," Joey broke in.

The Sylvanias stared at each other. It was a standoff.

A different voice. Ram's. "Do it in town or get punished. I'll even lend you my truck." Ram tossed a set of keys. They hit Larry in the stomach, then fell to the floor.

"Oh, all right," Larry said, putting on his jacket and walking toward the door. "You know what I'm going to dress up as?" he asked his brother before he went out. "You. So when people ask me what I am, I can say I'm an asshole. Get it?"

The pipe went around again, a sucking sound followed by a satisfied exhalation followed by silence, and they sat there, Squint and Ram, Joey and Cuzzy, happy, so very happy, that the game was momentarily forgotten, Larry was forgotten, and a pleasant time-lessness settled over them. To Tracy, who was standing in a corner, they looked stunned, each one of them frozen in place, their eyes open but unfocused.

"What are you staring at?" Ram demanded.

"Nothing," Tracy said, looking straight at him. "Literally."

"Good," Ram said. "Keep it that way."

Cuzzy was only vaguely aware of the exchange. Words were sounds, no more intelligible than the music Algie collected. Tracy was nearby. He remembered that and looked over and gave him a sloppy smile. He wished that Tracy would let up and live a little.

"You next," Ram said to Squint, "truth or dare?"

"Dare."

Ram rubbed his hands together, pretending to think. "I dare you to call 911 and report a stolen red Dodge four-by-four," he said, grinning.

Squint looked stricken. "But Larry—" he began.

"Do it or get punished," Ram said coldly. And then, softening a little: "We'll get it all cleared up in the morning."

A look of satisfaction settled on Squint's face, and he closed his eyes and smiled, imagining his brother coming out of the sheriff's office the next morning in a dress.

"The phone is dead," a voice said. Tracy's voice. "He can't call out."

"Then he needs to get in his vehicle and drive to town and find a phone," Ram said, as if talking to a child.

"You never said what the punishment was," Cuzzy said.

Ram pointed to the bottle of vodka. "All of it. Normally that sort of thing can produce brain damage, but in his case that would be impossible. Now get out of here," he said to Squint.

Then there were four of them, and the room seemed brighter to Cuzzy. The pots and pans overhead were lit by reflection, as were the horseshoes on the wall, the silverware in the sink. Everything had more definition and more color. Even Tracy's white face was whiter.

"Truth," Cuzzy said. he was tired of dares. "Let's do a truth."

"Whose truth?" Ram said.

Cuzzy waved his hand in the direction of his cousin. "Joey," he said. "Joey's truth."

"All right," Ram said. "Joey's truth."

Joey grabbed the first book he saw and put his hand on it. "I agree to tell the whole truth and nothing but the whole truth, so help me."

"Auden," Tracy muttered. "You're swearing on a copy of *The Selected Poems of W. H. Auden.*"

"Whatever," Joey said. "I'm ready."

Cuzzy was suddenly clearheaded. More clearheaded, he was sure, than he'd ever been in his life, and also more confused, and he wondered for a second if the two were connected, but then that second was gone. Here was Joey, his cousin, but what did "cousin" mean? What a strange word: "cou / sin." They had done a lot of stuff together. Stupid stuff. Driving around and smoking and listening to Joey's endless collection of Nirvana tapes. They *knew* each other. So when Cuzzy looked at Joey, he expected to see right down to the bone, and to the heart beating in its ribbed cage, but he didn't. What he saw instead was opaque, like the white of the eye, an eye without an iris or a pupil or an optic nerve. This was what he knew.

"Okay," Cuzzy said. "Did you, or didn't you, nail your sister?"

Quiet then. Pure quiet, except for the icy rain pelting the windows and roof. Joey's fingers, which had been drumming the table, stopped. Cuzzy could feel Tracy's eyes on his back, on his shoulder blade, to be precise, while everyone else looked at Joey.

"Truth," Joey said, drumming again.

"Truth what?" Ram said.

"I did it," Joey said. And then, after a long pause, "It wasn't like she minded. She only said that later."

Cuzzy looked away, embarrassed. It had been a giveaway question. A freebie. He'd thought he knew the answer, which was the only reason he'd asked it. If he didn't feel so good, so very goddamned good, he'd feel like shit.

"Dare," Joey said quickly. "I have a dare for Cuzzy." He looked mean then; he never looked mean. Joey was goofy. He was comical. He was the class clown. He was not mean. But he looked mean, mean and angry. And then his expression broke, and he smiled at his cousin, and he was back to being the way he always was, and Cuzzy exhaled, not realizing he had been holding his breath.

"I dare Cuzzy," Joey said, "to show us how he kisses Tracy. Tongue and all."

"Fuck you, Joey," Cuzzy said. "Fuck you."

"You don't get to choose for someone else," Tracy said quietly. "He has to choose himself, one or the other, truth or dare."

"Well," Ram said, "then we're just going to have to break the rules on this one."

Cuzzy glanced quickly at the bottle of vodka. It was over half full. He'd heard of guys losing consciousness when they drank that much. He'd heard of them dying.

"Don't drink it," Tracy's voice. Cuzzy's heart began to pound. He felt it in his forehead and his neck and along the inside of his leg, loud and fast and insistent.

"You want me to kiss you, don't you, Tracy?" he sneered. "Don't you." He wanted to know about Tracy, and now he did, and fuck him.

"Don't," Tracy started, but before he could say more, Cuzzy reached over and took the bottle of vodka and put it to his lips. His tongue snaked down the neck, then he drew back, then snaked down again.

"Like this," Cuzzy yelled. "You want it like this."

Tracy stood up then and reached for the bottle. "Give that to me, Cuzzy," he said calmly, as if it were a gun. "You're going to hurt yourself."

"Fuck you, Tracy," Cuzzy said, standing up and wheeling around defensively. He raised the bottle to his lips again and started drinking. A minute passed—or what seemed like a minute. His throat was burning, and his mouth, too, and Cuzzy liked it, he liked the way it felt, and he felt like he could see it carving a phosphorescent trail from his throat to his stomach. He looked up through the bottle to the ceiling and watched the liquid lowering, little by little. His mouth was a funnel. His throat was a drain. He was moving. He was sideways to himself.

"Stop it!" somebody was yelling. It hurt his head. Cuzzy dropped to the floor. He felt a hand tug on his sleeve and pull him up.

"Cut it out," Joey said, grabbing the bottle.

"It's my present," Cuzzy said. "Give me back my present." He crawled toward Joey and lunged for his legs. "Give it back," he shouted. Joey fell to his knees. He was kneeling right in front of Cuzzy. He looked like he was praying, and Cuzzy started to laugh. He bent over laughing, then looked up with tears in his eyes.

Joey's punch caught him under the left eye. Cuzzy blindly swung the bottle in Joey's direction and heard it shatter, and then he heard nothing. He was curled up and bleeding, and from the deep place where he had been sent, he could almost see the blood breaching the surface and spilling out over his bruised skin.

He didn't feel it when Tracy pulled him up and led him to the couch. He didn't feel Tracy tilt his head and prop it up with a pillow, or the washcloth under his eye stanching the blood. Pieces of glass spangled his boots, but he didn't see these, either. Where he was, there was no angularity. There was light, but it didn't illuminate anything.

"Dare. I have a dare for you," Tracy said to Ram, walking purposefully back to the kitchen. His voice was cold and detached and Ram, crouched on the floor next to Joey, sharing a joint with him, actually seemed afraid.

"All right," Ram said, recovering his cool. "A dare. From Tracy."

Tracy retrieved the book Joey had sworn on, *The Selected Poems of W. H. Auden,* and looked in the index. "Here," he said, passing Ram the opened book. "I dare you to read this to us."

Ram scowled. "I don't do words," he said.

"Don't or can't?" Tracy asked.

Ram ignored him.

"Don't or can't?" Tracy said again.

"Shut up, faggot."

"Is *that* what you think?"

"It's what I know," Ram sneered.

"Oh Jesus. You don't know anything."

"I know about your 'friend,'" Ram said, "the one who gave you the car."

"Brilliant," Tracy said. "That's just brilliant. And I know about your friend," he said, pointing at Joey. "Does that make you a—"

"And I know you, and you, and him," Joey said sloppily, pointing in the direction of the couch in the other room where, as if on cue, Cuzzy groaned.

Tracy wet a dish towel and went to him. One of Cuzzy's eyes was swollen shut, but the other was open. Tracy bent over and laid a hand on his forehead, then carefully wiped at a line of blood connecting Cuzzy's mouth to his ear.

"Don't," Cuzzy said sharply, trying to sit up.

Tracy stopped and regarded him sympathetically. "It's okay. It's almost done."

Cuzzy leaned back and let him finish.

"Here," Tracy said gently, "we've got to get these off," and loosened a boot and started to wiggle it off.

Cuzzy bolted up, his one good eye narrowed and his face full of contempt. "I told you not to touch me. Do not touch me." He pulled away, and the boot came off in Tracy's hands and thudded to the floor. Tracy bent down to get it, and when he looked up,

Cuzzy was insensible again, both eyes closed, mouth ajar, his head and right arm askew, as if arrested in motion.

"You need to leave now," Tracy said after returning to the kitchen. "The party's over."

"We don't think so," Ram said. "Me and Joey have been talking, and we want to play another game."

"Game time is over," Tracy said.

Ram stood up and put his hands on Tracy's shoulders. "It's called Ring Around the Pansy," he said. He pushed Tracy into a chair. "Did you like that?" he asked. "Did you like that, poetry boy, when I put my hands on your shoulders?" Ram pressed harder, pinching the skin on either side of Tracy's collarbone.

"Cut it out," Tracy said, shaking him off and standing up.

"She said 'cut it out,'" Ram said, looking Tracy in the eye. "The girl said 'cut it out,'" and drove the tip of his boot into Tracy's shin.

"Ow!" Tracy yelled. "Jesus." The pain arced and went straight to his stomach. He thought he might throw up.

"She said 'ow,'" Ram reported. Joey, who was peering into the closet, snickered.

Arms folded at his midsection, Tracy dropped dully into the chair, trying to catch his breath.

"Good girl," Ram said. He unbuckled his belt and started to pull it slowly from his pants. "You people are all scum," he said as the leather snaked around his waist. "Which I guess explains your friend's name." The belt was off now, and Ram was using it to cinch Tracy to the chair. For an instant Ram's arms were around Tracy's chest; if the camera had stopped right there, it would have shown Ram embracing him.

"*Mgnwengwe*" came into Tracy's mind from Algie's fifth notebook: "certain blessed sticks in Zambia representing human bones."

The definition was written across the page, separating two pictures from Angkor Wat called "Killing Field Study 1" and "Killing Field Study 13, 438," with some ambiguity about whether or not they were the same photograph. The eye played tricks. The same thing, twice, could appear different. And things that were different could be conflated and thought to be the same, too. Truth, even visual truth—maybe especially visual truth—was not assured. In that same instant Tracy considered bolting, or trying to bolt. Ram was behind him, and Joey was rooting around the utility closet and out of sight. Pull, break free, stand up, kick the chair, run. Tracy saw the whole sequence in his head. But when he tried to see it again, he couldn't. Instead, it was pull, pull, pull, and nothing. Or worse than nothing.

"Found it!" Joey called, stepping out of the closet with a roll of duct tape and tossing it to Ram.

"Yes!" Ram said, catching it. "Now, the first part of the game is called 'Shut the fuck up.'" He tore off a length of tape and slapped it across Tracy's mouth. Then he tore off a longer length, reinforced the tape over the mouth, then wound it around the back of Tracy's neck. "Very stylish," Ram said. "You people are all very stylish, aren't you?" He hit Tracy playfully in the arm.

"Where do you keep the rope in this place?" Joey called from the utility room. "I can't find it."

Ram chuckled. "Poetry boy is not exactly in a position to tell us," he said.

Joey poked his head out of the closet. "Whoa, Ram, that's awesome," he said, looking at Tracy. "No rope in here," he reported. "I'll look in the other room."

He was back in a minute. "How about this?" he asked, carrying a big drum whose head was held in place by a piece of jute that was laced up and down and around the wooden base.

"Perfect," Ram said, handing him a knife.

"Oh yeah," Joey said, cutting into the string from the top. "Oh yeah. You know what this reminds me of?"

"No, what?" Ram asked.

"Intestines."

"What?"

"Yeah, you know how your intestines are all coiled up in your stomach and don't look like much, but if you pulled them out, they'd be like a mile long." Joey unwove the string till he had a good five feet, and the drum skin shrank and separated from the bottom. "Here you go," he said proudly.

"Bend your arms at the elbow and put them up on the armrest like this," Ram said to Tracy, as if he had a choice.

It was a dondo drum, from Ghana—a talking drum. Pressing on the strings and banging on the goatskin head with a crooked stick would broadcast moods and feelings and information. War, for instance, or happiness. Or terror. Also from the fifth notebook, a handwritten receipt for this drum, opposite part of a transcript from a sign-language interview with Koko the gorilla, her handler, and a moderator at the National Zoo.

MODERATOR: Koko, are you going to have a baby?

KOKO: Pink.

HANDLER: We've had an earlier discussion about colors today.

KOKO: Listen, Koko loves to eat.

Bent and bound, Tracy's arms looked like goalposts. Algie had kept that drum by his bed. He loved to whale on it when he was happy.

"Now, the thing to know about this game," Ram said, standing back to admire his work, "is that you have already lost."

In one of Algie's notebooks—which one? Tracy couldn't remember—was a piece of graph paper that he had colored in with markers, boxes of blue and green and red and orange and yellow that overlapped and made other colors, brown and purple and black and shades of orange, shades of green. It was a gorgeous page, and Tracy could imagine Algie sitting cross-legged in some bus station, markers scattered close to hand, working on it; he could hear the scratch and squeak of the felt tips rubbed back and forth over the paper. "Out-of-Body Experience," it was called—he remembered at least that—and when you turned it over, there was a fluid map of the multiple identities of a girl named Rita, twenty-one in all, small babies and grown men and nine-year-olds whose fathers did not share them with their friends, as Rita's father did.

Could fear do the work of fever? Tracy prayed it could. He prayed and tried to regulate his breathing, in and out, in and out, steadily and surely, listening to that rhythm and remembering that it was the twelfth notebook, that map was in the twelfth notebook. His mind was working in slow motion and randomly, moving more slowly than Joey, who was walking around the house prying horseshoes from the walls, and less clearly than Ram, who was directing him.

"I want you to promise to find the tree house," Algie had said, and told Tracy how, when he was little, he would stand at the railing and look out at the tops of the trees and think he was seeing across the whole wide world, think he was seeing over oceans to other continents, where he would someday go. "That's what I learned when I went up there," Algie said, "that the world is bigger than me. I want you to see that.

"Promise," Algie said, and raised his hand weakly—he was almost gone—and Tracy promised. He took that hand, which was cold and the color of waxed beans, and brought it to his lips, and promised.

"The pitcher's box is right here," Ram explained, walking ten paces from Tracy's chair and drawing an invisible line across the pine planking with his toe. "No," he corrected himself. "I have a better idea," and he tore another length of tape off the roll and smoothed it flat upon the floor. "We pitch from here," he told Joey. "Feet behind the line, or it doesn't count."

Joey giggled and stacked the horseshoes in two piles behind the line. "It's four shoes an inning, right?" he asked. "Best two out of three?"

"How about first to a hundred," Ram suggested. "First ringer is three, second is six, arms or neck." He bent down and picked a shoe off one of the piles, then faced Tracy in the chair, shaking his throwing arm to loosen it.

"Wait a minute. Wait a minute," Joey said, and raced out of the kitchen, through the living room where Cuzzy still lay asleep or unconscious, they looked the same, and into the bedroom, looking for paper. There were notebooks on the desk, lots of them, and Joey pulled one away, opened the cover, and tore out the first page he found. "Notebook Seven," it said. "Algernon S. Black."

Joey turned the page over. Nothing. He grabbed a pen and drew a quick, unsteady line down the middle, dividing it into two columns. At the top of one he wrote "Ram," and at the other he wrote "Joe."

"Okay, I've got it," he sang out to Ram. "The scorecard."

In the kitchen Ram was warming up in earnest now, swinging the horseshoe up and down.

Tracy's eyes were open. He couldn't remember how to shut them.

Ram stepped up to the line. "Game one, Ring Around the Pansy," he announced, staring at the space between the top of Tracy's sweater and the silver tape that covered his mouth.

"This one's for three," he said, and let it go.

TAILINGS

"Residue separated in the preparation of ore," Colton. *It is toxic, for the most part, due to methods of extraction, especially because of the use of cyanide (the same stuff that's used in gas chambers). A warden at San Quentin, regarding execution by gas: "The eyes pop. The skin turns purple and the victim begins to drool." Pretty quick segue from the manufactured (the macadam) to the unfeigned (the drool). Is everything left behind automatically "waste"?*

He woke because he was cold, his feet especially. The fire was out, though Cuzzy hoped there might be embers enough to rouse a flame. Drumbeats of rain overhead, but otherwise the house was still. As he lay there, he took a quick inventory of his body. His head hurt from the inside out, but dully, and everything else seemed to be working all right. Even his swollen eye—he could almost open it. No kindling: *that* he could see. He was going to have to drag his sorry tail to the porch and grab some wood if he had any chance of warming up.

The kitchen clock said 3:24. In the morning, he guessed. The place was a mess. No one had done the dishes, a couple of chairs were upended, and the half-eaten birthday cake was still on the table. It could all wait, he told himself. Anyhow, it was his birthday. You shouldn't have to clean up after your own party.

It was freezing on the porch. The rain was sticking to the railings drop by drop, and light sneaking out of the house made it shine. Cuzzy quickly chopped some kindling from a piece of scrap, loaded it in his arms, and walked into the house, careful to avoid the places where the overhang leaked and the rain had puddled and iced up. He didn't want to slip, not on his birthday. Shouldn't have to slip on your own birthday, he was thinking. He shouldered the door open and was in the kitchen again, which was when he noticed that he had one boot on and one boot off: his steps were making a hobbled, peg-legged sound. He heard it and looked down and vaguely remembered Tracy pulling off the right one, and then making Tracy go away.

Why was there a piece of duct tape stretched across the floor? Cuzzy was standing on it, but it didn't mean anything to him. Had something broken?

The rain was getting louder; there was wind, too. But what was that sound he was hearing? What kind of animal made that sound? He looked around the room. Once he'd caught a weasel in here, gnawing on a mouse; only the mouse's tail, wagging back and forth across the weasel's lips, had been visible.

Cuzzy tried to follow the sound back to its source with his good eye, on the lookout for a patch of fur or an unconcealed and twitching nose. He was a decent hunter. He knew how to look. His mother could never find anything. Not her keys, not her reading glasses, even when they were resting on the bridge of her nose.

He let go of the wood. It crashed to the floor. "Oh God, oh God, oh God," Cuzzy said instead of breathing. He dropped to his knees and crawled under the table. There was Tracy, strapped to a chair that was tipped on its side, his arm bent upright at the elbow as if he were taking an oath. Cuzzy saw blood outlining his body, and horseshoes scattered there. He crawled closer, then stopped, unable to make himself look at what had become of the face.

Cuzzy backed up, stood up, and swaying, steadied himself on

the lip of the sink. He was going to be sick, he knew he was going to be sick, and he hung his head over a bunch of empties, but nothing happened. His mind was racing; there wasn't time to be sick. Get in the car, drive to Gus Meacham's, call the rescue squad. He said it: "I'm going to drive to Gus's house and call the rescue squad. It's going to be okay. It's going to be okay. Oh God, Tracy." He hoped Tracy could hear him. He couldn't make himself look. Cuzzy raced to the porch, then stopped short. No car. The car was not there. The dark sky was raining ice. He started to jog down the driveway. The wind was sending the ice sideways, like bullets. Run, Cuzzy coached himself. Faster. Ice. Watch out for the ice.

The woods were dark, and the road was slick. It was hard to see where the road went, and more than once he veered off it into the brambles, which set him right again. The road tended down—that he knew. But he couldn't remember anymore what down felt like.

Cuzzy didn't see the fallen hemlock, inert across the road, till he almost ran into it. To his left the woods were a wall of pricker bush, so he detoured to the right, down a quick culvert and up the other side. But the other side was steeper, and he couldn't make it. Too icy. He slid backward and landed at the bottom, where water had collected. His jeans and shirt were a wick. Before he could crawl out, he was soaked. His hair was already plastered to his head, his hands were wet and numb, and now his clothes were soaked through. Back on the road, shivering, Cuzzy fought his way through the hemlock as if it were an opponent, thrashing its branches and sharp needles till he was at last on the other side, gluey with pitch, his clothes torn and his skin, too, and crying, his tears the only warm thing.

He believed he had been running for ten or fifteen minutes, but he was exhausted; it felt much longer, and he was panting and could taste blood in the back of his throat, the same as when he breathed hard in winter air, and his bootless foot hurt, he could barely put his weight on it before springing off it again, and he was so cold the shivers drove right through him like contractions, five a minute, seven a minute, till he was shaking uncontrollably, and was he still on the road?

He thought he was, but it was so dark, and he could no longer feel what was underfoot, or hear it, and why were there so many trees to dodge, and he had to rest. Cuzzy slowed down and then stopped altogether. How long since he'd left the house? He had no idea. There was absolutely no moon, and the cloud cover was low. These things registered, and so did the way the birch tree on which he was leaning was glazed with ice, and how good it felt to lay his cheek upon it, and how warm he felt, finally, like it was going to be a bright summer's day, his birthday, if the sun would ever hurry up, he was sweating, that was the trouble, so he took off his flannel shirt and let it fall to the ground for the rain to cool him like those runners in Kenya, he wasn't sure how, but like them, and he was moving again.

He found the road. He couldn't run anymore. And what was the rush? He could barely remember why he had been running. He knew and he didn't know. He felt almost happy. But so tired. That thought arrested him. Cuzzy stopped and knew what he should do: he should sleep. He sat down in the road and let the cool rain wash over him. He lay back with his hands behind his head and opened his mouth to drink from the sky.

Jason Trimble got the call at nine minutes after four. Gus Meacham, hysterical, from the hospital. He needed the minister right away. Molly had fallen out of bed sometime in the night, and Gus had tripped over her, realized she was in trouble, and rushed her to Halcyon Falls still in his pajamas. No wallet, no health-insurance card. He needed the minister to bring them down. Jason pretended he was already up and drinking his coffee. He liked Gus and Molly Meacham. Still, he thought that sometimes people took the idea of "servant of the Lord" too literally.

The road was a skating rink. His tires were studded, but the car slid from side to side as Jason hung tight to the wheel, until he inched up behind the sander on the county road, its massive wheels sending grit onto his windshield like a hale greeting.

Whisper Notch Road wasn't half bad, either. Shoreham's tailings at work. Still, Jason's coffee sloshed in the cup holder, reminding him to take it easy. Make a mistake here and it was a long walk out. His high beams were on, and every so often he'd tap the horn to warn off any animal that might be thinking of jumping out in front of him. A couple of branches were down, but he was able to maneuver around them, and then his lights picked out something bigger, and some instinct, something, told him it wasn't another tree, and it wasn't a deer, though maybe it was. But then his high beams picked out a foot, and then a boot, and traveled up the body, over the jeans and over the shirt to a bare arm, crossed over the chest.

"Oh good Lord," Jason Trimble said, opening the car door before the car had stopped, and jumping out, dashing to the body. He knew that chin. He pushed the hair off the face. It was Cuzzy. Cuzzy Gage. Jason called his name. Cuzzy opened his one good eye and smiled.

"What are you doing here?" the minister asked dumbly.

"Sunbathing," Cuzzy said slowly, slurring the word.

He wasn't being sarcastic; Trimble could see that right away.

"Oh, sweet Jesus in heaven," he said, "you have hypothermia. You have hypothermia. We've got to get you out of the cold. Put this on. You have hypothermia." He was frantic. He handed Cuzzy his hat.

"But I'm hot," Cuzzy complained.

"Your mind is playing tricks," Jason said. "Can you stand up?"

"I don't want to," Cuzzy said petulantly.

"Get up, Cuzzy," Jason said sternly, and for some reason Cuzzy did, but then he couldn't walk.

The minister draped Cuzzy's arm around his shoulder. "We've got to get you warm," he said. In the car he turned the heat up high and blanketed Cuzzy with his raincoat. "You're soaked," he said.

Cuzzy looked at him cross-eyed. His pupils were dilated. His skin was waxy, with a bluish tint. He smelled of alcohol.

Jason made a quick calculation. It was an hour to the hospital in the best of times. This morning it might be more like two. They didn't have two hours, he was sure of that. He was chaplain to the rescue squad. He knew about hypothermia, how you had to warm people up slowly, how the guys on the truck would say, "No one is dead until they're warm and dead." Cuzzy wasn't even shivering.

"We're going to Gus's house," he said, but to himself. Cuzzy was somewhere else. His head was tipped back. His blue lips were drawn tight over his teeth. His breathing was shallow and slow.

The door was unlocked, but the stairs were steep. Jason struggled with Cuzzy's body, pulling it up carefully, in fits and starts, like a fish being hauled on a test line that might break at any second. The Meachams' ancient retriever gave a halfhearted bark when she heard the door open, then thumped her tail and struggled to her feet when she saw who it was.

"Hi, Tammy," Reverend Trimble said absently. The dog lay down right where she had been standing. Jason coaxed Cuzzy to the sofa.

"We have to take off your wet clothes," he said, again more to himself than to Cuzzy. He tried to remember what he had seen the rescue squad do: breathe up the nose. He thought he remembered that, and he leaned over and sent a stream of warm air from his mouth into Cuzzy's nostrils. But it wasn't efficient. He couldn't do that and get the clothes off, too, and he knew he had to get them off or else Cuzzy would freeze. Jason fought with the boot. It seemed to be soldered on. The laces were frozen. He wasn't going to get it off if they were frozen. He bent down and picked at the laces with the ends of his fingers, but it was no use. "Oh dear Jesus," he said, and pressed his tongue to the tongue of the boot until the ice turned liquid. He licked his tongue mostly clean on the back of his sleeve, and pulled the laces off the leather and the boot from the foot. Underneath the sock, Cuzzy's skin was a bright yellowish white. Jason put Cuzzy's foot in the pit of his arm, then couldn't, it was making him so cold. He turned to the other foot. It was cut up and bleeding and studded with tailings. The sock was shredded and came off in pieces. The jeans and shirt were harder. Both were stuck to Cuzzy's skin and didn't come smoothly. Jason worked jerkily, tugging, pulling, lifting, tugging, peeling. He had seen bodies at the mortuary before the morticians were done with them. This body looked like that.

"I'll be right back," Jason said when Cuzzy was undressed, and he went into the bedroom for a blanket.

He found it balled at the bottom of the bed, a tied quilt in the log-cabin pattern, worn but thick with batting. He carried it into the living room and was about to throw it on top of Cuzzy when he saw that Cuzzy had peed on himself. His thigh was wet, and so was the couch under him. "Oh good God," Jason said, tearing off his Red Sox sweatshirt and using it to dry Cuzzy. He threw it on the floor. "Come on," he said, and lifted Cuzzy and carried him to the bedroom and lay him on the bed. Then he went back to the other room and gathered up the blanket.

"Come on, Tammy," he coaxed the dog. She thumped her tail. "Come on, Tammy," he said more desperately. "Come with me."

The dog stood up, stretched, and looked at him. Then she lay down again.

"Come on," he said angrily, and went over to the dog, dropped the blanket on her back, and picked up the whole package, the blanket and the dog, and brought them into the bedroom and deposited them on the bed. Instinctively, the dog curled next to Cuzzy, pushing her hips into his. Jason put the blanket over them both. He was hoping that maybe Cuzzy would feel this and give him a sign, but he didn't. Somewhere in the house, a clock chimed. Jason Trimble looked at his watch. Five o'clock. He leaned over Cuzzy. "Here goes," he said and, tipping the head back to get a better angle, started mingling his own breath with Cuzzy's.

"God of Jesus, Matthew, Mary, John," he said quietly, expressing a stream of warm air. "Luke, Isaiah, Simon, Ruth." He named every prophet and disciple he could remember, then did it all again. Cuzzy's color was better. Either that, Jason thought, or I am getting used to the pallor of death. He put his fingers on Cuzzy's neck to check the pulse, counting out loud, but only to thirty-six. He tried again. There was a slight improvement: thirty-eight. How slow could a heart beat?

Jason picked up the phone—the same phone Gus had used to call him, he realized—and dialed 911. A dispatcher answered, a woman.

"Is this an emergency?" she asked.

"Of course it's an emergency, why else would I be calling?"

"I understand, sir, but I have to ask. We've got a lot of calls coming in tonight."

"I'm a minister," Jason said, as if that might let him jump the queue. "I've got a young man here who's hypothermic with a pulse under forty."

"Where is he?"

"I've got him in bed with a blanket on him. And a dog."

"That's good, that's good," the woman said. "Can you hold on? I've got an accident on the interstate." Before Jason could protest, she was gone, and he was listening to a public-service announcement about the fire hazards of Christmas lights.

"Sorry about that," the dispatcher said, coming back on the line. "Are you still there?"

"Of course I'm still here," Jason said. "And so is he. He needs an ambulance."

"I'll put you on the list," she said. "It might not be for quite a while. All of our vehicles are in service."

"He is going to die," Jason said.

"Do not panic," she said. "Try breathing up his nose."

"I did that."

"Do it some more. If you're not seeing any improvement, call back."

"Great," Jason said, "when?" But she had already hung up.

In fact, Cuzzy had begun to stir. When Jason squeezed his hand, Cuzzy squeezed it back. His good eye was open again, and the other one almost. Still, there was nothing present about him; he seemed a long way off.

"Look, Cuzzy," Jason started, "I don't know if you can hear me." His own voice sounded strained, as if he was on the verge of tears. He spoke to Cuzzy as if into a microphone. "This is Jason Trimble. I found you on the road. You have hypothermia. I am trying to help you. I am not sure if you can hear me. An ambulance is on the way. But it might not be here for a while. So I'm going to help you." He pushed the hair away from Cuzzy's face, where it had fallen again. Cuzzy made a small sound. He was trying to move his lips.

"What are you saying?" Jason said.

Cuzzy tried again.

"Horseshoes? Bloody horseshoes? Oh dear God," Jason said, and picked up the phone again.

"He's hallucinating," he told the dispatcher, a man this time. "Forty minutes? Yes, I know the roads are bad. What should I do till then?"

"Tracy," Cuzzy said with great effort.

Jason turned to him. "Let's don't worry about Tracy," he said more sharply than he'd intended. "Let's worry about you." Then, to the dispatcher: "Direct heat transfer? No, I haven't."

Jason Trimble hung up the phone and regarded the young man in the bed. His breathing was better, the minister was sure of it, and he wasn't quite as waxy, but Cuzzy was still underwater, still out of reach. This was Leo Gage's boy. The boy Leo Gage had held as a newborn, whose body he once knew. I can do this, he told himself. I can do this. He sat on the side of the bed and kicked off his boots. He unbuttoned his shirt and loosened his belt. Jason took off his shirt, and then his pants, and stood there, naked and cold himself, contemplating the bed. He drew back the covers and looked at Cuzzy's body, gray now, not white, and then looked away, to a picture on the nightstand of Gus and Molly Meacham. What we do for each other—those words came into his head, which was otherwise silent.

Jason slid down the sheets till his warm feet touched Cuzzy's cold and swollen ones, then he pulled up the blanket and settled it around them. He shivered, and whether it was from cold or from fear, he did not know. Dear God, he prayed, feeling every point of contact, every place where his skin touched Cuzzy's, and his own breath, cooled on Cuzzy's neck, coming back at him. He didn't know what to do with his hands, and then he did. Tentatively at first, and then with more authority, Jason put his own bare arms around the young man's muscular shoulders and drew him close. He felt Cuzzy relax into his embrace. He hadn't expected that.

CRYSTAL

"A body that is formed by the solidification of a chemical agent or a mixture and has a regularly repeating internal arrangement of its atoms and often external plane faces" (Youngblood).

From his bed, the bed Nora Trimble had made up in the study, Cuzzy could see the elm tree that dominated the parsonage lawn. People said it was the only elm in Stover to have been spared Dutch elm disease, and that growing over an old graveyard, it was somehow special and blessed. Cuzzy had no idea. All he knew was that he'd been watching it prosper for months as his feet healed after the surgeries. The buds had opened, and he could smell the new leaves through the open window as if the color green had a scent. He had been an invalid, and now he was not. After the toes came off and his balance faltered, Nora rigged low zip lines from the study to the bathroom and to the kitchen, and she wouldn't let a walker or crutches into the house. The doctors told him to be prepared to lose his foot, the left one, the one that had been wrapped in the boot, which cut off his circulation, and he went into surgery wondering how he was supposed to prepare for that. But when he woke up, his foot was still there—diminished but still basically there.

"You're down a shoe size," the surgeon joked, which was supposed to make him feel better. Nothing Nora Trimble had him do made him feel better, the stretches and the leg lifts especially, but she was relentless, and he liked her, and she was one of those women you didn't want to disappoint.

Nora adored her husband, Cuzzy saw that right away—didn't just love him but liked him, and laughed at his dopey habits without being mean, and kidded him out of his seriousness and piety as if they were clothes that could be removed with a little help. Jason Trimble wasn't a bad person—Cuzzy knew that now—and knew it as surely from watching Nora straighten her husband's glasses and blow eyelashes off his cheeks as he did from knowing that Jason Trimble had saved his life. At first it bothered Cuzzy that he owed his life to this man: he didn't want to owe Trimble anything. But Nora said it was not about debt, it was about collateral. "Your life is collateral for your life," she said cryptically, and when he asked what she meant, she told him to do another set of calf raises. "It's true that you are still among the living because of Jason," she said, counting down from fifteen, "but that does not mean he saved your life," and left it at that.

Nora made him get up early, and make the bed, and limp down the driveway for the paper. She said it was part of his therapy, though Cuzzy wasn't sure if she meant the walking or the newspaper. The headlines were still full of the case, which was going to trial soon. Holed up in the hospital for nearly a month, Cuzzy had been spared the brunt of the publicity, catching only glimpses of the television reporters using the Nice n Easy as their home away from home, and one time watching Ram's mother explain to *News at Noon* how her son didn't have anything against *those people*, even if he was raised to know it was wrong, what they did with each other. The lady even had props: two pieces of PVC pipe eight inches long, the same diameter, that she tried unsuccessfully to jam into each other. "See," she said, "it don't go."

The best story, though, was about Crystal and how she broke the glasses of a *People* reporter who was hounding her to pose for a spread on trailer life in Poverty.

"I don't live in Poverty," she said. They were in the Grand Union, in front of the frozen foods.

"It's close enough," the reporter said. "It just has to seem authentic to our readers." He proceeded to follow her down the cereal aisle, explaining how they were going to shoot in black and white to get the *Let Us Now Praise Famous Men* look.

"I can deal with that," she said. "*Famous* men."

"You know, if our readers saw how you people up here have to live," the reporter confided, "maybe something could be done about it. I really see this story helping you people."

The reporter didn't know what hit him. It was pink dog, square between the eyes.

In the papers, too, Cuzzy saw a picture of Tracy's father, and it surprised him how much he looked like Tracy. Michael Edwards, Jr., said the family was devastated and brokenhearted, "and it was for nothing. My son wasn't like that," as if Ram and Joey had gotten the wrong man.

In Algie's sixth notebook, on a page entitled "Consequences for Truth," were pieces of a transcript of an interview with Steve Biko, torn and glued randomly, over the words of the South African police officers who tortured him and denied it. Cuzzy imagined his own words like this, his own version of the truth torn in countless pieces: even he did not know how they went together. "It is not your fault," Jason told him. "What happened to Tracy is not your fault." But Cuzzy knew more about culpability than he had before; he knew that guilt could be cumulative, that all the small things you did, and all the things you didn't do, showed up on the same side of the balance sheet.

"Friendship is on trial here," the prosecutor told him. "Some people are going to find it hard to believe that you and Tracy were just friends. Sex, they get. Sex is a motive. But friendship is so intimate. And they are going to say, 'Why did an educated guy from the city want to be friends with a guy like you?'"

And why had he? Jason Trimble, sitting at the edge of the bed on one of the early days, when Cuzzy's feet were bandaged and he couldn't go anywhere, said that true friendship was the expression of grace. He said it was part of the mystery. But he didn't say which part.

The mail was delivered in big boxes, letters addressed to Cuzzy Gage, Poverty, just that, or to the hospital. Somehow people had gotten the idea that he had tried to stop it, and they wanted to let him know what they thought of that. For the most part he liked the nasty ones better than the ones that pretended to know him and his motives, the ones that said he should be nominated for an award. But he wasn't a hero, he knew he wasn't a hero, and neither was Tracy. Tracy was just dead.

People sent presents, too—stuffed animals and pictures of their vanished children, Bibles and hand-knitted socks. Nora opened these for him and sorted out what went to the Mission and what went to the trash, not because Cuzzy couldn't do this himself but because he couldn't bear to. The human need to connect exhausted him. What he wanted most was to be able to walk in the woods.

Still, sometimes there was comfort. "What the heck is this?" Nora said one day as she went through Cuzzy's mail. She held up a white bag embossed with EDISON COMPANY. Inside was a brief note: "You'll know what to do," it said. But did he? Cuzzy clutched the wax record so long it seemed it might melt, then he relinquished it to his nightstand, on top of *The Collected Poems of Wallace Stevens,* and dropped the marble, the one that Tracy gave him for his birthday, through the hole in the top. Only he knew it was there, and at night, when the lights were out, he tipped the cylinder so the agate rolled out and into his palms. He held it there, thinking about the places it had been.

"You'll know what to do." The trial was coming up, and he would get to demonstrate just how much of a hero he was not. How he'd done nothing. How he'd seen nothing. Even so, the evidence was solid: the scorecard Joey and Ram left behind, Tracy's car in Ram's possession, Tracy's blood on Ram and on Joey. The list was long. They would blame it on the drugs—on how Ram and Joey didn't know better. They would blame it on Tracy, who had invited them. They would say it was a game—that they were just having fun, that it was the drugs. Cuzzy was going to testify for the state. He only hoped they didn't settle before he could. The prosecutor said Cuzzy shouldn't do what he said he was going to do—he said the poetry thing might work against Tracy, but Cuzzy did not care. He was going to sit in front of that jury and read a poem he found dog-eared in the book Tracy gave him, a poem called "The Poem That Took the Place of a Mountain." He'd swear on it if he could.

There it was, word for word,
The poem that took the place of a mountain.

He breathed its oxygen,
Even when the book lay turned in the dust of his table.

It reminded him how he had needed
A place to go to in his own direction,

How he had recomposed the pines,
Shifted the rocks and picked his way among clouds,

For the outlook that would be right,
Where he would be complete in an unexplained completion:

The exact rock where his inexactnesses
Would discover, at last, the view toward which they had edged,

Where he could lie and, gazing down at the sea,
Recognize his unique and solitary home.

"Knock, knock, are you decent?" Nora Trimble called, and then she walked into the room anyway. Cuzzy was sitting on the bed stretching his metatarsal with a piece of rubber webbing.

"Very good," Nora said. "Do five more and then you should go. Jason is putting gas in the car."

Cuzzy was wearing chinos and a plaid shirt Nora had bought for him, and special support hose to help the blood flow through his feet. Shoes still hurt, but today he had no choice. Today he was going to drive.

"He is very nervous," Jason said as Cuzzy backed them out of the driveway.

"Yeah," Cuzzy agreed, grimacing. It hurt to brake.

The letter was hand-delivered. Jason gave it to him one evening after his weekly visit to Newkirk, and when Cuzzy read it, he expected a lecture about why he should go see his father, or at least the question: would he? But there was none of that, only Perkins's words running through his head again: "You'll know what to do."

"We need to take a detour," Cuzzy said, turning left when he should have been going straight. It was his first time driving since before it happened. The last car he'd driven was Tracy's. "Your bushings are shot," he said, shifting into third. "Feel how the chassis is shaking?"

The minister didn't know. Maybe it was the car. Maybe it was him. Maybe it was Cuzzy. Maybe it was the earth itself. He had lost his ability to say anything for sure.

They were off the main streets, and Cuzzy was slowing the car. "I'll be back," he said, stopping in front of Marcel and Therese's.

Jason nodded. Everything now had the capacity to silence him.

Cuzzy walked tentatively and deliberately, like a man on a tightrope. He couldn't count on his balance, but he wanted to.

There was music on in the house. Cuzzy heard it from the driveway. Crystal was not expecting him.

Cuzzy saw her through the window in the door. She didn't see him, but he saw her, Crystal, holding Harry. The baby was in her arms, and she was nursing him and dancing around the room. Her eyes were closed, and so were Harry's.

Their blindness arrested him, and arrested his hand in midair, before he could bring it to bear on the door. The sureness of her feet and her arms and her nipples. The circuitry of mother and child.

Cuzzy dropped his hand and turned to go. He saw that they did not need him, that they were just fine. He would tell this to Jason Trimble, who would understand.

From the passenger seat, the minister saw Cuzzy hesitate and turn and walk back. One step and then another, careful and studied. Jason averted his eyes; it was painful to watch.

And so he was not looking. He didn't see Cuzzy turn and retrace his steps. When Jason looked again, Cuzzy had mounted the front stoop and was gripping the railing. And then he reached out, and knocked.

ACKNOWLEDGMENTS

For their help with this book, my gratitude and thanks to John Glusman, Aodaoin O'Floinn, Gloria Loomis, Robb Forman Dew, Sara Rimer, and, always, Bill McKibben.